Anna's Chair

No one believed her until . . . .

Cindy L. Hamilton

"No eye has seen, no ear has heard,
and no mind has imagined
what God has prepared
for those who love him."
1 Corinthians 2:9

ISBN-13: 978-1722309220
ISBN-10: 1722309229

To Kate, Saylor, Preston, Asher, Silas, Patton, and Slaton

* * * *

Follow Jesus
and you are in for a lifetime
of adventure.

ACKNOWLEDGEMENTS

Several years ago, as I was fighting a year-long battle with cancer, God placed an idea in my spirit to write a story for teens and the young at heart—a story that would express my yearning to see the face of Jesus and have an even closer relationship with Him. As we walked through that season together, He taught me so many things through prayer, scripture, Christian music, books, and even visions. Jesus lifted me up to a higher level of intimacy, one where He was so real that I could almost reach out and hug Him.

God wants to reveal himself in personal, authentic ways. *"So, the Word became human and made his home among us. He was full of unfailing love and faithfulness. And we have seen his glory, the glory of the Father's one and only Son."* John 1:14

About a year later, I came across a news report about a missionary family, Brad and Kim Campbell, and their girls. Here was my story!

In 2012, they had sold all their possessions and moved to South Sudan with the *Keeping Hope Alive* Ministry. The Campbells worked at an orphanage in Malakal taking nine orphans under their wing. On Christmas morning, 2014, rebel Sudanese forces overtook the city. The Campbells and the orphans huddled under their beds as gunfire erupted around them. They escaped with their kids to an ad hoc U.N. Camp outside of Malakal. The Campbells refused to abandon the orphans even though food and water became extremely scarce.

Ultimately, the authorities would not let the Campbells take the orphans out of South Sudan, so Brad, Kim, and their girls had to leave without them. But not without promising to rescue the nine children. They stayed in a country close by trying to work through all the red tape to get their kids out. A caretaker at the orphanage finally manages to escape with the children, taking them on a perilous and expensive journey that ended in another country in Africa.

The Campbells joyfully reunited with the children in Ethiopia. Since then, they have expanded their mission work through *Keeping Hope Alive* ministries. They work with street kids in Romania, refugees in Greece, and are hoping to soon open an orphanage in Gambella, Ethiopia. They have begun their own ministry, *Gather*, with the blessing and help of *Keeping Hope Alive*. https://www.gather1.org

I want to thank the Campbells for their ministry and allowing me to use their story for my inspiration.

Cindy Hamilton

Soli Deo Gloria – Glory to God Alone

CHAPTER ONE

No one believed her.

Adults smiled, patted her on the back, and said, "Anna, that's nice, you have *such* a wonderful imagination." She tried to explain. She really did, but what did they know? Finally, Anna gave up.

Max believed her. He was there the first time it happened, and the strange thing was—he didn't even bark, and Max barked at everything. He just lay there with his beautiful, golden brown eyes and gazed up at her from the bed. Did she dream it? It was so long ago. She was only six years old. But, now she was sixteen—and it was happening again. *How did she even begin to explain?*

* * * *

"Anna. Anna James!" As Anna entered the cafeteria, her best friend, Grace, called out to her.

It was the first day of their last quarter as tenth graders at Johnson High School. Spring break was behind them, and summer was a long two months away. Anna turned toward her friend and smiled. With a you-won't-believe-what-I've-got-to-tell-you grin on her face, Grace hurried toward her. Anna stopped at the door of the cafeteria to let Grace catch up.

Grace always had something exciting to share with Anna. She had this contagious enthusiasm that radiated from her. Everyone liked Grace. What wasn't to like? She was smart, friendly, kind; quick to smile and give an encouraging word.

She had gorgeous, curly, chestnut brown hair, pulled up today in a bouncy ponytail. Her eyes were light, periwinkle blue, mischievous behind large tortoiseshell glasses. She was adorable. It would be so easy to be jealous of Grace, but she was also very down-to-earth and completely unaware of her beauty.

Grace's sister, Shelby, joined them in line for breakfast. Shelby was the antithesis of Grace. She was an "I see the glass half-empty" kind of girl. She usually had a scowl on her face, looked on the negative side and questioned everything. She was a loner and hung out with Grace only when she felt like it. Even at that, Shelby was ferociously loyal to her sister. Today, she wore a black T-shirt with some weird symbol on the front. She had dyed her hair black and streaked it with blue. She always wore her hair pulled high in a ponytail. Shelby and Grace were twins, completely identical and then totally not. They lived with their mom, Maria. Their dad died a year ago in a tragic accident.

Shelby glared as a boy stepped in line in front of Grace. "Hey, no cuts."

With a shrug, he backed away, raising both hands in surrender.

You didn't mess with Shelby.

Grace ignored the interruption, smiled at the boy and apologized. She turned to Anna and blurted out, "You will never, never, ever guess who has moved in beside us."

Shelby groaned, rolled her eyes, and shook her head.

Grace continued, "The cutest two boys you have *ever* seen, that's who."

"Really?" asked Anna.

Grace paused and glanced around. Suddenly, she squinted her eyes and lowered her voice to a whisper. "There they are."

Anna turned her head and spotted two boys coming their way. As they joined the end of the line, one of them smiled at Grace and waved. She blushed, turned her back to them and said, "Okay, he just smiled at me."

"Hey, they *are* cute," said Anna. "What are their names?"

"David and Jonathan Knight—they're MKs."

"MKs?" Anna raised her eyebrows at Grace.

"Missionary kids—their dad and mom are missionaries, and they've moved back to Johnson for some reason. They also have an adopted sister from Ethiopia."

A beautiful girl walked up and joined them in line. She was stunning, tall and slim with ebony skin and lovely brown eyes. She said something to the two brothers, and they both laughed.

"Is that her?"

"Yeah—her name is Favor," Grace said, putting her hand to her heart. "It means 'beautiful inside and out.'" Grace did tend to be dramatic at times.

"How do you know this?"

"Oh, yesterday, after they moved in, I went over and met her. Wait 'til you hear her talk—she has the coolest English accent."

Anna glanced over Grace's shoulder. She lowered her voice. "So—which one's which?"

"The tall, handsome one is David, and the short, cute one is Jonathan."

By this time, it was their turn to order breakfast. Anna chose a biscuit and sausage, orange juice, and fruit and followed Grace and Shelby to find a table.

"Let's invite them to sit with us," Grace said.

Shelby groaned again and sat down at the nearest table.

"Are you sure they'd want to sit with us?" Anna asked.

To be honest, boys, cute boys, made her heart race and caused her to blather and turn beet red. These two guys were *especially* cute. Anna wished she had her friend's confidence. Grace had no trouble speaking with boys.

Grace ignored both girls and called out to the three as they came close to their table. "Would you guys like to sit with us?"

David answered, "Sure, why not?"

Jonathan grinned, plopped his tray down, and said, "Hey."

He was short and wiry. Blonde hair fell to his mischievous green eyes. His brother, David, was as opposite to Jonathan as Grace was to Shelby. He had short-cropped auburn hair and freckles. David was tall, and if you judged him by the smile on Grace's face, very handsome. Favor sat down gracefully between her brothers and smiled.

Grace introduced Shelby and Anna. "This is my best friend, Anna James, and my sister, Shelby Mercer—well, I guess you already knew her last name, since she's my sister and all." Grace smiled her adorable smile.

Jonathan regarded Shelby and then Anna and asked, "So, what grade are you two in this year?"

Not sure if Shelby would answer, Anna blurted out, "We're all in tenth grade—Shelby, too, I mean—of course, she is since she and Grace are twins." *Oh, no.* Anna's cheeks began to slowly burn, so she quickly picked up her milk carton and took a sip. Shelby barely nodded, took a large bite out of her bagel and just stared at him. She was obviously not going to say anything.

Unfazed, Jonathan continued, "So am I—in tenth grade, that is. David is in eleventh, and Favor is a senior."

"Why've you moved to Johnson?" asked Grace.

Favor smiled and glanced at her brothers. "We're on furlough with our parents. Our family started the *Come and See* ministry in South Sudan about five years ago. We're back in the states to raise support both financially and spiritually. We hope to go back to Sudan or Ethiopia as soon as possible."

"What's the *Come and See* ministry?" Anna asked.

Favor hesitated, glanced once again at her brothers as if to get their permission, and then focused intently on each one of the three girls. Finally, she asked, "Do you really want to know?"

Curious, Anna asked, "Why would we *not* want to know?"

Favor's eyes bore into hers, and Anna shifted

uncomfortably on the bench.

A guilty feeling flooded over Anna as she checked her own intentions. Most of her friends were pretty superficial. Anna had to admit that she, too, was guilty. She jumped in and out of social media with all the latest stories and events. She found herself moving from one account to another. *Did she really care?* But here in front of her were Favor and her brothers—real people with a real-life story, not characters behind the screen of her iPhone.

Anna squarely met Favor's gaze and said, "Yes, yes, I do want to know."

Grace also nodded in affirmation.

Favor eyed Shelby and raised her eyebrows. Shelby gave a reluctant nod.

This may have been a weird coincidence, but at that very moment, the noisy drone of voices in the cafeteria dimmed. Anna knew somehow if they—*she*—said yes, their high school life would take a 180-degree turn that would completely spin her, Grace, and Shelby out of their comfort zones.

Pleased, almost relieved, Favor smiled at them and said, "Well, the name came from the New Testament. When people were curious about something Jesus said, he would tell them, 'Just come and see.' Our family ran a coffee shop in Malakal, and every day we met amazing Sudanese people. When one of our regulars asked questions about Jesus, we would say, 'come and see.' About a year ago, we met a man by the name of Jafaar, the director of the orphanage in Malakal. He and his wife, Zofa, and her brother, Luka, became our best friends."

Anna, Grace, and Shelby sat speechless as Jonathan explained how his family often went to the orphanage on weekends to play with the kids and help where they could. About a year ago, four orphans arrived who stole their hearts. There were Ulan and Achan, seven-year-old twins, and Lala, who was eight years old. Jonathan said she was a beautiful little girl with "the sweetest smile you could ever imagine." And then there was Tut, the man of the family at fourteen years old and fiercely protective of his brother and sisters. Their mother, Abi, was a tea lady in the streets of Malakal.

"Tea lady?" Anna asked, intrigued.

"Yes, she sold tea each day out of her cart," Jonathan said. "There are a lot of women who do this to make a living for their families—tea is a very popular drink in South Sudan. But one day, the police put a stop to it. They came and arrested her—and Abi never came home. The four kids ended up at the orphanage."

Favor continued their story. "They often came to our apartment for overnights. At first, they were extremely shy and wary of us, but it wasn't long before they relaxed and fit right into our family. They were like our very own brothers and sisters, and our parents thought about adopting them." Favor had to stop her story at that point because the bell rang for their first-period class, and Mr. Hall, the principal, walked by and encouraged everyone to hurry to class.

As they grabbed their backpacks and trays, Anna said, "I'd really like to hear more about your ministry and the orphan kids."

David grinned at her and said, "Well, let's eat lunch together, and we'll tell you more about it."

"Great, let's meet at the picnic tables outside the cafeteria," said Anna. "First one there saves everyone a seat." Anna and Grace had two classes together, Algebra II and Pre-AP Literacy. Anna was pleased that Jonathan was in their first-period Algebra II class. He sat on the other side of the room from them. Hoping to still talk to him at lunch, Anna caught his eye, gave him a quick wave, and then tried to focus on the teacher as she wrote equations on the Smart Board. It took every brain cell Anna could muster to understand math, so it was imperative she pay attention.

Their second period together was literacy. This class was another story. It was Anna's favorite because she loved to write. Anna's dad said she was born with a crazy, overgrown imagination. He often smiled at her, shook his head, and said,

"Anna, I'd like to get inside that head of yours one time to try and figure out how your brain works." Grace struggled with literacy as Anna struggled with math, so they helped each other.

For the next two class periods before lunch, Anna listened to the same old rules and procedures. The teachers went over them *ad nauseam* at the beginning of each quarter. As the teacher droned on, Anna's thoughts turned again to Jonathan, David, and Favor.

What was it about these three? Were they for real?

They weren't like any kids she'd ever known. There was something curious, remarkable even, about them. When they spoke to her, their eyes convinced her that she was the most important person in the world at that time. The three siblings reminded Anna of someone else—someone she'd met years ago during a tough time in her life—someone she would never forget.

So—back to the beginning of this story. The part where no one believed her.

CHAPTER TWO

It had been almost ten years to the day since Anna's life turned itself on its head like one of her lopsided, ungraceful cartwheels. Anna thought she'd put it all behind her—you know, as adults told her to do—because she was so young when it happened. "Get over it, Anna. Move on, Anna. It will be okay, Anna." But did a kid ever really get over something like that? Maybe, she just pretended to in order to make the adults in her life feel better, but did they ever really understand how it affected her? She didn't think so.

Anna's little brother, Ben, was four years old, and she had just turned six. Their mom worked in the city as a buyer for a large department store, which meant she was away a lot, traveling to and from Dallas and New York. They loved it when she came home from a trip because she always had something for them, but they missed her, too. It was their Dad who cooked the meals and read the bedtime stories at night because their Mom was usually too tired or distracted to spend much time with them when she was home. She was always on her cell phone calling one buyer or another.

They had recently adopted a long-haired dachshund puppy. Anna named him Max. He was a ball of energy with a beautiful red coat and inquisitive brown eyes. He followed her around everywhere and they became best friends. She adored him. Her mom, however, was not so crazy about Max. She was not too happy when he had an accident on the floor or barked too loudly.

Anna would never forget that night—it was Dad's thirtieth birthday. He decided to cook one of his delicious celebration dinners—tender, spiced meatballs covered with his homemade spaghetti sauce and sprinkled with shavings of fresh parmesan cheese. Of course, he always baked bread to go with it. The sweet aroma of homemade bread wafting through the kitchen always brought her back to that night.

As Dad popped the bread into the oven, he glanced at the kitchen clock on the wall and said, "Mom's plane gets in at 5:00 so she should be home soon. A home-made meal will be a treat for her since she eats out all the time when she's away." Anna and Ben wanted to make something for Dad's birthday, so they both got out paper and crayons and created their masterpieces. They were so proud of their creations and placed the birthday cards beside his plate at the table.

Five o'clock came and went, and they hadn't heard from Mom. She always texted when her plane arrived. At six o'clock, Dad called her number, but only got her answering machine.

"All right, guys," he said, "Let's eat, and we'll keep Mom's dinner warm in the oven."

Disappointed again, they all sat down to dinner. Ben gave Dad his card and sang an off-key version of "Happy Birthday." Anna joined in and laughed at Ben's terrible singing.

Later that evening, after they'd gone to bed, Mom's voice drifted from her bedroom. Anna hopped out of bed and ran into the hall to give her a big hug, but then stopped short—Mom was crying. *Why was she crying?* Curious, Anna padded over and put her ear to their bedroom door.

"John, I'm so sorry."

"Evelyn, you don't mean this."

"I don't know what else to say, John. I love him. It's over between us."

Without another word, Mom opened the door and hurried out into the hall. She paused and noticed Anna for the first time. "Anna, honey, you need to get back in bed. I'll see you tomorrow." She knelt and pulled Anna to her. Anna would never forget the sweet smell of her mom's perfume as she kissed her. She released Anna, walked down the hall to the front door, grabbed her purse and keys, and left.

"Mommy?" Anna cried. She ran toward the door and stopped. Confused, Anna turned toward her daddy and asked, "Where is Mommy going?"

Dad walked over and picked her up. He held her close in a ferocious hug.

"Daddy? Why are you crying?"

"It's okay, honey. Let's get you back to bed. You'll see Mommy tomorrow, I promise." Dad tucked her into bed snug and tight the way he did every night. When he got through, Anna resembled a mummy. Only her eyes moved as she barely peeked out above the blankets. He reached over and kissed her forehead and then picked up Max and snuggled him in close.

"Good night, Anna. I love you, Doodlebug. Good night, Max."

"'Night, Dad," she said, her voice muffled under the covers. Max had already closed his eyes and drifted off to sleep.

The next day, Dad sat Anna and Ben down and explained. "Anna . . . Ben . . . Mom is moving to another house, but you will go and stay with her on weekends and holidays."

Ben didn't understand, but Anna did. She was the big sister, and she knew these things. Well, at least she pretended that she did.

Several nights later it happened for the first time—an encounter, a visit—Anna didn't know what to call it. She and Dad had stayed up later than usual that night. He had told her he had a difficult time going to sleep, so she wanted to keep him company. About nine o'clock, he said, "Anna, we've got to get you to bed, young lady."

Every night Anna and Dad had a favorite nighttime ritual. He read her favorite story, said their prayers, and tucked her in nice and tight. After dad left her room that night, Anna couldn't sleep. She lay in bed and listened to the creaking and popping of their old house. She heard a sound. *Was Max snoring?* She reached over and placed her head on Max. *Nope, not him.* She lay back down . . . there it was again. This time, Anna slipped from her bed and padded out to the hall. The sound was louder now. Curious, she followed it to the living room. Anna walked closer. Her dad lay face down on the carpet. He was praying.

"Lord God, help me, please help me, I can't do this. I can't face this. God, what am I going to do?" He balled up his fists and hit the floor. "God, where are you?"

Frightened and confused, Anna ran over to him, knelt and bent her face close to his. He was completely unaware of her presence. "Daddy, get up, get up. What's wrong with you?" She called out to him even louder, "Stand up tall, Dad. Stand up tall." Anna grabbed hold of his shirt and pulled. *Why won't he get up?* "Dad, Daddy get up." She started to cry.

He laid motionless for a moment and then as if in a daze, pushed himself up off the floor to his knees and focused on her for the first time. "Anna? Oh, Anna, I'm so sorry I frightened you." He wrapped his arms tightly around her. After a moment, he released her. "I promise . . . I *will* stand up tall. God will give me the strength—give *all* of us the strength we need to get through this." With that, he got to his feet, reached for Anna's hand, and walked her back to bed.

As she snuggled down under the covers, Anna couldn't go back to sleep. Her six-year-old self couldn't understand what was happening to her mom and dad. Could it be her fault? She and Ben were always arguing about something and that really made her mom mad.

Mom would yell at them, "You two get on my last nerve." Other times she would just get mad, slam the door, and say, "John, I'm going for a walk. You deal with the kids."

Anna lay in bed and thought about her mom and dad. Suddenly, she had a great idea and sat straight up almost knocking Max off the bed. Her Grandmother Smith said Jesus was always with her and he would listen to her prayers.

That's what I'll do. Anna smiled, kicked off the covers and slipped out of bed. She knelt on her pink shaggy carpet, folded her hands together and bowed her head against the beautiful smiley-face quilt Grandmother had quilted for her when she was a baby.

"Jesus? *Jesus*?"—she said it louder the second time—"Jesus? Are you there?"

There was nothing. Maybe she wasn't praying the right way. Anna folded her hands a different way, closed her eyes tight and tried again. "Jesus?" She listened for a minute and then said, "Would you help my mommy and daddy? Please?"

"Here I am, Anna," a voice said from the other side of the room.

Startled, she poked her head up above the bed. The voice came from her big, overstuffed rocking chair. The room was dark except for her nightlight in the corner. Slowly the room lit up as if someone had turned on a dimmer switch. He materialized in front of her like Hans Solo in Ben's favorite Star Wars movie. An iridescent radiant energy encircled him. Even her American Girl doll, Sally Primrose, and her beloved old bear, June, glowed as they sat beside him in the chair. Anna inhaled deeply and drew in the most wonderful, sweet aroma. Max raised his head and sniffed at the air. For some reason, she was completely unafraid. She got up off her knees, crawled onto the bed and grabbed her blanket. She stared at Him.

"Hello," she whispered.

He smiled at her and whispered back, "Hello."

He didn't look like the pictures in her children's Bible. He had short-cropped hair and a neat beard, and he wore a white t-shirt and jeans. He did have on sandals, though.

"Where's your robe?" Anna asked.

He laughed and said, "Oh, I haven't worn that in a while."

"Why are you here?"

"You asked for my help."

With her childlike innocence, Anna asked the age-old question: "So, are you gonna make my mom and dad get back together? I prayed to you about it, you know."

With a sad smile, Jesus shook His head and said, "Anna, I never make anyone do anything they don't want to do, but I can promise you this, I'm here for you and I will never leave you."

"Are you gonna leave my mom?"

"Nope."

"Are you gonna leave my dad?"

"No, Anna."

Satisfied, she crawled back under the covers.

"Good night, Anna."

"Good night, Jesus."

As the light in the corner dimmed, she closed her eyes and drifted off to sleep.

The next morning at breakfast, Anna tried to tell Dad about Jesus.

"Daddy?"

"Yes?"

"I talked to Jesus last night."

"Oh yeah?" he said. He spooned cornflakes into his mouth, chewed, and then swallowed. She just sat and stared at him until finally, he smiled that condescending smile that adults sometimes have for kids and said, "Must have been a dream, Anna." He picked up the cereal box and asked, "More?"

He didn't believe her. Oh, well. That was all right. Even at six years old, Anna already knew adults sometimes got it wrong.

Jesus didn't appear in her room again after that one time. Mom and Dad got a divorce, so she guessed that Jesus was right. He wouldn't make anyone do anything that they didn't want to do.

Ten years later, Anna was still trying to make sense out of all of it. She had a long way to go.

CHAPTER THREE

When the bell for lunch rang, Anna jerked in her seat and realized that she'd been daydreaming again; something she tended to do right before lunch. Anna chalked it up to low blood sugar or, more likely, the boring class.

"Anna—earth to Anna." Impatient as always, Grace stood beside her desk and waited for her friend to gather her things.

"Come on. It's time for lunch and I'm starving."

"Me, too. Let's go." Anna grabbed her backpack, and they hurried out into the hall.

"Hey, Anna, Grace, wait up." Jonathan pushed his way through the crowded hall and caught up with them. "So, breakfast was pretty good this morning. What's for lunch?"

"Wait a sec." Grace pulled a menu out of her backpack, studied it for a moment, and said, "Hmmm . . . we're having burritos and cheese dip—one of my favorites."

Grace loved to eat, and she was always hungry. She had a crazy metabolism that allowed her to eat anything and not gain an ounce.

Anna grimaced and held up her lunch bag. "Always bring my lunch. Trying to eat right, you know?" *Where was the justice in this world? Oh, well.*

Grace made a face to show what she thought about Anna's lunch choice.

Jonathan grinned. "Well, I'm hungry for whatever."

It was a beautiful, warm spring day. Anna squinted as they walked outside into the bright sunlight. David waved to them from a picnic table on the far side of the courtyard. Favor and Shelby sat beside him laughing about something.

When they sat down, David, Jonathan, and Favor began talking about their family and why they were here in Johnson. As Anna chomped on her apple, sipped Fiji water, and listened to their conversation, it struck her how totally cool these kids were. They had such an easy camaraderie between the three of them like they were each other's best friends.

When there was a lull in the conversation, Shelby spoke up and said, "So, tell us more about what happened in . . . where were you, now?"

Surprised that Shelby had asked this question, Grace cut her eyes at Anna and raised her eyebrows. Anna shrugged, took another bite of her apple, and smiled at the Knights, waiting for their answer.

"Malakal," said Favor. "We used to live in Malakal."

"Yes, the city was in the new country of South Sudan," David offered.

"Was?" Anna asked.

"There was a rebel uprising, and all of the people in the city were forced to flee to a United Nations refugee center," he said.

After a pause, Jonathan's face hardened, and he said, "The city as we knew it is dead and gone."

Stunned at his fierce reply, Grace asked, "So . . . were you there?"

"What about the four kids? The kids at the orphanage?" asked Anna. There was a long pause, and she didn't know if he would answer.

Jonathan hesitated, glanced over at Favor and David, and then back at Anna. "Yes—they're still there."

"We were at the orphanage the night it happened—Mom, Dad, and the three of us," said David. "It was Christmas Eve, and we'd taken presents over to the orphanage. The kids were so excited and couldn't wait to open their gifts. We were teaching them a Christmas carol when we heard gunfire. A shot burst through the window and hit the wall on the other side of the room. We grabbed our four kids and followed Jafaar and the others into the back bedroom and piled mattresses and suitcases up against the door."

"We thought we were going to die that night," said Favor. "We could hear the rebels shouting, and we were so afraid that they would come inside. We'd heard about the horrible things that the rebels had done. All we could do was hope and pray that they wouldn't find us. Ulan and Tut tried their best to comfort Achan and Lala and keep them quiet." She closed her eyes for a moment and then continued. "I can still see them huddled together in the corner of that room. All night long and the next day, we listened . . . gunfire . . . mortar shells exploding around us. The building would shake when one landed near us—" Favor's voice trailed off as she took a deep breath.

Stunned, Anna, Grace, and Shelby didn't know what to say. As they listened to this unbelievable story of terror, their classmates laughed and cut up around them. It was surreal.

Grace was the first to speak. "How'd you get out of there?"

"Well, thankfully, the rebels weren't after us, but after each other. We stayed in our safe place until the next afternoon when the shooting died down. Mom and Dad told us that we'd have to make a run for it to the United Nations base close by, so we each grabbed what food and supplies we could and made our first attempt to escape."

"Yeah," Jonathan said, "that was a bit hairy. As we walked down the road, we heard gunfire, and at the same time, a mortar shot went over our heads. We didn't know if they were shooting at each other or us, so we turned around and ran back to the orphanage. After about two hours, Dad told us that we had to try again." Jonathan paused, and his face reflected the painful memory. "We gathered together in a circle, held hands, and prayed that God would protect us."

"That time we were able to make it to the back gate of the U.N. base. It was crazy. There were thousands of Sudanese people trying to enter. A U.N. worker told us to go around to another gate, so we did, but all these people followed us."

"A man tried to hand me his child to carry inside for safety," said David. "I didn't know what to do. After about an hour, we were all allowed to come inside."

The bell rang for fourth-period before they could ask any more questions. Anna told the Knights that they all lived within a mile of the school and tried to walk as often as the weather allowed. The group agreed to meet up in front of the school at the end of the day so that they could walk home together. The afternoon dragged on, and Anna couldn't focus on the lessons because all she could think about was what the Knight kids had shared with them. Anna had been a bit envious as she sat there and listened to their story. Her life seemed so boring compared to theirs—nothing like that happened in her ordinary teenage world, at least nothing that remarkable.

Anna sat at the back of the room by the window in her seventh period psychology class. This was an unusual spot for her, since she tended to like to sit at the front in her other classes. She didn't know if it was the teacher or the subject, but she often found herself daydreaming in that class. She'd stare out the window and wish for the bell to ring so she could just go home. That afternoon, it was even more difficult to pay attention. Anna thought about her life in comparison to the Knights'. She'd never been in danger, always had plenty to eat, a nice house, and good friends. All she had to worry about were her grades . . . what college she would attend . . . well, there *was* the ACT test coming up in April that concerned her, but hey—that's nothing life threatening. Her parent's divorce was a big deal, she guessed, at least to Ben and her, but that happened a long time ago and wasn't so unusual since half her friends came from divorced families. She vaguely remembered the visit she had with Jesus that horrible week when Mom left Dad for Tom, but that was ten years ago, and truthfully, Anna wondered if it was just a dream because nothing like that had happened since. She went to church and Sunday School and learned all about Jesus. But the Knights? Anna knew her faith was nothing like theirs—that's for sure. Chin in hand she stared out the window. *What would it be like to have that kind of faith—to live that kind of life?*

"Anna? Would you kindly answer the last question?"

At the sound of her name, Anna's hand slipped from underneath her chin, and she jolted back to the present.

"Ma'am? I'm sorry?" Anna tried to engage her brain back to the subject at hand.

"The last question, would you answer it?" Mrs. Stout repeated.

Thankfully, the 3:30 bell rang and rescued her.

Anna held her breath and ducked her head as she passed by Mrs. Stout at the door.

Her teacher scowled at her and said, "Anna, I need you to pay attention tomorrow."

She let out her breath with a whoosh. "Yes, ma'am."

She promised herself that she would pay more attention in Mrs. Stout's class the next day, but all she could think about that afternoon was the Knights. She couldn't wait to hear the rest of their story.

CHAPTER FOUR

The weather was beautiful that spring afternoon. Anna enjoyed the warmth of the sun as it soaked into her dark t-shirt. She waited for her friends at the flag pole. Grace joined her first and the Knights walked out soon after. Lighthearted, they walked together past the buses and the car line toward Palm Street. They had to dodge kids on bicycles and skateboards and little elementary kids who pushed around them and ran down the sidewalk. As they walked, the friends talked about their classes and the upcoming baseball game Friday night against their rival Wakeland High School. Johnson played Wakeland every year for the bragging rights to the Spring Classic trophy. The winner proudly displayed this trophy until the next year's Spring Classic. David and Jonathan said they'd like to attend a baseball game, so they decided they'd all go together.

As the group stopped at the corner, a little boy ran in front of Anna, tripped, and sprawled out on the sidewalk. He wailed and thrashed his arms in the air. His friends laughed at him and ran away. He howled even louder when he caught sight of his skinned and bloody knees. Jonathan and Favor walked over and knelt beside him. Favor laid her hand on his shoulder, and they both bowed their heads for a moment.

If Anna hadn't seen it with her very own eyes, she would not have believed it. She watched as the little boy stopped crying and stared wide-eyed at the two beside him and then down at his knees. Anna followed his gaze. There was no blood, no skinned knees—no injury at all. What?

"You okay, little fellow?" David asked.

Solemnly, he nodded his head and stood up as if nothing had happened. Then, with a huge smile, he dusted off his shorts and ran off, yelling at his friends to wait for him.

Anna and Grace stood dumbfounded. Didn't know what to say.

"So, what just happened? That little guy was so angry and hurt. His knees—what did you do?" Shelby asked suspiciously.

"We prayed the name of Jesus," said Favor as if it was the most natural thing in the world.

Shelby grimaced. "That's it?"

David grinned and then said matter-of-factly, "Yes. Where we come from, the name of Jesus is the most powerful word that we could ever say. His name heals the sick, calms the storms, opens doors—we've seen it happen over and over."

"Well, we've never seen anything like that around here. Why not?" asked Shelby.

Jonathan shrugged his shoulders. "Honestly, we don't know why. Maybe it's because people in Sudan have such a simple, childlike belief in what Jesus can do—they just believe."

Before Shelby could open her mouth to make some sarcastic reply, Anna jumped in to change the subject and asked, "Is your family here to stay?"

As they came to a stop at the crossroads of Palm and College, David said, "We're here until we accomplish two things. One is to plan a battle strategy, and the other is to get people to help us." Determined, he said, "We're going back to get those kids."

Wide-eyed, Grace stammered, "Wha—what do you mean, a *battle strategy*? War, guns and ammo—that kind of thing?"

"Not that kind of war," David said. "They *do* have guns in Sudan, but that's not the weapons that we need. We fight with weapons that are different from those of the world. Our weapons have power from God."

"Yes, that's the way we win," said Jonathan. His eyes flashed. "Our enemy isn't the Sudanese rebels—our enemy is Satan himself. He's out to kill, steal, and destroy. We won't let him have our kids."

A cold chill ran through Anna. This was all a little too much for her to understand, so, she just said, "Well, I guess I'd better get home. Dad's going to wonder where I am. I'll see you guys tomorrow."

Anna walked into the house a few minutes later. Ben and her dad pounded out pizza dough in the kitchen. The smell of the warm, spicy sauce made Anna's mouth water. Those two prided themselves in their pizza making abilities and enjoyed creating unusual new recipes. Of course, Max was at their feet with his tongue out hoping for a taste of anything they might throw his way.

"Hey, you," Dad said. "How was your day?"

"Well . . . it was certainly interesting," she said. "I met the coolest kids today. They moved into town last weekend."

"Oh, yeah?"

"Yeah, they're missionary kids, here with their family for a while."

Dad pushed a ball of dough and a pizza pan toward her. "Like to help?"

"Sure."

Anna went to the sink and washed her hands. She dipped them in flour and began to spread the sticky dough around the pan. As they worked, she told Dad and Ben all about the Knights' life in Sudan and their mission to get back to South Sudan and rescue the four kids.

Dad and Ben were both great listeners, and she could share anything with them. Even so, Anna paused.

"A weird thing happened when we walked home today." She explained how the little boy had fallen and skinned his knee. She hesitated for a moment. "Dad . . . Ben . . . if it hadn't happened right before my very own eyes, I wouldn't have believed it. But . . . Favor and Jonathan prayed for him, and God completely healed his knee. I mean, it was bleeding, and it just stopped. There was nothing there."

"Are you sure you saw what you thought you saw?" asked Ben.

Ben was Anna's stabilizer, her questioner—he kept her grounded.

Dad stared at her for a moment. "Hmm, it *does* sounds strange," he said. "Surely there's an explanation. You know, I'd like to meet these kids and their parents. I'll invite them over for dinner one night. Speaking of that, let's get these pizzas in the oven—I'm starving."

Anna's stomach growled at that exact moment. "Me, too!"

After dinner, Anna took Max to her room to do homework. She always tried to get algebra out of the way first since it was her hardest subject, but tonight, Anna couldn't concentrate. She sighed, closed her book and stared blankly at the wall. Everything that had happened that day played over and over in her mind.

What did they mean about battle strategy? What kind of help did they need?

When no answers came, she opened her book again and tried to put it all out of her mind. Mr. Jones would be after her tomorrow to answer one of his annoying algebra questions, and Anna had better be ready.

"Knock, knock," came a voice at the door.

"Come in."

Ben stuck his head in the room, grinned, and said, "Finished with your homework? I was wondering if you needed any help with your math."

Ben was the math genius of the family. Even though he was twenty months younger than Anna, they were only a year apart in school, but he was light years ahead of her in math.

Anna nodded her head. "Yes, I do. I absolutely cannot figure out why algebra uses x, y, and z instead of numbers.

Drives my brain crazy. Hey, would you check my answers? Not sure if I got them right."

"Sure." Ben took the paper from her and plopped down in her chair, right on top of her old teddy bear.

"You're sitting on Ted," she said.

"Sorry, Ted," he said as he pulled the bear out from under him.

"Like my new chair?" She'd just finished redecorating her room in shades of blue and peach. The chair was a gift from her dad—periwinkle blue, sleek and modern—so totally different from her old rocking chair. She loved it.

'Yeah, it's cool."

Anna depended on Ben for a lot of things, not just help with her algebra homework. They may have been brother and sister, but they were also best friends. They'd argued and fought at times, but Anna and Ben had been through so much together. If it weren't for Ben, she couldn't have tolerated weekends with her Mom or their annoying stepdad, Tom. They'd reversed roles. Ben was so young after Mom left that at first, he depended on Anna as his big sister. When they'd go over to Mom's on the weekends, he'd crawl into bed with Anna at night after Mom went to her room. When he cried out in the night or woke up with a nightmare, Anna would reach over and put her arms around him and help him go back to sleep. But now, he was the one who comforted and calmed Anna when she'd had it up to there with their stepdad, Tom, and his attitude.

Let's just say that Tom and Anna did not get along very well. When she was at Mom's, Anna tried to ignore Tom, but it wasn't always easy. He tended to tell her what to do and that got on her nerves. He was the kind of guy who thought he was always right. Ben had a way of dismissing Tom, but that was difficult for Anna to do. She knew that her relationship with Tom bothered Mom, but she just couldn't help herself. Ben was the peacekeeper, so he was the one who dealt with Mom—and Tom. Anna appreciated him for that. The two spent every other weekend with Mom as well as half the summer. They just endured the visits. Their mom was okay; she tried. But honestly, they were at the age that they'd rather spend time with their friends. Anna's overly-active conscience told her that wasn't right, but it was what it was.

"Hey, looks good. You figured it out." Ben handed the paper back to her and grinned.

He got up to leave and then hesitated and sat back down in her chair. "I have a question for you." Ben was not usually so serious.

"Okay. What's up?"

"I've been thinking about the new kids that you met today . . . and that little boy. He hesitated as if he were afraid to voice his thoughts. He knitted his brows. "The little boy—his knee—he was healed? Are you *sure*?"

"All I know is what I saw, Ben. They prayed for him, and his knee was completely healed."

Ben attended church with Anna and Dad, but it was only because Dad gave him no choice. It's not that Ben didn't believe in God—he did. At least Anna *thought* he did. Sure, she had questions about her faith, but honestly, it's like Ben didn't really give much thought to God at all. God just wasn't a priority.

Max whined and jumped up against Ben's leg. Automatically, he reached down and scratched Max behind the ears. After a moment, Ben grinned up at Anna. "I want to meet these new friends of yours."

"Okay, I know you'd like them a lot. Hey—why don't you come with us this weekend? We're going to watch Johnson beat Wakeland."

"Sure—sounds like a plan." Ben stood up. "Guess I'll go to bed. Good night, Anna."

"Night, Ben."

CHAPTER FIVE

After Ben went to his room, Anna stuffed her homework in her backpack. She gently picked up Max and placed him on her lap for his nightly ear rub.

Max had been Anna's best friend for over ten years. When she was at the house, he rarely left her side. His muzzle had grown gray in the last couple of years, but he still had a lot of pep in his short legs. He thought he was still a young pup, and Anna would never tell him otherwise. She had noticed, however, that he spent a little more time during the day curled up asleep on his bed. They still had some great conversations. Max had grown even wiser over the years.

"Max, I know you're all comfy, but you gotta go potty one more time before we go to sleep," she said.

Max groaned as Anna picked him up. She cradled him in her arms and walked outside to the backyard. As she waited for him to do his business, Anna peered up into the sky at the millions of stars flickering over her head. A thought came to her that these same stars shone over the four kids that the Knights wanted to go back and rescue.

"You need to help them, Anna," a voice inside of her head said.

"What can *I* do?" she thought.

"I'll show you," the voice said.

Anna shrugged off the crazy thoughts rolling around inside of her head. "Come on, Max, let's go to bed—I'm so tired."

It didn't take long for her to fall asleep. Anna dreamed that she was in Sudan with the Knights. They were searching for the four kids but couldn't find them. There was gunfire all around as they ran from building to building. They called out the names of the four orphans. It was dark and suffocatingly hot. Sweat dripped into their eyes. Terrified, the four ducked into a small storage hut to catch their breath. There, huddled in a corner, were Tut, Ulan, Achan, and Lala. Their eyes cried out and begged for help. They had just grabbed hold of the kids when a rebel soldier pounded on the door.

Favor prayed, "In the name of Jesus, we ask for protection."

They all began to pray, "In the name of Jesus, in the name of Jesus." As the rebel's pounding intensified, Anna woke from her dream and sat straight up in bed. Her heart pulsated in her ears.

"Anna, it's okay." A soft light shimmered and illuminated her room. Anna turned her head toward the voice. Jesus sat once again in her chair, her old raggedy bear squashed in beside him. Anna stared at him and reached up to place her hand over her heart to quiet it. Max whined, stood up, and shook his head and body. His tags clinked together in the quiet room. Memories flooded in—memories of ten years ago—it all came back to her. Anna thought she'd remembered it as a dream, but there he was . . .

"Jesus?"

He smiled. He wore the same white t-shirt and jeans, but this time he had bright-colored Chacos on his feet.

An inexpressible peace flowed through Anna as she continued to stare at him. "I had a bad dream," she whispered more to herself than him.

"Yes, I know."

"Wha—what was that all about?"

"You were searching for the kids," he said. His voice calmed her.

"The soldiers—did the soldiers get them?"

"No, they're okay now, but they're still in danger."

"What can I do?"

"I need you to pray, Anna."

"But Jesus, I live here, and they're thousands of miles away."

"No, you don't understand. We're not fighting against human beings but against the wicked spiritual forces in the heavenly world, the rulers, authorities, and cosmic powers of this dark age."

She had no clue.

He sensed her confusion and smiled. "You don't pray against the soldiers in Sudan—you pray for this family in the heavenlies. Your prayers empower the strong angels to fight for them."

"But honestly, I don't know how to pray like that," she admitted. "I'm in tenth grade—sixteen years old. Can you teach me how to pray?"

"Better yet, would you like for me to show you?"

Anna stared at Jesus for a moment. *Did she want him to show her? Of course, she did.* Anna smiled at him and slowly nodded her head.

With a twinkle in his eyes, he said, "Well, come on, then." He reached out for her hand, and without hesitation, she grabbed hold.

A strange, tingly sensation pulsed throughout her body as Anna stepped from the physical into the spiritual realm. All the heaviness and confusion left her mind as she drank in the pure delight of this new world. There were no words in her vocabulary that described the experience as she held tightly to Jesus' hand.

Instantaneously, he transported them both to the same dark and horrifying place from her dream, but this time, Anna bore no fear. The kids still cowered together in the corner of the room. Favor prayed out loud, "In the name of Jesus." The same soldier pounded on the door. He turned and yelled curses into the night. In the shadows, dark and murky beings squirmed like a wad of snakes, curling, and hissing.

Jesus smiled at Anna and squeezed her hand. A dazzling light swirled around the room so intensely that she had to shade her eyes with her other hand. At that very moment, an ungodly and horrific shriek pierced the air from one corner of the room. Startled, Anna leaned back against Jesus and gripped his hand even tighter. As she did, a radiant and visible energy immersed the room, cleansing it from the evil within. Four colossal and extraordinarily beautiful beings appeared and bowed toward Jesus. He nodded. The angels lifted their swords, and the pounding on the door stopped. There was complete silence.

Wide-eyed, Anna whispered, "Where did they go?"

"They have left us for a while."

As Jesus spoke, they were instantaneously back in her room. Once again, Anna found herself curled up on her bed beside Max. Jesus relaxed in her chair.

"Wow." That was all she could say. Anna had no other words in her vocabulary. "Wow." Sometimes that word totally said it all. She gave Jesus a pitiful, questioning smile.

"Do you understand the power of prayer, Anna?" he asked.

"It all seems so impossible."

"It's impossible with human beings, but not with God. All things are possible for God. It's all written down in my Word to you."

Anna drew in a deep breath. "So, what do you want me to do?"

Jesus stood and walked over to Anna, took her two hands in his, and smiled down at her. He gazed straight into her eyes and spoke to her very soul. "Anna, you're a warrior. The Holy Spirit will empower you to be all that I need you to be. Do not worry about anything—He will guide and direct you. You will know what to do, what to say, and above all, how to pray for those four kids. Do not be afraid. I have commanded your guardian angel to stand beside you."

"Guardian angel?"

"Yes, you met him in the room with the kids."

Anna's eyes grew wide. "My guardian angel? That's really cool."

He smiled, his eyes sparkling with good humor. "He's always been with you, Anna, just as I have."

"Wow." There was that word again. "I really need to work on expanding my vocabulary," she said.

"Now I need for you to get some rest because tomorrow it all begins. Keep your eyes and ears open. Things are starting to happen."

Anna, and Anna loved her. Her heart broke when Grandmother Smith died of cancer four years ago.

She picked up the worn, dog-eared Bible and opened it to the first page. Curious, Anna began to read.

My Dear Anna,

The time will come when Jesus will teach you from His Word. I have prayed for you from the time you were a baby. You are in for the adventure of your life.

Much love,
Grandmother

With the Bible in her hand, Anna walked into the kitchen to find Dad cooking breakfast.

"Dad?"

"Hmm?"

"Did you know this Bible was for me?"

He furrowed his brow and puckered his mouth like he did when something puzzled him. "You know, I vaguely remember Grandmother Smith said something like that, but honestly, after she died, I packed up her books and never got around to going through them. I thought I packed that one away, too, but I must have stuck it in the bookshelf."

"Uh-huh. Well, is it okay for me to take it to my room?"

"Of course, honey. Come on back down as soon as you can. Your French toast will be ready, and you want to eat it while it's hot."

"Sure, Dad," she replied.

As she walked up the stairs, Anna thought about how this was too bizarre and coincidental to be true. So much had happened in the last couple of days. She couldn't seem to wrap her brain around it.

As Anna brushed her teeth, her phone vibrated. It was a group text from Grace to Shelby and her. She quickly rinsed out her mouth and picked up the phone.

Grace: "Hey!"

Anna: "Hey!"

Shelby: "Why are you texting me, Grace?"

Grace: "Because you won't talk to me! You're such a grouch in the morning!"

Anna: "What's up?"

Grace: "Are we still going to the game Friday night?"

Anna: "Sure. Ben wants to come, too."

Grace: "Cool"

Anna: "Let's be sure and invite the Knight kids!"

Grace: "K!"

Shelby: "Hello? Are you guys leaving me out?"

Anna: "Hey, Shel! Of course, not!"

Grace: "I guess my sister has decided to talk to us!"

Anna: "LOL. I've got to go eat breakfast. See you guys at school."

Grace: "CU2"

* * * *

An hour later, as Anna walked into the gym, she ran into Favor and Jonathan.

"Hey, guys," she said.

"Hey, Anna," they both said at the same time and then laughed.

"Are y'all still up for the baseball game this weekend?" she asked.

"Sure. We haven't been to a baseball game in years," said Jonathan.

"The ballpark is not far, so we can easily walk there," Anna said.

"What time?" Favor asked in her beautiful accent. "We can't leave until after six because we're going to try and skype the kids that afternoon after school."

"Really?" asked Anna. "How can you do that?"

"The kids are at a United Nations refugee camp that has Internet access that works sometimes, and sometimes it doesn't," Jonathan said. "We tried to talk to them a couple of days ago, but the call wouldn't go through. We hope to try and connect again Friday night."

"You know, I'd like to meet your kids," said Anna.

"You would?" Jonathan asked. "Great!"

"Why don't you come by the house before the game?" Favor offered. "Hopefully, we'll be able to connect. Our parents would love to meet you."

"That would be awesome. Thank you so much. Would it be okay for Grace, Shelby, and Ben to come?" Anna asked.

"Of course," Jonathan and Favor said at the same time.

"Anna . . ." Favor said. She hesitated, glanced at Jonathan, and then back to Anna. "We know you may not understand this yet, but God told our family that he would send us warriors, prayer warriors, to help us fight to get our kids back. We know who they are now."

Anna shivered and rubbed away the goosebumps that suddenly ran down her arms and then up the back of her neck. Should she tell them about her visit? She swallowed hard and was about ready to open her mouth when the bell rang.

Relieved, Anna said instead, "See you guys at lunch?"

"Sure," said Favor.

That day and the rest of the week passed uneventfully. On Friday, Anna even survived Mr. Jones's algebra class. To her surprise, she scored a B on the weekly quiz. Ben would be so proud of her. Who knew?

"Good job, Anna," said Mr. Jones.

He smiled proudly as he handed the test back to her. Anna figured that he was proud of himself, too, that his teaching finally got through to her. She ducked her head and caught Grace's eye across the aisle. She grinned and gave Anna a thumbs up.

Late that afternoon, Anna and Ben walked over to Grace and Shelby's house. They were both out on their front porch, swinging on the porch swing. Seeing them, Grace jumped up off the swing and almost caused Shelby to fall out. She grabbed hold, scooted to the middle of the swing and gave her sister a dirty look.

Ignoring her, Grace said, "Hey, guys. Let's go. They said they were going to try and connect at 5:00. It's 1:00 in the morning in South Sudan, but that was the only time the kids could get to the computer."

Mr. Knight answered the door with a welcoming smile. "Come in—come in. I'm Mr. Peter."

In the South, young people tended to call adults by their first name with a Mr. or Miss or Ms. in front of it. They introduced themselves, and Mr. Peter led the three girls and Ben downstairs to the basement where everyone had gathered around the computer.

Grinning, Jonathan motioned for them to come over. His mom, Ms. Ruth, was talking to four sleepy-eyed children who smiled back at her from the other side. The kids huddled together so that they could all see the monitor, each one with a huge, beautiful smile on their face.

Anna moved in closer to hear what they had to say.

"How are things going, Tut?" Ms. Ruth asked.

Tut respectfully nodded his head. "We are well, ma'am. Lala was very sick with the fever last week. We were worried about her, but she seems to be better now."

Lala giggled and covered her mouth with her hand.

"Is that so, Lala?" Ms. Ruth asked, concerned.

"Yes, ma'am," she whispered.

"We will pray for you, Lala," Ms. Ruth said.

Lala beamed and bowed her head in respect.

At that, Mr. Peter and David walked over beside Ms. Ruth to talk to the kids. They each took their turn and asked questions about what was going on at the refugee camp, the food, the weather, and if they needed anything. Jonathan and Favor then moved in to say hello.

After a short while, Favor said, "We want you guys to meet our new friends here in Johnson." She motioned for Anna and the others to step up to the monitor. "This is Anna and her brother, Ben, and her friends Grace and Shelby."

As Favor introduced them, Anna noticed Tut staring at her. He turned to Lala and whispered something. "Yes," he said. "We know of Anna."

Favor glanced at Anna, puzzled, and then back at Tut. "How do you know her?" she asked respectfully.

"Jesus has shown her to us."

What? Anna's heart skipped a beat, and her face started burning. Okay, now things were really getting weird. Shelby scowled and stared at her in disbelief. Anna just shrugged her shoulders and didn't say anything.

Favor didn't seem surprised at all to hear this. "What did he show you?"

"She was with *him*," said Tut, "but we did not know her name until now."

"She was praying for us," Lala added. Her face lit up with a beautiful smile.

Even Ulan and Achan nodded their heads.

What was Anna supposed to say? She smiled and mumbled something like, "Gladtomeetyaguys."

As Anna stepped away from the computer, Shelby grabbed her arm and hissed, "What was that all about?"

Anna shook her head. She didn't understand it herself, so how could she explain it to Shelby?

Despite Grace's efforts to get her to come to church, Shelby refused to even talk about it. Grace and Shelby's dad had died a year prior in a motorcycle accident. Shelby's faith died at the same time. After the accident, she wore nothing but jeans and black t-shirts and even dyed her hair black. Grace, however, survived by growing in her faith. While Shelby blamed God for her father's death, Grace grabbed hold of him and wouldn't let go.

Anna turned away from Shelby's grasp and stammered, "I . . . I don't know. I really don't know."

"Well, I'm out of here." She turned to go.

"Where are you going, Shel?" asked Grace.

"I'm going home." With that, Shelby walked out of the room.

CHAPTER SEVEN

Shelby stormed out of the house, angry. She didn't even know why. She hated it when things happened that she didn't understand or that were beyond her control. She reached the street and started to jog. Running helped clear her mind and settled her spirit. It cleansed her. She knew that she was unreasonable back there with her friends, but sometimes, she just couldn't help herself. What in the world was with these Knight people? Who did they think they were with their God this and their God that? None of it made sense to her at all. But, to be honest, she didn't like herself very much when she acted the fool. Of course, she'd never admit that to Grace.

She hadn't always been that way—not until last year. Not until *after* her dad died. As she jogged, she thought about how things had been before the accident. She'd been a daddy's girl. She readily admitted that. While her sister loved their dad, Grace spent most of her time with their mom since they liked the same things—shopping, make-up, girly stuff. But Shelby? She enjoyed nothing better than to hang out with her dad and his motorcycles. She loved everything about them—the noise, the smell of the wax and the grease, and, of course, the riding—that was the very best part.

She'd never forget when her dad bought her very own miniature bike for her tenth birthday, much to the dismay of her mom. He'd also bought the coolest pink helmet to go along with it. Her mom about had a fit, that was for sure. But her dad was a stickler for safety. He sat her down and talked about all the rules and responsibilities of owning a motorcycle. When

Shelby was fourteen, she couldn't wait to get her beginner's permit—not to drive a car, but to ride a bike. Dad had promised her that when she turned sixteen, if she was responsible, made good grades, all that important stuff to parents—he'd buy her a motorcycle. But here she was, sixteen years old, and her dad was gone.

Shelby's dad had been the president of the local motorcycle club, Rides, which had members from all walks of life. Every fall at Pinnacle Mountain, the group sponsored the Rides Rally, a fundraiser to help the local children's hospital. Shelby had enjoyed helping her dad plan the Rally every year by handling the social media.

It was a stupid, pointless accident that caused her dad's death. Shelby had been riding with him at the time. The most popular ride during the rally was the Pinnacle to the Greers Ferry Loop. This organized ride always started at sunrise and ended up back at the Pinnacle around noon for barbeque from the Pink Pig. There were stops along the way with food, prizes, and activities. Shelby and her dad always rode the route the day before the rally to make sure everything was in place for the participants. She'd enjoy the time alone with her dad before all the hustle and bustle began.

When they took off that morning, it promised to be a cool, gorgeous October day. As the sun rose, they mostly had the road to themselves, which was a good sign. The ride took them through beautiful, golden valleys dotted with cattle grazing in still, green pastures. Trees canopied the roads with stunning gold and red leaves. Shelby remembered stopping at a breathtaking overlook.

"Look, Shel," he said, "take it in. Take in all of God's glory."

Shelby didn't say anything but drank in the beauty of the scene in front of her.

"This is just a taste of what Heaven will be like," he said stretching his arms wide.

They both stood and gazed out to the valley, until her dad reluctantly said, "Okay, let's go."

It happened a few miles from that overlook. They were coming around a curve when they noticed a car off to the side of the road. A woman stood beside it signaling for help, obviously upset. As Dad waved toward the woman and slowed down, another car came around the curve from behind and hit them. They were both thrown from the motorcycle. Shelby ended up in a muddy ditch that softened her landing, but her dad landed on the hard asphalt.

Everything after that was a blur. She didn't remember a lot of what happened. Her dad died on the way to the hospital. Shelby's cries only added to the screams of the sirens. By the time the ambulance reached the emergency room, the sheriff had called her mom. She and Grace were waiting when Shelby stumbled out of the ambulance. She fell into their arms, devastated and inconsolable. Shelby had a broken arm, but the doctor sent her home that afternoon. She was heartbroken and couldn't or wouldn't leave her room except for the funeral a couple of days later.

At first, she kept telling herself that it hadn't happened—there was no way that her beloved dad was dead. Then she became angry— so angry—angry at God, at herself, even at her dad. She was angry at her mom and Grace and didn't even know why. She could not understand how God could take away her dad, one of the good guys—and even now, a year later, she still grieved. Her mom sold her dad's motorcycle, hoping that with it gone, they could start to heal. But Shelby seemed to sink deeper and deeper into her grief and depression. She was a mess, and she just couldn't dig herself out.

* * * *

A couple of months before, Shelby had met someone who caught her eye and helped her forget—for a little while, at least. One day as she walked home, she was about to cross the street when directly in front of her was the most impressive and magnificent motorcycle that she had ever seen. It was low-slung, jet black with an iridescent red flame that streamed along the side and glowed in the afternoon sun. A tall guy sat astride it dressed in black leather with black boots and a black helmet that covered his face. She noticed a red insignia on his jacket, but she couldn't make out what it was. He raised his hand in greeting, and she stopped a safe distance away from him. Something was compelling about the guy—but her natural instincts told her to beware.

"Hey," he said.

Shelby didn't say anything at first, but the bike totally mesmerized her. Finally, she said, "Cool bike."

"Thanks." He put down the kickstand, crawled off and removed his helmet.

Shelby stared at him for a moment. He was not handsome, but he had a captivating presence. His eyes seemed to bore into hers as she stared. Breaking the stare, she caught sight of a jagged red scar along the side of his forehead. At the end of the scar, close to his temple, was a small tattoo, a pointed star. She couldn't seem to take her eyes off it.

With an unabashed smile, he reached up and slowly rubbed his forehead and introduced himself as Lou.

"Hey, Lou."

He glanced down and lovingly patted the motorcycle. "Like it?"

Shelby drew nearer, transfixed by the beauty of the machine. She thought about her dad and how he would have been impressed, too. She shook aside her reservations and walked up to the bike to check it out.

"I'm Shelby," she said as she walked around the motorcycle. "This bike is amazing."

"You want a ride?"

Shelby stepped back. She hadn't ridden or even been this close to a motorcycle since the accident. "Nope, don't think so."

He smiled and said, "Okay, maybe another time. See ya around."

At that, he got back on his bike, turned the key and saluted her as it roared to life. She stood and watched as he disappeared down the street.

Lou was at the same place the next day and the next. It only took about a week before Shelby tossed caution to the wind and hopped on the bike behind him. Mom and Grace would not approve, but they didn't have to know. She just didn't care anymore.

* * * *

With all of this on her mind, Shelby jogged along the old railroad trail until she came to the end of it and had to stop, exhausted and wheezing. Holding her side, she bent over and tried to catch her breath. Finally, as she straightened up, a voice called out to her, "Hey, you look tired. Need a ride?"

Shelby was tired, not only because of the run, but weary of trying to make sense out of her life. She could find no good answers to her questions. It was all too painful. Sometimes, she thought she'd like to just give up.

"Hey, Lou," she said. "You know what? I *am* tired. I'd love a ride. Can you drop me off at the baseball game?"

Lou grandly swept his arm toward the bike and bowed. "Your chariot awaits, my lady."

CHAPTER EIGHT

Anna watched Shelby storm out of the house and thought her reaction and departure after the strange encounter with the Sudanese kids was a little over the top even for Shelby.

"What's with Shelby now?" she asked Grace.

"Oh, she's just being Shel," said Grace. "You know how she gets sometimes. It's okay. I'll talk to her later."

Favor walked up to them. "Anna, Grace, is everything all right?"

Shrugging off the mood in the room after the confrontation with Shelby, Anna smiled and said, "Yes, thanks. It was great to meet your kids."

Ms. Ruth called out from the kitchen, "I've got plenty to eat. Would you all like a sandwich before you go to the game?"

"Yes." Of course, that was Grace. She was always ready to eat.

"Thank you, Ms. Ruth. That would be great. Ben and I didn't have supper before we left," Anna said.

"Good. Hey, Jonathan, would you get the drinks? David and Favor, grab plates and utensils."

A few minutes later, they all sat around the dining table and held hands as Mr. Peter prayed, "Father, together we ask that you bless those around this table and our kids in Sudan. Protect them, Lord. Help us to reunite with them as soon as possible. I pray that you bless Anna and Ben as well as Grace and Shelby. Thank you for bringing their friendship into our family. Bless this food to the nourishment of our bodies and help us never to forget how fortunate we are to have all of this. In the name of Jesus, Amen."

After a chorus of amens, Ms. Ruth passed the lunch meat and bread and they made their sandwiches.

When everyone had fixed their plates and began to eat, Ms. Ruth said, "Wasn't it great to talk to the kids? I'm worried about Lala, though—she acted like she didn't feel very well. Do you think she's getting the care that she needs?"

Mr. Peter patted her hand. "We trust that she's in God's care until we get to her, Ruth."

"Yes, you're right. God has taken care of them so far, hasn't he?"

Ever the inquisitive one, Grace asked, "Mr. Peter, can you tell us more about what happened to your family in Mala—where were you?"

"Malakal," he finished for her with a smile.

Anna was glad Grace had asked that question. There was so much more that she wanted to learn about the Knights and their life in South Sudan. An urgency welled up inside her. *What made these people so special?* She had to figure them out.

"Dad, we told them about Christmas night and trying to get to the UN evacuation center," said Jonathan.

"Yes, we did get inside the base, but the conditions were terrible," Mr. Peter said. "We had little food and water between the nine of us even though the UN workers tried to provide for us whatever they could scrounge up."

David took a bite of his sandwich, chewed, covered his mouth, and then said, "Dad held a church service that first Sunday inside the camp. We were all so grateful that God had brought us to the camp safely. The room was full of people singing and praising God. Sudanese people sure know how to celebrate."

"Remember Lala and Achan dancing around the room?" asked Favor.

Jonathan and David burst out laughing, and Jonathan said, "I don't think I have ever seen anything like it."

CHAPTER SIX

The next morning, Max woke Anna by licking her face. When she opened her eyes, he wagged his tail and his warm brown eyes pleaded with her to start the day.

"Okay, Okay, Max, I'll take you outside."

As they walked out into the backyard, a gentle south wind wrapped itself around her. Anna took a deep breath, stretched out her arms and breathed in the rich, sweet fragrance of new spring—one of her favorite times of the year. Cleansing the cobwebs out of her brain, she spoke out loud to reassure herself. "Anna, was it a dream? Did it happen? Are you going crazy? No, I'm not—I remember everything."

Then she whispered, "Hello? Jesus? Angel?"

Silence.

Anna stood quiet for a moment and listened; then shrugged and said, "Nope—nothing. Come on, Max, let's go in the house."

Back inside, she paused beside the bookshelf in the den. There in plain sight was Grandmother Smith's Bible. Her grandmother was very contemporary for her time. She switched from the King James Version years ago to this parallel Bible with the Good News Bible on one side and the New International Version on the other. Anna remembered her grandmother so clearly, sitting in her prayer chair, her little dachshund, Ruby, curled up beside her, reading this very Bible. After Mom left, she was like Anna's rock, someone to turn to, talk to, who cuddled and rocked her when she cried. She loved

Anna sat and listened. She'd never been around a family like the Knights. Were they for real?

"Yes, the joy of the Lord was certainly in the camp that day," said Mr. Peter. "He got us through a lot of long, hot days and nights, didn't he, kids?"

There was a pause, and then Jonathan explained that they had to sleep in a small room which they had to share with fourteen other people. He said the room was so hot and crowded, but no one, not even the little kids, complained. They worried that the food supply was running low and they didn't know where to obtain more.

People had become suspicious of them and wondered if the family had received special favors, so, they knew they had to leave as soon as possible—but how could they abandon the children? Tut and his brother and sisters were in danger because they were from the Nuer tribe. The Nuer and Dinka tribes were in a fierce civil war, and the family feared that leaving the kids might have been a death sentence for them.

Their parents tried to convince Jonathan, David and Favor to fly out on one of the evacuation flights. No way. They figured that Jesus had put their family together, and they'd all stay or they'd all go.

"As you can guess, we all stayed," said Mr. Peter. He reached over and put his arm around his wife.

She smiled at him and said, "For ten days, we tried to obtain travel documents for the four kids, but the office where they generated the documents had been destroyed in a bombing. Then we appealed to the local governor, and he informed us that the kids were South Sudanese, and they were not our problem. He wouldn't give them permission to move to a safer place in the country much less move with us to the states—it was so frustrating."

Mr. Peter said, "One afternoon, while I was sitting outside trying to catch a bit of fresh air, Tut found me and said he needed to talk. He was so serious—I knew he must have had something important to say to me. He did—he assured me that he'd take care of his brother and sisters if we left them."

Mr. Peter shook his head, took a deep breath, and continued. "He's intelligent and mature—way beyond his fourteen years. Honestly, I didn't know what to say to him. I just wondered to myself how were we going to leave those kids to who knows what? I prayed that God would give me a clear and definite answer, but it was one of the most difficult decisions that we have ever had to make. We could only trust God from there on. It was heart-wrenching."

By that time, Anna's mind tried to process, without much success, everything that the Knights had shared with them.

Grace kept saying over and over, "Oh wow, oh wow."

Ben listened quietly, captivated by their story. They'd all learned about missionaries in church, but they'd always lived far away in some strange country. The Knights were missionaries that they could get to know personally. Anna had never met any people like them.

Mr. Peter said, "We didn't want to do it, but we had to leave the kids behind and fly back to the states. We hope to help them from here until God brings us back together."

"We've been raising money for if—*I mean when*—we get the kids out," said Jonathan. "We're also working with a group in Kenya to airdrop food and water close by the camp. We just heard the other day that an air transport had dropped one thousand pounds of food and supplies close to the UN camp. That made us feel a little better."

Never afraid to say what was on her mind, Grace asked, "So is Tut the only one taking care of the children?"

Favor said, "Do you remember us telling you about a man named Jafaar—the director of the orphanage? He and his wife, Zofa, are fiercely protective of them. We spoke to them online before you all got here. We're praying that God will give us a plan to get them all out of South Sudan."

"Yes," said Mr. Peter, "I sat down and talked to Jafaar for a long time before we were evacuated. We discussed several possible ways that we might reunite with the kids. Once they arrived at the camp, it was very difficult—and dangerous—to leave. They would have to travel without any official documents, but Jafaar was determined to make that happen. We gave him all the money that we had for their journey. We'd already discussed with him about helping us start an orphanage somewhere else, in another country—one that would serve other Sudanese refugee children. He and Zofa were very excited about all the possibilities. It would take a lot of money to make that happen, but who knows what God has planned?"

Anna listened and tried to absorb everything that the Knights said about their story, South Sudan, the four kids, Zofa, and Jafaar. She remembered Jesus's voice in her ear, *Anna, I want you to help them.*

What happened next to Anna was weird. It was like she was in the middle of a music video. As music played in the background, the story unfolded in front of her. As the Knights shared their story—Anna experienced a strange sensation. She stood off to the side as an observer and not a participant. Anna's heart fluttered when it hit her. Jesus had chosen *her* and placed *her* slap-dab in the middle of the Knight's story. She knew without any doubt that God would use her to do much more than pray for them. Somehow, Anna would help the Knights reunite with their South Sudanese kids.

But why me? How am I going to make that happen? No—how are we going to make that happen?

CHAPTER NINE

There was silence around the table as the group munched on their sandwiches. Anna glanced at her phone and noticed that it was getting close to game time. She held it up and said, "Looks like we better go if we're going to get to the game on time."

They all talked at once, gathered up the plates and cups and made their way to the kitchen. "You kids go on. I'll take care of cleaning up from here." Ms. Ruth insisted.

"Thank you so much for supper. It was great to meet y'all," Anna said.

Ms. Ruth came over, hugged her and whispered, "I think we'll see a lot of you in the future. Thank you." She turned toward Ben and Grace and gave them both a hug, too.

The ball field was a short distance from the house, so they decided to walk. It was a beautiful, warm spring evening. The spicy smell of new-mown grass and sweet jasmine filled the air. Cars full of people backed up down the street waiting to park. There was always an excitement in the air when Wakeland played Johnson in any sport.

Ben, Jonathan, and David wanted to beat the crowd, so they walked on ahead, eager to get in the ballpark and find everyone a good seat. Anna, Favor, and Grace lagged, talking about all kinds of things—mainly girl things. Favor had so many questions about American teenagers.

She asked about fashion, music, and what they did for fun. She especially had questions about the youth group at church.

"Come with us next Wednesday night to our Xcite Group," Grace said. "We have so much fun, and you'll love our group leaders."

"Yes," Anna said, "we're always doing something crazy, but we learn so much about being a Christ-follower."

"I'd like that very much, and I know that my brothers would, too."

Anna checked out the crowd streaming through the gate. "Well, I guess we'd better hurry and catch up with the boys."

As they approached the gate to get into the park, Grace stopped so fast that Anna almost tripped over her. Grace scowled.

"There's Shelby. I thought she went home."

"Where?" asked Anna.

"In the parking lot. Over there—by the fence."

Shelby had her back to them, talking to a strange guy.

"Who's that?" asked Grace.

"I don't know him," said Anna.

The guy was tall, dressed in blue jeans and despite the warm temperatures—a raggedy-looking motorcycle jacket. He had dark hair pulled back in a greasy bun at the back of his head. Shelby said something, and he laughed and reached up to pat her on the shoulder and then stepped back and leaned against a black Harley Davidson motorcycle.

Grace narrowed her eyes toward Shelby and the guy. "Well, I'm going to find out," she said.

Anna and Favor followed Grace as she threaded her way through the maze of cars. When they reached Shelby and the guy, Grace stopped abruptly, stood with her hands on her hips and said, "Shel, I thought you were going home."

Shelby hadn't seen the girls walk up, but the guy did. He raised his eyebrows and smirked at them.

Shelby turned around and frowned at her sister.

She shrugged and said, "I changed my mind." Shelby jerked her thumb at the guy and said, "He gave me a ride."

Grace stared directly at him. "Who's your friend?"

Shelby gestured toward him with her typical nonchalance. "This is Lou. We've—we've been sort of seeing each other." She placed her hand on his arm defiantly.

"Seeing each other?" Grace sneered. "Does Mom know?" she asked accusingly.

Anna's eyes flew from Grace to Shelby and then back at Grace. They just stared at each other.

"Well," said Grace, "she'll know now, won't she?"

"Yeah, maybe."

Lou raised his thick black eyebrows, crossed his arms and leaned back against the motorcycle. He didn't say a word.

There was something about this guy that gave Anna the creeps. She didn't know whether it was the smirk on his face, the scar on his forehead, the weird tat on his temple, or the way he stared at them, but, he made her skin crawl.

She took a step back and stammered, "We . . . we're going to miss the game if we don't hurry."

Favor stared at him and then said, quietly but firmly, "Kwa Jina la Yesu."

Anna didn't understand a word she said, but by the scowl on Lou's face, for some reason, it seemed like he did.

"Shelby, come on," said Grace, grabbing hold of her arm.

"Hey, let go," said Shelby. She jerked away from Grace and then turned toward Lou and said, "See ya later."

As they walked toward the gate, Anna couldn't stand it and turned around for one last peek at Lou.

"Where'd he go?" she said out loud.

Everyone stopped and turned to look—he was gone, motorcycle and all. Shelby, her posture rigid, just stared with a vacant expression on her face. Anna glanced over at her and shivered.

"You okay?"

Shelby still didn't move.

Anna shook off another chill. "Forget him. Let me text Ben to see where they're sitting." Her phone pinged and she glanced down at it. "They're in the bleachers over by the concession stand. Let's go watch the ballgame."

The game had already started when they found the guys sitting about halfway up the stands, already totally absorbed in the game. Because of the crowd, Shelby had to squeeze in beside Ben and the guys, and Anna, Grace, and Favor sat a couple of rows down below them.

The game wasn't very exciting for the first six innings. The teams were so closely matched that it was 0-0 at the top of the sixth.

A little bored, Anna tilted her head toward Favor and asked curiously, "Favor, what did you say to that guy back there with Shelby?"

Grace leaned around Anna and said, "Yeah, what did you tell him? Whatever you said, he sure didn't like it."

Favor stared out toward the field and didn't say anything. Anna wondered why she didn't answer and asked one more time. This time she turned toward Anna and Grace and said, "Kwa Jina la Yesu. In my language that means, in the name of Jesus."

"Why did you say that?"

"He is not good," she said with a vehemence that seemed so unlike her. "Sometimes you must call on the name of Jesus for protection."

"Well, I know that I didn't like him, that's for sure," said Grace. "I've got to find out more about him from Shelby."

"Your sister must stay away from this guy—he is evil."

The game picked up from there. By the bottom of the sixth inning, the score was Johnson one and Wakeland one. At the top of the seventh, Wakeland came alive and scored two more runs before they got three outs. Johnson was up last to bat, and at the bottom of the seventh, the crowd jumped to their feet. It was the top of the batting order, and two Johnson guys got base hits. The crowd went nuts, and then two more came up to bat and struck out. With two players on base and one last out, John Davis stepped up to the plate. He was a great shortstop but didn't have the best batting average. Anna could feel everyone around her hold their collective breath and then let it out after he swung and missed the first two pitches. The next two pitches were balls, so it was now two balls and two strikes. She grabbed hold of Favor and Grace's hands for the next pitch. The pitcher let loose the ball, and John smacked the perfect home run. It sailed out of the ballpark, and the crowd went absolutely crazy—the final score was Johnson 4 and Wakeland 3. Anna, Favor, and Grace jumped up and down, high-fiving all the people around them. Anna glanced back over her shoulder toward Shelby and the guys, and they were going nuts, too. She was glad to see Shelby have some fun for a change.

After the game, Anna, Favor, and Grace met up with Shelby and the boys at the concession stand. Since it was so late, Anna sent out a text to her dad to tell him that she and Ben would be home soon. As they walked down the street after the game, horns honked, and cars whizzed past. People stuck their heads out their windows and hollered. Their voices echoed back from the large oak trees along the road. A full, buttery moon hung high in the sky reflected against a wisp of thin, silvery clouds.

Favor walked beside Anna, quiet-like. Neither one of them said anything, until Anna asked, "Favor?"

"Yes"

"The baseball game was fun and all that, but how important is it in the scheme of things? Who cares? Here we are celebrating this victory, while at the same time, halfway across the world, four kids are fighting a battle—a battle for their very lives. How can I even wrap my mind around that? I want to help them, but how? What can I do here in Johnson, USA?"

Favor didn't say anything at first, but then she spoke, "We can't limit God, Anna. When I was a little girl, my grandmother taught me how to weave baskets. They were so intricate and beautiful, but she started with ugly strips of plain, brown grass. Everything is important to God. He has a plan—a mysterious plan—one revealed to us in scriptures. He weaves all things together to create perfection.

"All things?" Anna asked and shook her head. "Even baseball games?"

Favor was quiet for a moment. "Who knows, maybe he even works through a baseball game. What is important is that we're open to serve God wherever he plants us. We each must walk our own journey. God placed you right here in Johnson for a reason. You can't go to Africa, Anna, but God can still use you here."

The conversation turned to other things, but Anna's mind kept going back to what Favor had said. "God can use you here." *So, what can she do?* There was that question again—the one she asked Jesus. *What can I do?*

CHAPTER TEN

Still high on adrenaline after the game, Anna's mind flipped from one thing to another as she got ready for bed. She thought about all that had happened in the last five days—meeting the Knights and their Sudanese kids, Shelby and that creepy guy, Lou, the excitement of the win over Wakeland, and of course, the visit. Up until now, she lived the typical teenage life, attended school, hung out with her friends at the mall—just tenth grade ordinary. Honestly, Anna had no idea what to make of it all. *Overwhelmed? Oh, yeah.*

"What do you think, Max? What do you think?"

When Anna was alone with Max, she kept up an ongoing stream of conversation with him. Talking to Max helped her process her thoughts. He would focus his beautiful brown eyes on hers, cock his head and wag his tail. Max just *got* her. She smiled, reached down and rubbed his silky ears—he loved that.

"Thanks, Max. I think so, too. Come on, let's put your short self in bed."

She picked him up, placed him on her bed and then crawled in after him. Anna fluffed up her pillows and snuggled into the covers. Max edged over, swirled up warm against her and promptly fell asleep.

Anna sat back against the pillows, laid her hand on his head, and stared over at a poster on her wall. It was a cool picture of her favorite Christian rock band, The Righteous

Descendants. There was a scripture at the bottom of the poster that said, *For I know the plans I have for you," says the Lord. "They are plans for good and not for disaster, to give you a future and a hope. In those days when you pray, I will listen. If you look for me wholeheartedly, you will find me.* They won a *Dove Award* for a song based on that scripture. It was one of those songs that got stuck in your head and played over and over. Anna closed her eyes and sang the chorus quietly to herself.

"Plans for good and not disaster;
For a future and a hope.
When you pray—I will listen.
When you pray—I'll be there."

So many thoughts bounced around inside her head. What's real—what's not? Who knew? It was all so very confusing. Anna glanced over at her nightstand where she'd placed Grandmother's Bible that afternoon. *I wish I could talk to Grandmother. She always helped me think through things . . .*

She reached over and picked up the Bible. Anna settled back into the pillows, opened it and began ruffling through the pages. A thin, crinkly piece of paper fluttered out and onto her bed. It was that old-fashioned and transparent stationery that Grandmother used to write on when she wrote to her friend in France. Anna asked her about it one day. Grandmother had chuckled and said the paper was thin so that she wouldn't need to pay so much for postage. She always tried to save money one way or the other. Anna carefully opened the fragile sheets and recognized Grandmother's beautiful handwriting. As a former schoolteacher, she wrote neatly, each letter perfectly formed. Amazed, Anna realized that it was a letter to her. She began to read:

January 13, 2012

Dear Anna,

I guess that by the time you read this, you have grown into quite a beautiful young lady. As a little girl, it was clear that God had his hand on you. There was something sweet and innocent about you that could only have come by a special touch from Jesus. You had his heart.

Anna, you always had so many questions. From the time you could talk and follow me around, you repeatedly asked me this and asked me that. Many times, I felt that my answers were so inadequate, but you would just smile and pat my hand, and then ask more questions. It was clear that God had something extraordinary planned for your life.

You were so young when your mama left, but you were able to bring all of us such joy, comfort, and even peace. I remember you and I praying together one day, and you prayed, "Thank you, Jesus, for coming to visit me." Curious, I asked you about it, and you smiled your innocent smile and said, "Jesus talks to me." I believed you.

Well, Anna, that gives me such a sense of peace to know that when I am gone, He will always be with you. He said he would never leave you or abandon you.

There will be times in your life when discouragement and fear threaten to overwhelm you, but Jesus will always be there. He said he calls you his friend because he has made known things to you. He chose you—You, Anna, to produce beautiful fruit. Whatever you ask in Jesus' name, He will give you. That is very, very exciting.

I won't have the privilege of seeing you grow up into the lovely and Godly woman that I imagined that you would become. But, please know that the prayers that I have sent up for you and Ben will continuously be circulating between heaven and earth. There will come a time when we will be together again forever and ever. Won't that be incredible?

In the meantime, I want you to know that I love you with all my heart, and I am so proud of you.

In Christ's love and mine,
Grandmother

Anna had to reread the last two paragraphs several times because of the tears that blurred her vision. The last ten years had taken a toll on her family and as the "big sister," she was supposed to be the responsible one, but sometimes? Sometimes she got tired of that person, and all Anna wanted to do was hide in her room with Max. So much had happened that broke her heart—her mother left them, and her grandmother died of breast cancer.

She worried about the kids in South Sudan and even Shelby and her unhappiness. Anna leaned over and buried her face into Max's warm, furry body and cried great heaving sobs that went on and on until finally—it was over. She straightened up and glanced around. She hoped that she might see Jesus sitting across the room in her rocking chair, but it was empty except for the old teddy bear and Sally Primrose. Anna lay back against her pillows and stared at the ceiling devoid of all feeling and emotion. But, as she continued to stare, a quiet peace engulfed and filled her empty brain. Where did that come from? Exhausted, she leaned over once again, gathered Max in her arms and fell asleep.

Sometime in the night, Anna dreamed that she stood outside of the United Nations compound. Her hands grabbed hold of the barbed wire fence as she peeked through it. The four kids were on the other side. Achan and Lala cried as Ulan and Tut reassured and comforted their sisters. Anna tried, but she couldn't reach them. Feeling an ominous presence behind her, she turned around and caught sight of Lou and Shelby. He turned his face up toward the sky and laughed, a hideous sound that vibrated through the barbed wire.

Shelby stood nearby, her face contorted in horror. She shrieked at Anna. "Help me, Anna. Oh, God! Help me!"

The kids howled the same thing, "Help us, Anna. Help us."

Lou continued to laugh, and the hideous sound filled the air with a visible blackness.

Anna's heart thudded in her chest and into her ears. She began shouting at him, "In the name of Jesus. In the name of Jesus."

Lou scowled at her and said, "Stop that, Anna. He can't help you."

"In the name of Jesus. In the name of Jesus," she continued screaming at him.

Slowly, little by little, Lou began to melt in front of her eyes.

Anna turned away from him and noticed Ulan, Achan, and Lala huddled together under Jesus' right arm. His left arm circled Tut's slender shoulder as he calmed and comforted all of them. Tut stood tall and strong beside Jesus. Jesus glanced over at her and smiled his beautiful smile and gave her a thumbs up. Smiling back, she thought, *did Jesus really give me a thumbs up? It's a dream, right?*

Tut beamed at her and mouthed, "Thank you."

Anna searched for Shelby. She was gone.

CHAPTER ELEVEN

Anna woke up Saturday morning as Max stirred beside her. Sunlight streamed into her room, and she realized that they'd both slept later than usual. Max was an early riser, so Anna had to be also, but it was already eight o'clock.

"Hey, Max. Thanks for letting me sleep."

He stood up, shook all over and sneezed two times.

Anna reached over, gently cupped his head in her hands, and gave him a quick kiss. "I think you're allergic to the morning. You always sneeze when you wake up."

Max wagged his tail and Anna laughed.

"Come on. I'll let you outside."

Anna grabbed her robe and her phone and walked down the stairs to let Max out into the yard. As she walked out the backdoor, her phone dinged with a text message from Grace.

Grace: "Hey, Anna! Let's plan something fun today!"

Anna: "What do you want to do?

Grace: "I dunno. Any ideas?"

Anna: "Mall?"

Grace: "No money."

Anna: "Walk to the Dairy Bar?"

Grace: "Did that last weekend."

Anna: "Hey, I know! Let's climb Pinnacle Mountain!"

Grace: "We haven't done that since last fall. I bet the Knight kids would like to go, too."

Anna: "Especially David? Wink, wink—hmm???"

Grace: "Just don't know where you're going with that!"

Anna: "How about Shelby? Do you think she would want to go?"

Grace: "She's still in a snit, but I'll ask her."

Anna: "Hey, I'm starving. Got to eat breakfast. Talk to you soon."

A few minutes later, Anna followed her nose to the kitchen. She stopped at the door, breathed in deeply and quoted Grandmother, "Oh my stars and good heavens—what is that delectable aroma?"

Dad was frying bacon and flipping his famous Saturday morning pancakes—the best pancakes in the entire world.

"Good morning to you, too." He chuckled and piled her plate with the hot, buttery discs of deliciousness and three pieces of crispy bacon, cooked the way she liked.

Anna drowned the pancakes in warm maple syrup, sighed with pleasure and took her first bite. Savoring it for a sweet moment, she muffled, "Hey, Dad, would you take a group of us to the Pinnacle today?"

"What was that you said? Try that again without a mouth full of pancakes."

Anna took a gulp of milk to help swallow the pancakes, took a deep breath and tried again. "Grace and I thought it would be fun to climb the Pinnacle today, and we were wondering if you'd take us?" She swallowed one more time and coaxed him with a smile. "You know you're always ready for an adventure." Anna's friends loved her dad. He was their go-to guy when it came to take them places.

"Oh, yeah?"

"We want to invite the Knight kids to come along."

"I might be able to arrange that."

"Arrange what?" Ben walked into the room. His unruly hair stuck out perpendicular to his head and it appeared like he just got out of bed—which he probably had. The first thing on Ben's mind when he got up in the morning was food.

"Dad's driving us to the Pinnacle. Do you want to go?"

"Sure, sounds like a plan."

"I tell you what, we should finish with our climb about two o'clock and everyone will be starving. Why don't I slap together some sandwiches, chips, and drinks, and we'll have a picnic at the bottom of the Pinnacle?" Dad said. "I'll throw in some granola bars to hold us over until we eat lunch."

Anna texted the group after she finished her breakfast and went upstairs to get ready.

Two hours later, everyone gathered in Anna's front yard. Dad packed a picnic basket, drinks, Frisbees, and sunscreen in the back of his SUV.

Anna, Shelby, Grace, Jonathan, and Favor piled in the back while David sat up front with Dad. Several miles down the road, David turned around and said, "We have more news this morning about the kids."

Everyone in the car stopped talking, all eyes and ears riveted on David.

"Dad talked to Jafaar early this morning. Last night there was a skirmish inside the UN compound. Two of the rival groups began fighting with each other with machetes and small arms. Several people died. Our kids are in danger."

The car was silent as the reality of what might happen to the kids suddenly overshadowed the joy of the morning.

Grace asked, "So, the kids . . . are they okay?"

"Yes, everyone is fine, but we know now that we have to get them out of South Sudan as soon as possible."

Anna remembered the beautiful brown eyes and sweet smiles of the four kids. "But how?" she asked.

"We have a plan, but it's a dangerous one," David said. "Jafaar and Zofa will journey with the family. They must escape from South Sudan, but we're not sure which direction they will go, either to Uganda or into Ethiopia. Whichever way, the trip will be treacherous and long for all of them, especially the youngest. But, they must leave now before everything gets worse. There is something important that we must do when we get to the top of the Pinnacle."

"What's that?" Anna asked.

"We're going to pray."

Silence filled the car for the rest of the drive. Anna thought about the trip ahead for the kids and all the dangers that they would face during their journey.

When they arrived at the park, the group unloaded the car and gathered around David. "This is what I want us to do. When we reach the top of the Pinnacle, we're going to pray. Our family trusts that when you pray in the name of Jesus and believe, he will answer that prayer. We can't be with the kids physically on their journey, but we can be there in spirit. That's as powerful or even more so."

When they started to hike up the Pinnacle, the boys raced on ahead while Anna and Grace walked together. Shelby hiked alongside Favor, and Anna noticed that they were in deep conversation. Dad quickly fell behind.

He called up to them from the third switch back, "It's okay, I'm okay, don't worry about me."

Anna laughed down at him, waved and yelled, "You can do this, Dad!"

Hiking was easy at first but soon became more difficult as the trail twisted and turned around and over rocks and boulders. It was unusually warm for March and the sun beat down on their heads as they hiked. Anna and Grace had to stop often to wipe the sweat out of their eyes and catch their breath.

"I've got to get in better shape."

She giggled and said, "Why don't you sign up with me to join the track team?"

Anna groaned and mumbled, "Yeah, like that's going to happen."

As they neared the top, the sun disappeared, and storm clouds rumbled in the west. Ben, Jonathan, and David reached the summit of the Pinnacle first. They hollered and encouraged everyone to come on up. Finally, Anna and Grace stepped over the last boulder and reached the boys. Anna caught her ragged breath and gazed out at the magnificent valley view.

"Wow." She willed her breathing to slow down as she drank in the splendor of the panorama.

"Where's Dad?"

Amused, Ben said, "I think we lost him a little way back."

About ten minutes later, Dad stumbled up over a rock. He grabbed hold of his side and bent over. "Okay, every year this gets harder and harder."

Ben and Anna chuckled, walked over and gave him a drink of water. "You okay, old man?" said Ben.

Dad could only nod.

David gave everyone time to catch their breath. He motioned for them to gather around. They stood in a semi-circle, held hands and gazed out over the edge of the bluff. As thunder rumbled in the far distance, a soft north wind began to blow and, thankfully, cooled off their sweaty bodies.

They bowed their heads as David prayed, "Father God, we come to you and ask for protection for our brothers and sisters. Send your angels to stand guard around them, guiding Jafaar in this dangerous journey. Keep them safe and reunite them with us very soon. In the name of Jesus. Amen."

At the end of the prayer, Anna lifted her head. She sucked in her breath. A magnificent being stood right behind David. He was heads taller, a giant man clothed in white and gold. His skin was as black as his clothes were white. He had an iridescent, rainbow-like staff in his right hand. He raised it above his head. A strong gust of wind blew up around the group and filled the air with dust and debris. The clouds parted, and a gilded light streamed down from above illuminating the particles like gold dust. Wide-eyed and delighted, they watched as the golden specks drifted back to the ground, sparkling in the light. Amazed, with arms outstretched, they caught the glittering flakes in their hands, and then—poof!—they vanished along with the beautiful angel being.

Anna stood for a moment in awe. *What had happened?* She turned toward Ben.

"Whaa . . . what was that?" Ben asked.

With a quizzical expression on his face, Anna's usually rock-steady, practical dad sat down hard on a nearby boulder.

He caught her eye and could only throw up his hands, raise his eyebrows, and shake his head. Anna sat down and leaned her head against his shoulder.

"Okay . . . I . . . I . . . what was that?" Grace said with wonder. She held out her arms and peered down at them. "Did I have . . .?"

Shelby backed away from the group and turned to sit down on one of the boulders, her face pale, bewildered even. Grace walked over and sat down beside her. She tried to put her arm around Shelby, but she shrugged it off.

"Did you see him, Shel? Did you see him?"

"I don't know—I don't know, Grace."

Favor stood away from them, her eyes closed, and her face turned to the sky.

A crack of thunder sounded in the distance.

"Hey, guys," Dad called out. "We better get off this mountain before we get soaked."

They turned to hike back down the mountain—all that is except Shelby, of course.

"Come on, Shel," Grace said. She stood with her hands on her hips. Shelby sat motionless and stared out across the valley. "Shelby, let's go. We're going to get wet."

Grace grabbed Shelby by the tail of her hoodie, urging her to move.

"Please."

After a streak of lightning lit up the sky, Shelby finally got up and followed Grace. Anna waited for them at the top of the trail, and they hurried back down the path—the easy one this time—to the base of the mountain. About halfway down, it began to pour. By the time everyone reached the bottom, they were all laughing and soaked to the skin.

Dripping wet and chilled to the bone, the group gathered under a picnic pavilion. As usual, Grace was the first to speak her mind.

She turned to Favor and asked, "What? *What* just happened on the top of the Pinnacle?"

Favor spoke in her quiet but firm voice. "It has begun."

CHAPTER TWELVE

With a jolt, Tut opened his eyes and sat straight up on his makeshift pallet. *Was that gunfire or thunder?*

Another crack rattled the building and sent his heart racing.

Raining in March? The rainy season is two months away. What is happening?

Jafaar was up and moved hurriedly around the room while Zofa picked up blankets and Luka woke up the other three kids.

His voice calm yet urgent, Jafaar whispered to Tut, "We are leaving. God has sent a thunderstorm. Hurry! We must hurry. At six o'clock they open the gate for the supply truck. I pray that the guard's attention will be on the truck and not on us."

Achan rubbed her eyes, walked over and placed her small hand in her brother's. "Tut, I'm scared."

"I know, little sister, but you must be quiet. Baba will tell us what to do."

In less than five minutes, they had gathered at the door. Jafaar turned toward the group and said, "Zofa, I will lead. You and Ulan follow behind me. Luka, you stay in the middle. Lala, grab Achan's hand. Tut, you will bring up the rear. We must try and stay together. It is pouring rain outside, and we pray that the guards will be more concerned about their comfort than about us. You must move quickly and not lag. Do you understand? One more thing, and this is very important. If anyone separates from the other, make your way to the river."

"Where along the river, Baba?" Tut asked.

"We will meet at the washing jetty."

Tut and the children knew it well. They had often played along the banks while their mother laundered their clothes.

Tut studied the faces of his brother and sisters. "We are ready, Baba."

Zofa held Ulan's hand while Lala stepped up and reached for Achan's. Luka caught Jafaar's eye and nodded.

Jaffaar gave all an encouraging smile, opened the door and ushered the group outside into the violent storm. The wind caught their clothes and belongings and whipped them around and around. Torrential rain fell in sheets almost blinding them. Hands clasped tightly together, they hugged the building and moved as a group toward the closed gate. They would have to wait for a while until a truck arrived and the guard opened the gate. Drenched and miserable, they crouched behind a stack of wooden pallets.

At last, headlights shone through the gate and a truck honked. With a quick glance toward heaven, Jafaar prayed out loud, his voice lost in the storm. "Father, protect us."

The rusty gate swung out wide and the truck drove through and stopped at the guard house. Zofa stood behind Jafaar. They squinted through the rain and watch as the soldiers walked over to the vehicle. It was time. Jafaar squeezed Zofa's hand and she, in turn, passed it down the line through each person until it got to Tut at the end. Slow and steady, they moved as one toward the opening. At the same time, the truck shifted and drove into the camp. As soon as the vehicle began to move, the group took the opportunity and stumbled quickly forward.

"Stop!" The soldiers had spotted them.

"God help us," Jafaar prayed out loud. He grabbed Zofa who held tightly to Ulan's hand. They ran blindly through the rain and prayed that they were heading in the right direction. Squinting through the deluge, Jafaar turned back and stopped. It was raining so hard by this time, that he couldn't see anyone else until Luka bumped up against him.

"Where are Tut and the girls?" he yelled.

"I've lost them," he shouted back at the top of his voice.

Helpless to do anything, Jafaar yelled back, "Hopefully, Tut is with them, and they'll meet us at the river."

* * * *

Tut tried to swallow his panic. He was right behind the two girls when Achan tripped taking Lala down with her. He pulled them both up to their feet and yelled, "Run!"

He took off after them as a bolt of lightning flashed and struck so close that he could feel the tingle through the soles of his feet. A loud crack of thunder sounded as a downburst from heaven hit him as he ran for his very life, pelted by the torrential rain. He could only pray that the girls were still in front of him.

Rat-a-tat-tat.

Gunfire? Tut ducked instinctively and loped forward. He hoped that he was running the right way. He tripped, regained his balance and continued to sprint through the brush. He stumbled over something in his path. It was Achan and Lala. Achan was crying and holding her leg.

"Tut, something hit my leg. It hurts so bad! Help me."

Tut scooped her up and yelled at Lala. "Come on. This way."

As they ran, a massive, giant of a man, his skin as dark as night, stepped out in front of them and blocked their way. Frightened, Tut stopped abruptly, almost dropping Achan.

"Do not be afraid," the man said. His voice rang clear; easily understood above the din of the thunderous rainstorm. "You must follow me."

Tut hesitated for a moment, but they had no other choice. He motioned for Lala to follow, and they trailed the man through the brush.

"Where are Ulan and the others, Lala?" Tut yelled.

She'd clearly heard the giant man in the storm but couldn't make out what Tut had said. She put her hand to her ear. He yelled again.

"I don't know, brother," she yelled back.

Abruptly, the rain stopped and replaced the deafening din with total silence except for the sound of water dripping. The early morning sun filtered through the trees. The rain-soaked leaves caught the light and sparkled like diamonds.

The big man stopped, turned around and pointed toward the west. "You must follow this wadi for about a kilometer. Do not veer from it. You will find the river from there." At that, he walked away and disappeared into the bush.

"Wait," Tut called after him. "Who are you? Where did you come from? Sir, don't leave us, please."

Exhausted, Tut sat Achan gently on the ground and plopped down beside her.

"Tut, my leg hurts."

"Let me look." He leaned over to examine her leg. "I think a bullet just grazed it."

Tut ripped the sleeves out of his shirt. He wiped the blood from the wound with one sleeve and wrapped her thin calf with the other.

"It won't be long, sister. We will find Jafaar and Zofa, I promise. We must keep walking. Can you hop on my back?"

"Yes, I can," she said.

As they continued, Tut remembered the large man's warning to stay in the wadi. With Achan on his back, he had to tread carefully because of the roots that twisted toward the water at the bottom of the ravine.

About an hour later . . . could it be? Yes! Familiar voices! With a cry of complete joy, they rushed toward the sound. Their family rested on two massive flat rocks by the river. When Jafaar spotted them, he yelled and jumped to his feet. Ulan ran toward them. "It's Tut! It's Lala! It's Achan!"

Everyone laughed, hugged and talked over each other.

"Are you okay, Achan?" Zofa asked.

Achan managed a weak smile and nodded.

Concerned, Zofa gently removed the bandage that Tut had placed on her leg. She reached into her bag and pulled out a cloth scarf. She dipped a corner of it into the river and gently cleaned off the dried blood around the wound. At that, Achan began to sob, not that it hurt so much, but because she was so glad to be safe. Zofa wrapped the scarf around Achan's leg, and then pulled her into her arms and rocked her.

Drained and reassured that Achan was all right, Tut walked over and sat down on a rock beside Luka. He drew in a visible breath and then let it out. They made it. It was so good to be back together. For a while, he thought they would never see each other again. Overwhelmed, Tut placed his face in his hands and tried to hold back the tears. Jafaar sat down on the other side of him.

"You did well, my son."

His head still in his hands, Tut shook his head.

"I was terrified, sir."

"We all were, Tut."

Finally, he dropped his hands and said, "Honestly, Baba, we were so lost. We had no clue where we were or where we were going. I had Achan on my back and Lala was behind me. We ran—blinded by the rain—if it hadn't been for that man . . ."

Curious, Jafaar asked, "What man, Tut?"

"A man stopped us on the path and pointed us in this direction. He was the tallest man that I have ever seen—must have been over seven feet tall. Ask Lala and Achan. They saw him, too."

"If you say you saw a giant of a man, I believe you."

Tut felt more at peace after his talk with Jafaar. He walked back to the group, followed by the two men.

Jafaar addressed everyone, "Our journey has begun. The soldiers may shrug their shoulders and forget about us or they might come after us, so we can't stop too long and take that chance. I cannot lie and tell you that the rest of the journey will be easy. There are many dangers ahead, but if we stay together and pray, with God's help, we will make it safely to the border. The rainy season begins in two months. That does not give us a lot of time to travel. Zofa, Luka, and I are very proud of all of you. God has his hand on us already."

Tut directed his gaze at his family and then back at Jafaar. "Baba, I speak for my brother and sisters. We are destined and determined to make this journey. We understand and recognize the difficulty and the dangers." He turned back toward his brother and sisters. "We can do this. We are ready." Wide-eyed, Achan, Ulan, and Lala solemnly nodded their heads in agreement.

CHAPTER THIRTEEN

Sunday morning, Anna woke up early with Max licking her ear.

"Ugh, Max, don't you want to stay in bed this morning?"

She turned over and buried her head under two pillows. Max whined and dug under the pillows and nosed her. Anna grumbled as she sat up on the side of the bed, slipped her feet into furry rabbit house shoes, and pulled on her robe. She lifted Max down off the bed and he hit the floor running, excited about his new day. She shuffled down the stairs and followed him to the kitchen door.

"How can you be so energetic this early in the morning, Max? I wish I were more like you."

He ignored her. Wiggling all over, Max waited as she opened the door and then, howling to the high heavens, he streaked out to the patio to chase a squirrel that dared to come into his yard. Anna shook her head and smiled, shut the door and went back upstairs.

She sat on the side of the bed and picked up Grandmother's Bible. Grandmother had written all through her Bible. She'd highlighted scriptures in different colors, bookmarked them, and jotted down notes along the margins. Curious, Anna turned to one of the bright colored bookmarks. It opened to John, chapter fourteen.

"I tell you the truth, anyone who believes in me will do the same works I have done, and even greater works, because I am going to be with

the Father. You can ask for anything in my name, and I will do it, so that the Son can bring glory to the Father.

Grandmother had written a note beside this scripture that said, *Jesus will do anything that I ask in His name only if He will be glorified.* She had highlighted the words *so that the Son can bring glory to the Father.*

Is that true? Anything? Greater works? Anna had to admit that she didn't know what that meant. So many people were more spiritual than her, and they didn't always get what they asked for . . . *or did they*? Where did that thought come from?

"Did they, Anna?"

She could have sworn an audible voice spoke to her.

"Hello?"

There was nothing but silence.

"Wait and see."

Okay, there it was again. Anna stood up and hugged the Bible against her chest and began to pace around the room.

"I know it's you, Jesus. Talk to me, please. I need to know about all of this. I'm in the middle of a pretty serious situation here with the Knight kids and Shelby and . . . my . . . my life is so crazy now, Lord."

Tick—tick—tick—only the annoying sound of her bedside clock. Anna plopped back down on the bed and sat as still as possible, straining to hear. Nope—nada—zilch. She opened the Bible one more time hoping to get an answer, but nothing made sense.

"Hey, Anna. Who ya talking to?" Ben yelled through the door.

"Uh . . . no one, Ben."

"Well, Dad said to get dressed. We're going to be late for church."

Anna glanced at the clock and yelped, "Oh my goodness. I'll hurry."

"Yeah, right. That's a first."

Anna had made plans with the Knight family to meet them at church since it was their first time, so she couldn't be late—but, she *did* want to look cute. Anna smiled to herself and thought about Jonathan—would he even notice what she was wearing? At least she could give it a try. Guys didn't pay much attention to her, at least not the way they noticed the "popular" girls. Sometimes, Anna had to admit that she was envious of those girls. It would be nice if a guy asked her out on a date (which hadn't happened) or kissed her (which definitely hadn't happened). Guys considered Anna as a friend. They'd talk to her about their girlfriends or if so- and-so would go out with them. Maybe, it would be different with Jonathan—he certainly wasn't like any other guy that she'd ever met. A girl could only hope, so back to that cute outfit.

Anna ran to the closet and rummaged through her clothes. "No, no, no—yes, yes, yes." She grabbed a cute jean skirt and a striped tee.

What do I wear with this?

Grandmother always said accessories made the outfit. A girl wasn't dressed without them.

"Hmmm, what do you think, Max? How 'bout that polka dotted scarf with my new jeweled converse shoes?"

Of course, Max agreed. She finished dressing and added a pair of yellow, dangly earrings and a darling Dachshund pin for her shirt. She hurried to the bathroom, brushed her hair into a high ponytail, swished a little blush on her cheeks, and applied mascara. As she brushed her teeth, Anna walked over and checked her outfit in the full-length mirror. She ran back to the sink, rinsed her mouth and glanced down to make sure she hadn't spit toothpaste on her T-shirt. Satisfied, she spritzed on a yummy new fragrance and slipped a sweater over her shoulders to complete the look. Anna couldn't resist one last glance in the mirror. Smiling at her reflection, she turned and skipped down the stairs.

Dad and Ben waited for her at the front door. Dad pushed a Pop-tart into one of her hands and a mug of milk in the other. Grateful, Anna smiled her thanks and munched on her breakfast as she walked to the car.

"You look very nice this morning, Anna," Dad offered as he opened the door for her since her hands were full.

Mumbling through a mouthful of cinnamon Pop-Tart, Anna tried to get out "thank you," but it came out "flankflu."

She gulped down the milk to help swallow the dry pastry, finished her breakfast and sat in silence for the rest of the trip. Anna thought about the scripture that she'd read this morning. *When you ask me for anything in my name, I will do it . . .*

The parking lot was almost full when they arrived, so they had to park at the far end of the lot.

"Come on, Dad," Anna urged, quickly getting out of the car. "Church is just about ready to start. We're late."

"I wonder why?" mused Ben.

"Okay, okay, I know. I made us late," she admitted.

Anna spotted the Knights as soon as she, Ben, and Dad walked in the door. They stood over in the corner, talking to the youth pastor, Pastor John. Jonathan waved, and Anna walked over to greet them.

Pastor John said, "Well, guess it's about time to start. I'd better get up front."

They followed him into the sanctuary and found a group of seats right in the middle.

Grace had recently started singing with the worship team. Up on stage, she grinned and waved at Anna as the lead pastor, Pastor Eric, stepped forward to open the service. Anna scanned the crowd but didn't see Grace's mom or Shelby.

Anna mouthed to Grace, "Where's Shelby?"

Shelby had promised her sister that she would come to church that morning. Grace shrugged and shook her head as if to say, "I don't know."

As the service began, Anna glanced at the bulletin and noticed that Pastor John was preaching. His youthful perspective always left her with something to chew on for the rest of the week. The sermon series for March came from the book of Acts. As Pastor John preached on the healing of Tabitha from Acts nine, Anna listened, totally captivated by the story of Paul raising Tabitha from the dead. Something resonated inside of her when Pastor John concluded the sermon with, "Do you still believe in miracles?"

With that thought in her mind, the praise team stepped back up to their microphones and the congregation entered into praise and worship—admittedly, Anna's favorite part of the service. The music always transported her to a different place. Anna closed her eyes and allowed her mind to focus on the glory of God. She always pictured Jesus sitting over in the corner during praise and worship. He would smile, tap his feet and even get up now and then and walk among the worshippers. As the music swelled, tears welled in her eyes and rolled down her cheeks. Anna grabbed several tissues from a box stuck in the chair in front of her and swiped at her face. People around her fell to their knees and cried out to God. Drawn by the Spirit, Anna walked to the altar at the front of the room and bowed down, and, as she did, someone kneeled shoulder to shoulder beside her and began to pray. She recognized the voice—Ms. Ruby. Ms. Ruby was in her 80's, a bona fide woman of God. Her prayers had touched people in this church for several generations. She operated in the gifts of the Holy Spirit, especially a gift called "the Word of Wisdom." The pastor explained that this special gift from God enabled a person to share spiritual wisdom and discernment with another.

"Lord, thank you for Anna. Thank you for her sweet spirit. Her heart yearns for you, Lord. Open her eyes to understand this new journey. She has questions, God. She needs answers, and I know that you speak with her. Thank you for using her in this rescue. Give her courage to fight against the evil one who wants to steal her confidence and joy. I pray that your name will be glorified in this."

Anna realized this was an answer to her prayer from earlier that morning. She reached out and took Ms. Ruby's hand as she continued to pray. "Lord God, Anna asks a lot in your name. I pray that you will answer her prayers directly and specifically. This is important to your kingdom. Keep her safe, Lord. Protect her in Jesus' name. Amen."

Anna said her own "amen" and reached over to help Ms. Ruby up off her knees.

"Thank you. I needed to hear that, Ms. Ruby. Things have happened this week that have left me confused and scared, and, honestly, I don't understand any of it." Tears sprang to Anna's eyes and she dabbed at them. *Why am I crying?* She was a mess.

Ms. Ruby smiled and reached out to hug her. "Child, God has an amazing life planned out for you. You are his blessing. I promise, things will turn out just the way God wants them to. What he starts, he finishes."

Anna smiled back through her tears and took Ms. Ruby's hand. "I have some special friends that I want you to meet. Ms. Ruby, we need a prayer warrior just like you."

A few minutes later the service ended. Anna and Ms. Ruby walked out hand in hand to the foyer. Anna spotted the Knights by the coffee station.

"There they are," she said.

They walked over to the Knights and Anna introduced Ms. Ruby to everyone. Mr. Peter explained to her about their ministry and the children in South Sudan.

"Would you join us, Ms. Ruby? Your prayers would mean a lot to us."

Her eyes twinkled as she took his hand and said, "Sweet Jesus, I already have."

At that moment, Grace walked out of the sanctuary. She greeted everyone with her cute smile then pulled Anna off to the side. "I don't know what happened to Shelby. I was so excited because last night she promised she'd be at church this morning, but . . . oh, well." Grace threw up her hands "Obviously, she never showed. Mom dropped me off early for practice, but she had one of her migraines, so she decided to go back to bed and not come to church. Before I left, Shelby told me that she'd get a ride and would come to the 11:00 service. Who knows? She wasn't in the best mood this morning when she woke up."

"Maybe next Sunday, Grace," Anna said.

Grace bit her lip, something she tended to do when she was frustrated, and said determinedly, "I don't know—something's just not right—and I'm going to get to the bottom of it."

CHAPTER FOURTEEN

Tut was dreaming. He walked toward something, but what was it? An oppressive darkness swirled around and threatened to engulf him. In front of him, a dazzling, iridescent light shimmered and pulsed with all the colors of the rainbow. As he moved toward the luminescence, a curtain of roiling, fetid darkness engulfed him once again. His friends, the Knights, and that girl, Anna, were in his dream. Over and over, they called out someone's name.

He shouted to them, "Do you need help?"

"Yes. Come and help us."

As Tut joined the group, a brilliant light burst forth over their heads illuminating the sky as if it were broad daylight. They stood on the edge of a cliff, a dazzling light above and behind them and darkness beneath them. He noticed a girl. She stood a short distance away from them. Her back was to him at first, but when she turned, he caught a glimpse of her face. It was the angry girl who stood beside Anna the other night when they skyped with the Knights and their new friends. The same blackness churned around her. Beside her stood a young man, dressed in a black, raggedy jacket. The man took hold of the girl's arm and pulled her away from them toward the abyss. At first, she went willingly, but as Tut and the group called to her, she struggled with the young man and then—they vanished into the blackness.

"Tut. Tut. Wake up." Someone pulled on his arm.

Startled, he struck out and began to kick with his legs.

"Tut. It's okay. It's Jafaar." Tut opened his eyes to see Jafaar kneeling beside him.

"You had a bad dream."

Tut sat up and tried to focus his eyes, the girl's image still fresh from the dream.

"The girl—she disappeared. We must find her."

"What girl, Tut?" asked Jafaar, confused.

"I dreamed that a man in black dragged that angry girl away. She struggled . . ." Tut's voice rose in panic. "He pulled her over the cliff."

He placed his hand on Tut's shoulder and said, "We will pray for her—God has given you this dream for a reason." Jafaar gave Tut's shoulder a reassuring squeeze and said, "Now, I must wake up the children."

Unable to shake his dream, Tut slowly stood up and walked over and sat down beside Zofa. As the children began to stir, Zofa laid out the food that they had jammed into their bags yesterday morning.

She apologized to Tut. "I know there is not a lot. Perhaps we will find a place along the way to purchase more food."

The children stumbled over to Zofa and sat down. Still tired, their eyes glazed and unfocused, she handed them each a piece of the flatbread called Kisra.

"Oh, how I wish for a hot cup of kakady." Tut's mouth watered as he conjured up in his mind the delicious, sweet tea that their mother used to fix for them each morning.

Tut noticed that Achan only stared at her bread but did not eat.

Concerned, he asked "How are you feeling today, Sister?"

Achan smiled wanly. "It hurts."

In her no-nonsense way, Zofa said, "Let me look at it."

Tut watched protectively as Achan straightened out her leg for Zofa to examine. She gently poked around the wound and said, "I will make a paste of calendula—that will help with any possible infection."

Zofa was well known for her herbal remedies and always carried a pouch of herbs with her. It was the first thing she grabbed before they escaped the United Nations compound. She made a paste of the dried flowers and gently applied the poultice to Achan's wound. The little girl grimaced but did not make a sound until after Zofa finished tending to her. At that, Achan let out her breath with a whoosh and a brave smile. Zofa hugged her.

"It will begin to feel better today, little sister. You must eat."

As they ate, Tut asked, "Where do we travel, Baba?"

Jafaar tore off a small piece of bread and gestured with it in his hand. "My plan is to follow the River Nile south to Juba and then into Uganda where we will find safety. There is a big hurdle in front of us, however—The Sudd.

Tut's heart sank—he knew of the Sudd. It was a vast, swampy low-land region of South Sudan, full of crocs, mosquitos, and disease. Many South Sudanese refugees who traveled into the Sudd died along the way.

Jafaar caught Tut's concerned eye and then said to the group, "Yes, to be honest, it is dangerous, and we have a very long journey in front of us. At times we will leave the river and travel south along the road when we can, but eventually we must find a boat or a barge to take us south because, of course, we cannot walk through the Sudd. Let's pray for God's protection today."

Tut and the rest of the family joined hands and bowed their heads as Jafaar prayed. "Lord, we ask that you go with us today as we travel toward safety and freedom. Protect and shelter us. Surround us with your angels. And Lord, we pray for the angry girl in Tut's dream. She, too, needs your protection. Send your angels to release her from the evil that threatens to destroy her. In Jesus name. Amen."

After a chorus of amens, the little group gathered their meager belongings and set out, kicking up puffs of dirt along the dusty path. Tut and Jafaar walked quietly side by side for a while. Tut had so much on his mind—it zoomed from one thing to another. First his dream about that angry girl in black. What was that all about? His people believed that when a person was alive, their soul roamed around during sleep. Death meant that their soul hadn't returned to their body. Dreams were very frightening at times—they worried him. From that thought, his mind jumped over to his brother and sisters and the journey ahead. They were his responsibility. He had been the one who took care of them after . . . the memory still felt raw and saddened him.

His mama, Abi, was a tea lady. She sold tea on the streets to support her children after his baba, Kamal, drowned in the White Nile during a skirmish with a warring Dinka tribe. Everyone loved his mama. He could still close his eyes—and if he concentrated long enough—picture her. Unfortunately, as time went by, that picture grew fainter and fainter. She was sweet as well as beautiful, drawing many customers to her little tea stand. He and his brother and sisters rode the bus with her each morning to stake out a tiny square of sidewalk where his mama would set up her portable teacart, and hopefully, if God blessed them, under the shade of a tree. Ulan's job was to gather the charcoal while Tut lit the fire. The girls would set up the precious silver teakettle, fetch the water, and lay out the spices, cups, spoons, and sugar on the tray. Unfortunately, the authorities thought it unseemly for a woman to work, notably by herself. The Health Ministry cracked down on many of the tea ladies and proclaimed that their wares were unclean. The police began to hassle his mama, threatened to take away her cart and jars, and demanded bribes. Of course, she had no money for bribes, so one day the police came and took their mama away. They waited on the street until dark, not knowing where to go or what to do. Heartbroken and afraid, Tut gathered his little brother and sisters together and they returned to their tumbledown shack along the river. Their mama never did come home. Several months later, Jafaar befriended Tut, and after hearing his story, invited them to the orphanage.

As they walked, Jafaar sensed that Tut needed to talk. "You are troubled, my son?"

Tut stared straight ahead, his head high. "Yes, Baba. I am."

"What troubles you?"

Tut didn't say anything for a moment, grateful that Jafaar did not hurry him to speak. Finally, he said, "I worry about my family. I want more than anything to arrive safely and reunite with the Knights." Tut dipped his head toward the ground and then back at Jafaar. "Will that happen, sir? How do we find them? I promised my brother and sister that we would."

"Do you have faith, Tut?" Jafaar asked.

"Faith, sir?"

"Do you remember when we met that first time?"

Tut smiled and nodded his head. He would never forget that day. He often scavenged for food in a dumpster outside of a restaurant close to the shack where he and his brother and sisters lived. His mother had been missing for over a month and it was up to him to find food for the family. That morning, the little girls had asked Tut to find them food, so he was determined to bring back something for them to eat. They were starving. A policeman found him and some of the other children foraging in the dumpster and chased them away. He sat down on a nearby curb and cried. What would he tell his sisters and brother? About that time a man walked up and sat down beside him. He asked Tut to tell him his story. No one had ever cared before. That man was Jafaar.

Tut had tears in his eyes as he remembered, "My brother and sisters were hungry, and that policeman made me so angry." Just the thought caused anger to boil up once again inside of him.

"Yes, you trusted enough to confide in me," said Jafaar. "And then, I asked you if you wanted to go with me to the orphanage."

Tut shook his head slowly. He would never forget that day. "I didn't want to go," he said honestly, "but then I thought about my brother and sisters, and I knew that it was best for them."

"What did you want for them, Tut?"

Tut reached out and shredded leaves through his fingers as he walked by a low hanging bush. He brought the fragrant leaves up to his nose and inhaled deeply. "Every night, Lala and Achan would kneel beside their pallets and pray that God would send them a family." Tears came to his eyes and he brushed them away angrily. "They missed our mama. They needed a mama. Ulan acted like he didn't care, but I know he did. He was only seven, but he'd seen too much in his short life. He needed a mama, too."

"Did you have faith that God would answer your sisters' prayers, Tut?"

Tut blinked at him, surprised at the question.

Jafaar smiled. "You had faith that I would take care of you and your family. You didn't know who I was or where you were going, but you placed your trust in me. That was faith, Tut. You can still trust God. He cares more about you more than you can even imagine."

"It's still hard, sir."

"Yes, I know, Tut. I know."

CHAPTER FIFTEEN

After Anna and Grace walked out to the parking lot and said their goodbyes to the Knights, Grace pulled her phone from her purse and said, "I'm going to text mom to see what happened to Shelby." She waited a few minutes and then shook her head. "Mom's probably still in bed. Let me see if I can text Shelby." There was no response, so she tried to call her. Still nothing.

Uneasy, Anna asked, "Was Shelby at home when you left this morning, Grace?"

"Yes, I had to be at church early for practice, and she and Mom were in the kitchen eating breakfast when I left. I asked her if she was coming to church, but she wouldn't answer me. Shel was in one of her moods, you know? I asked her again—she snarled at me and said to get out of her face—and yes, she would be at church. Of course, Mom didn't say anything," Grace said, annoyed. "She just leaves Shelby alone when she's like that."

"Dad will give you a lift home. I'm sure Shelby decided not to come this morning."

On the way home, Grace said, "I don't feel good about this. I don't know what it is, but . . ." Before she could finish her sentence, they drove into her driveway.

"We'll walk in with you to make sure everything's okay," said Dad.

Grace called out to her mom when they stepped through the door. "Mom? I'm home. Where are you? Mr. John and Anna are here with me."

"Out here, Grace." Her mom, Ms. Maria, must have felt better because she was on the patio reading the Sunday paper.

"Mom, have you seen Shelby?" Grace asked as soon as she walked on the patio. Her face mirrored the concern in her voice.

"Oh, that nice young man came by and picked her up to go to church about 8:45 this morning."

"What—nice—young man, Mom?" Grace asked slowly.

"The guy you met at the baseball game the other night—Shelby's new friend."

Grace had told her mom about Lou and Shelby—she had to, but she hadn't really described his appearance. Her so-called allegiance to Shelby had kept her from giving her mom too much information.

Grace's eyes opened wide and she cut them over at Anna who grimaced, closed her eyes and shook her head—surely, not Lou. Shelby's mom would never have allowed her to go off with someone who rode a motorcycle or dressed like that.

"Can you describe him, Mom?"

"Well, he was very clean-cut and handsome even. He was tall with dark hair. And oh, he was so polite." She thought for a moment and then added, "He had a scar on his forehead."

Anna's mind raced. *Couldn't be the same guy with her the other night. He wore that awful jacket and had that greasy man bun.* It was dark, so she didn't notice if Lou had a scar or not.

Anna knew when Grace began to panic because her voice always rose a pitch higher when she did. "Mom, what was his name?" she squeaked.

"Let me think—hmmm, it started with an L." She paused for a moment . . . "Larry? Leon? Lou? Yes—that's it. Shelby introduced him as Lou. She said you knew him."

Anna's eyes widened, and she glanced at Grace. All color had left her face. She whispered, "Anna, it's him. What do we do?"

Concerned, Grace's mom said, "Girls you're starting to frighten me. Surely that young man did not mean any harm to Shelby."

"Okay, let's not panic," Dad joined in. "Do you want me to call the police, Maria?"

"I . . . I don't know, John. I don't know what to do."

Suddenly, Anna jumped up. A compelling voice spoke within her, *Anna, you're in a battle, remember? You must pray.* The voice was so strong and forceful that she cried out loud, "Wait!"

Alarmed, everyone turned toward her.

"We have to pray. We have to pray now," she yelled. Anna blushed because this was so not like her. She took a deep breath and said as calmly as she could, "I'm sorry I yelled, but it is imperative that we go to battle right now."

Without another word, the four of them held hands, and Anna began to pray. "Father, God, we stand in agreement knowing that when two or more are gathered together, you're there. Your Word also says, *if two of you agree here on earth concerning anything you ask, my Father in heaven will do it for you.* So, right now, we pray for Shelby. We pray safety and protection for her, Lord. Bring her back to us quickly and safely, in Jesus name."

At that exact moment, a malevolent force encircled the group and tried to tear their hands apart. They gripped their hands tighter and continued to pray, "In the name of Jesus—In the name of Jesus—In the name of Jesus."

Finally, the force was gone. Just disappeared. Mouths agape, they could only stand and stare at each other.

Grace whispered, "What . . . was . . . that?"

"I . . . I . . . I don't know," said Anna.

Ms. Maria was a bit freaked out—to say the least. "What do we do? What do we do?" She paced the floor. "What do we do?" Her voice rose, "What just happened, John?"

Dad walked over, grabbed her by both arms to steady her and said in a soothing voice, "Maria, I'm not sure, but let's wait a little while longer. If Shelby doesn't come home soon, I'll call the police."

All they could do was wait, but thankfully about thirty minutes later Shelby walked into the house and hollered, "Mom? Grace?"

Grace and her mom both jumped up and called out at the same time. "Shelby, we're back here."

When she walked through the patio door, everyone stood for a moment, so relieved that all they could do was stare at her.

"What? What's going on?" said Shelby.

Grace ran up to her and gave her a big hug. "Shelby, are you okay? We were so worried about you."

Annoyed, Shelby stepped back away from her and said, "Yeah, I'm okay. Why?"

"Well, when you didn't come to church, I didn't know what happened to you—and then, Mom said you went off with Lou."

Shelby, suitably embarrassed for a moment, said, "Oh yeah, he was going to take me to church when . . ." Shelby broke off.

"When?" her mom questioned.

"Well, I don't know," Shelby retorted. "We kind of got to talking, you know? It was really kind of weird. Then his car broke down on the way. He said he had a friend who would come by and pick us up."

"Where did this happen?" asked Anna.

"Actually, we were at the cemetery," said Shelby.

"The cemetery?" Grace's eyebrows rose.

"Yeah, like I said, it was kind of weird."

Anna sensed there was a lot that Shelby wasn't telling them.

"Shelby—how did you get home?" she asked, frustrated now.

"About thirty minutes ago, Lou and I were standing out by the road waiting for his friend, you know? A strange car drove up and stopped. I assumed it was Lou's friend who was going to take us home,"

Grace's voice rose an octave higher and she asked, "Did you get in the car with this guy?"

"Well, no. At the same time, Ms. Ruby drove up in her old, white Cadillac. She stopped the car, rolled down the window, and ordered me to get in—that the Lord said I needed a ride home. Lou told her that *he* would bring me home, but Ms. Ruby would have none of it. She demanded that I get in—I mean, Ms. Ruby can be really bossy when she wants to—so, Lou left me there and got in the car with his friend and took off. Like I said, it was weird."

As she listened to Shelby's story, Anna thought to herself—*thirty minutes ago? We were praying thirty minutes ago. This was not a coincidence.*

"I don't know what the fuss is about," by demanded. "Why don't y'all leave me alone and get out of my life."

"Shelby, what is *wrong* with you?" asked Ms. Maria, angry this time.

"Nothing." Shelby raised her voice, "Absolutely nothing."

At that, Shelby stormed off the patio and into the house.

Embarrassed, Ms. Maria apologized. "I'm so sorry. What can I say? Thank you all so much for coming over and praying with me."

Dad reached over and put his arm around her shoulders. "It's okay, Maria. It's okay."

She smiled, tears pooling in her eyes. "It's hard without their dad here."

"I know—I understand."

She lowered her eyes, smiled, swiped at her tears and said, "Yes, I know you do."

After an awkward silence, Dad said, "Well . . . uh . . . okay . . . Come on, Anna. I'm starving. Let's find your brother and get a bite to eat."

Saying their goodbyes, Anna hugged Grace. "See you tomorrow, friend."

CHAPTER SIXTEEN

When the sun hung high in the African sky, Jafaar motioned for the family to stop beneath a large acacia tree. They had left the river for a while and followed a dusty road heading south. An old wizened man sat on a stump under the shade of the tree. His eyes twinkled with good humor as they walked up to him.

"May we rest here, old man?" asked Luka.

"Yes, it is good. This tree provides welcome shade for a weary traveler," he said. "Sit—come and sit a while."

Tut stopped and eyed the man with suspicion. Jafaar walked up to greet the old man with a handshake and a tap on the shoulder. A soft groan caused Tut to turn his head. He caught the grimace on Achan's face as she gratefully sunk to the ground. He knew that her leg hurt her, but she was not one to complain, so it was good that they had stopped for a while. He sat down between Achan and the old man. Ulan and Lala sat down beside him.

The old man spoke to Achan. "You are hurt, little sister?"

Achan was usually very shy, but she surprised Tut and answered the old man. "Yes, old father, I am."

The man did not say anything to her, but just nodded his head. He regarded Tut for a moment. "Where do you travel?" he asked.

Tut glanced at Jafaar who gave him a curt nod. "We are trying to get out of South Sudan, sir."

"Do you understand that this road is very dangerous?" the old man said.

"Yes, there are soldiers everywhere," said Tut.

"That's true, but"—he pointed a bony finger toward the road, "there are also mines hidden along the way."

Alarmed, Tut's eye widened. "Mines?"

Tut knew of the dangers of hidden mines. He had seen for himself men, women, and children maimed by the horrible remnants of civil war.

Jafaar placed his hand on Tut's arm and asked, "How do you know of this, old man?"

"It is known. You must be very careful."

Tut's stomach growled out loud, and he grabbed hold of it. It seemed like he was always hungry. Zofa once told him that he had a hollow leg that her food could never fill.

"Are you hungry my friends?" asked the old man.

"I am always hungry, old father," said Tut.

"Then, you must eat," he exclaimed. His face lit up and he smiled a toothless smile at everyone. "May I join you?"

Embarrassed, Zofa furrowed her brows and said, "We have barely enough for today, but somehow . . . God will provide."

Pulling out the meager fare, she laid it out in front of them and called for everyone to come and eat.

"May I pray?" asked the old man.

Tut exchanged glances with Zofa and she said, "Of course."

As each one bowed their head, the old man prayed, "Lord of the Universe, Giver of All Things, we thank you for this food. We ask that you multiply it for us, God. Give us sustenance and strength for our journey. In Jesus name. Amen."

The family opened their eyes and gasped in surprise. "H . . . how, can this be? What happened?" asked Tut. What was meager before had multiplied. He reached out and picked up a piece of kisra. Tut grinned and took a tentative bite—it was thin, a little sour, moist and delicious as if it had just come off the top of a griddle. He motioned for everyone to eat. Eyes closed, he savored another bite and then another until he was no longer hungry. Everyone ate their fill, with bread left over. Tut remembered a story Jafaar had told him about Jesus feeding five thousand people on just two fish and a couple of loaves of bread. Amazed still, he realized that this very story played out in front of his family.

When the old man had finished eating, he said, "I must take leave of you, my friends. I wish Godspeed on your journey. Remember my warning to stay clear of the road." At that the old man slowly got up from the ground, picked up his walking stick and ambled back toward the north.

Tut stared at the old man's back until he disappeared around the bend in the road. *Who was that old man and what had just happened?* He rubbed his stomach with satisfaction, smiled and lay back against a fallen log. All Tut needed to know was that God was indeed good.

Soon, Zofa dozed off in the noonday heat as the two younger girls leaned up against her and slept. Ulan curled up in a ball nearby. Unable to sleep, Tut got up and sat down beside Luka and Jafaar. They had squatted under a nearby tree to talk, their voices low so as not to disturb the younger kids. Jafaar had drawn a map in the dirt to show Luka possible routes that they might take. They discussed the dangers and possibilities of each one, especially after the old man's dire warning about the mines.

Tut listened in on their conversation for a while and then interrupted politely, "How do you decide? How do you know where to go?"

"That is up to God," said Jafaar.

"But how do you know what God has to say?"

"You must listen, Tut. You will know." Jafaar sat for a moment and then said, "I remember a conversation that I had with Peter Knight soon after Zofa and I had accepted Jesus as our savior. I knew that the future was perilous for us now that we were Christian. Peter asked me if we were ready for the adventure of our lives, and I told him that we were. He gave me a scripture that I memorized and have recited over and over since then."

"What was it, Baba?"

"Do not be afraid or discouraged, for the Lord will personally go ahead of you. He will be with you; he will neither fail you nor abandon you."

Tut tilted his head toward Jafaar, twisted his mouth, and slowly nodded. Encouraged by Jafaar's words, he leaned back against a tree, closed his heavy eyes for a short moment and napped.

Taka, taka, taka. Startled, Tut jolted awake. *Taka, taka, taka.*

Recognizing the sound of machine gun fire in the distance, Jafaar roused the group. "Hurry, hurry. We must go."

Quickly they gathered their belongings. "Where to, Baba?" Tut asked hesitantly. Jafaar bowed his head for a moment. Then lifting his head, he stared into the distance past a group of trees and said with certainty, "We haven't veered that far from the White Nile—perhaps a half of kilometer to the west. We must move away from the road and the dangers here and make our way back to the river."

"Perhaps now God will send us a boat," said Tut.

Jafaar smiled at all of them and said, "Yes, like the infant Moses floating down the River Nile, maybe God will provide a way for us, too."

Jafaar led the way with Tut and Luka bringing up the rear. The going was slow and tedious as they trekked toward what they hoped was the river. Tut flinched as the sound of gunfire, and then an explosion sounded too close for comfort.

Two hours later they stopped to rest. The gunfire and explosions had ceased, so they decided it was safe enough to take a break.

Jafaar glanced up at the sun. "It can't be much further." He smiled at the bedraggled and exhausted group. "I am very proud of all of you. Luka, I need for you to stay here with everyone while Tut and I go a little further to see if we can spot the river."

Exhausted, the rest of the family sat down for a much-needed rest.

An hour later, they returned, big smiles on their faces.

"The river is only a short distance away," said Tut.

"Yes," said Jafaar. "We'll camp along the river tonight and set out again in the morning."

That evening, they gathered around a small fire along the riverbank.

"Do we have bread, Mama?" asked Tut.

Hesitantly, Zofa reached in to pull out the food leftover from lunch. Amazed, she noticed that there were even more leftovers in her bag.

"Thank you, Jesus," she whispered.

Her eyes shone as she picked up a piece of it and held it up like an offering. "The Lord has provided for us once again. Thank you, Lord, for this feast."

They stared mesmerized into the pleasant fire and munched on the delicious bread, too weary to even speak. As the flames reflected on the tired faces of the group, Tut thought, *God is good—He is good.*

Mirroring those thoughts, Jafaar spoke up, "Look what God has provided for us. We have a long journey ahead, but God has already shown us that he will not leave or forsake us." Reassured, the group once again settled in for a long night.

As Tut lay back on his pallet, he put his hands behind his head and squinted up toward the North star and listened to the soft babbling of the river. In quiet times like these, his thoughts often turned to his mother. She enjoyed quoting old Sudanese proverbs and telling stories. She was the wisest person he ever knew, and he missed her so much. If he had difficulty sleeping, his mama would wag her finger at him and say, "*that which prevents you from sleeping is of your own making.*" She always knew if he had done something that he shouldn't have. He thought about the trip ahead of them. No matter what, he knew that his brother and sisters were his responsibility. When he doubted his ability, his mama would say, "Tut, *do not let what you cannot do turn your head away from what you can do.*" He smiled into the dark. He knew in his heart that his mama was smiling back at him.

His mind wandered to the girl in his dream the other night. Why did he keep thinking about her? He could still see her terrified face as she disappeared into the blackness. His heart raced as he thought about her even now. He placed his hands across his heart and prayed that God would give him a peace about the girl. At last, with the stars as his nightlight, he closed his eyes, felt peace soak into his spirit . . . and drifted off to sleep.

CHAPTER SEVENTEEN

Ping. Ping. Ping.

Anna stirred from a thick, delicious, early morning sleep. She groped blindly for her phone.

Ping. Ping. Ping. The phone blew up.

She squinted at the phone and picked it up. It was a group text from Grace to all the Knight kids and her.

"Great idea! Great idea! Can't wait to talk to y'all today." :-) :-) Grace always punctuated her texts liberally with exclamation points and emoticons.

Anna groaned and plopped back down on her pillow. What in the world was Grace's great idea? Max nudged her and whined.

"I know, I know. You want to go outside."

An hour later, Anna walked into the kitchen to the smells of one of her dad's tasty breakfasts. He loved to cook and enjoyed trying out some new recipe on them.

"Good morning, all," Anna said.

His mouth full of French toast, Ben mumbled something that she couldn't understand.

"What was that you said?" she grinned at him and sat down at the table.

Anna reached for the plate of sausages, hot and crispy, just like she liked them. Spearing several, she then filled her plate with three golden pieces of French toast sprinkled with powdered sugar and poured hot Maple syrup over it all. Anna sighed with pleasure. She took a moment to say a quick blessing and then forked the deliciousness into her mouth. *Oh, joy*. She did love a good breakfast.

Ping. Ping. Ping.

Anna glanced once more at her phone. She rolled her eyes.

"What's up, Sis?" Ben asked.

"It's Grace. She's got some great idea to tell me about at school today. She's been texting nonstop since I woke up."

Ben grinned. "Hmm, one of Grace's great new ideas, huh? Remember when she decided that y'all needed to protest the principal's new food menu? Standing out in front of the cafeteria with signs didn't exactly get you on the right side of Mr. Hall."

"Yeah, Mr. Hall was not amused."

"And then, calling the White House and yelling at the President because he said something about reducing her grandma's social security check? Not cool."

Anna's mouth twitched. "The Secret Service doesn't exactly like for you to yell at the president."

"And what about the time that Grace found a litter of orphaned kittens on her way to school and decided to sneak them into her backpack for the day."

Anna laughed and almost choked on a piece of French toast. "Yes, Mr. Owen kept stopping his lecture on the Battle of Gettysburg to ask what that meowing sound was. He thought someone's phone had gone off, or that someone was watching a YouTube cat video."

Ben shook his head and forked another piece of sausage and French toast onto his plate.

With a quick glance toward the kitchen clock, Anna stuffed one last bite of sausage into her mouth. "Yikes. I'm late. I've got to go brush my teeth and get to school."

Ben mumbled something with his mouth full. He nodded and motioned with his fork that he would be along soon.

About fifteen minutes later, Anna didn't even get through the front door of the school before Grace pounced on her.

"I thought you would never get here," she said.

"Okay, what's up, friend? What's your newest and greatest idea?"

Grace grabbed Anna by the arm and pulled her over to a bench by the principal's office. She yanked her down hard and said, emphasizing every single word, "Okay—what—if—we—started—a—YouTube—channel." She sped up and finished with "that helped raise money for the Knight kids in South Sudan?"

"YouTube?" Anna was clueless.

"Yes, you do know what a YouTube channel is, don't you?"

"Of course, I do," she snapped, "But, I don't know where you're going with this."

Patiently, as if talking to a child, Grace continued. "Listen, the kids at school don't know anything about South Sudan, do they? So . . . let's tell them." She said it as if it were the simplest thing in the world.

"But how? I don't want to throw cold water on your idea, Grace, but how do we get them to watch this channel? To follow us? There are a million and one YouTube channels on the internet."

"I don't know," she said impatiently. "I haven't gotten that far yet. But, we have to start—somewhere," she pleaded. "Even the most popular YouTubers had to start somewhere."

For a moment, Anna just stared at Grace and tapped her mouth as she was prone to do when thinking. "You know, that absolutely might be a great idea—and fun, too."

With a smug smile, Grace said, "I told you it was a great idea, didn't I?"

Anna gave her a quick hug. "Yes, it is." *How do I say "no" to Grace?* she thought.

Right then the bell rang, and they both headed to class.

That afternoon as the group walked home, Grace shared her idea with the Knight kids. Anna noticed Shelby trailing behind, lost in her own sad world. "Shel, I want you to hear this, too," said Grace. "You can help us."

Reluctantly, Shelby joined them as they stopped for her to catch up.

"Okay . . ." Grace lifted both hands, her palms outstretched toward them and gestured as she explained. "I want us to imagine not just reaching the kids at our school about South Sudan, but all over the United States—hey, even the world."

Grace's voice rose and ended in a high squeak.

They all smiled—all except Shelby.

David scratched his head. "That does sound like something we could do to get the word out."

Anna glanced over at Shelby. She scowled and mumbled, "So what do you need me for?"

Grace said, "Shel, you're the best at technology. You can help us. You helped dad with the Rides Rally . . ." Her voice trailed off.

Shelby's face had turned red.

"Oh, I'm sorry, Shel. I didn't mean to . . ."

Anna winced because she knew the Rally reminded Shelby about the accident that killed her dad—and her part in it.

The friends sucked in a collective breath as they waited for Shelby's answer.

She inspected her fingernails for a moment. "Yeah . . . yeah, maybe I could do that."

Anna let out an audible breath. "Well—okay. Soooo . . . what now?"

"We need facts, information, pictures, stories, anything you can think of about the Sudanese people," said Grace.

"We can do that," said Favor.

"A lot of kids subscribe to YouTube channels, we want ours to be different . . . cool . . . a favorite," said Grace.

"What do we name it?" Anna asked.

After a moment, Jonathan spoke up. "How about *Come and See*?"

Anna stared at Jonathan until it dawned on her. "Oh . . . that's the name of your ministry in South Sudan, isn't it?"

Jonathan grinned and winked at Anna.

She blushed. She hated it when she blushed. Anna had to admit that she liked Jonathan a lot. Maybe even had a crush on him.

Red faced, she stuttered, "Th . . . at's a great idea."

Grace ignored her. "Yes. I love it. And when we're ready for a rollout, we can spread the word through social media and ask everyone to share it with their friends."

"So, where do we start? I don't even know the first thing about how to begin or what we need to do first," Anna said.

It was exciting to think about the big picture, but the actual process suddenly seemed overwhelming. Anna thought about other projects that she and Grace had begun over the years and never finished because of that very same reason.

"We'll take one thing at a time," said Grace. "If we come up against a roadblock, we'll just stop and go a different direction."

"Well, friend," Anna grinned at her admirably. "That is very mature of you," she said a little tongue in cheek.

Grace laughed and hit Anna on the shoulder. "You're thinking of all those lemonade stands where we tried and failed miserably, aren't you? This is going to be different, Anna, I can just feel it."

Following their conversation, Favor smiled and said, "So, how about if David, Jonathan, and I start by talking to Mom and Dad tonight. We'll have more information than you could ever use or need."

After another pause, Shelby said in a low voice, "Let me sign us up for YouTube. Then we need to find a camera, and we're good to go. I've got some cool editing software on my computer that we could use."

Anna stared at Shelby. She seemed excited about this, at least as excited as Shelby could ever be. Impulsively, Grace reached over and gave her sister a big hug even though she knew she'd hate that.

Shelby scowled at her, embarrassed. "See you guys later." And then she walked off.

Grace rolled her eyes and threw her hands up in the air.

"Okay, there's one thing that we have to do first," said Jonathan

"What's that?" Anna asked.

"We've got to pray."

"Oh, of course," she said.

So, right at the corner of College and Palm, they all grabbed hands as Jonathan prayed. "Lord, this is yours. We pray that you give us your creative mind in helping us to get the word out about our brothers and sisters in South Sudan. Father God, this has got to be great, and we know that you are a great God. We thank you in advance. In the name of Jesus. Amen."

The friends lifted their heads just as a soccer ball landed right in the middle of their circle.

"Whoa—what was that?" asked David.

Just then, the same little boy who Favor and Jonathan had prayed for last week, ran up, grabbed it, and then with a huge grin, called out, "Sowwy, guys." and scampered off.

"Well, okay, then. I think we have some work to do," said Grace.

CHAPTER EIGHTEEN

Early the next morning, Tut woke to Jafaar singing a traditional African morning song.

Get up. Wake up. God has created a beautiful day.
Wake up. Get up. This day is created by God.
Get up. Wake up. God has created a beautiful day.
Wake up. Get up. This day is created by God.

Mumbling, the other kids began to stir. Still drowsy, Tut lay still for a moment listening to Jafaar, until finally, he groaned like an old man, sat up sleepy-eyed and squinted at the group. The other kids had a difficult time waking up, also, still tired and exhausted from yesterday's journey.

It was a beautiful African morning; the sun sparkled on the Nile as fish boiled up to the surface feeding on the millions of insects flying above its waters. His stomach growled and Tut wished that he had a fishing pole to catch some of the delicious Nile perch for their breakfast.

He turned toward Zofa. "Do we have food, Mama?" asked Tut.

As the other children gathered around, Zofa peeked into her bag. By the expression on her face, he knew that their breakfast would be meager that morning.

"Only a little bread," she said.

As Zofa laid the kisra on a log beside them, Ulan picked up a small piece of bread and said, "Tut, we are out of food. What do we do now?"

"We wait, little brother."

"How long?"

Tut smiled at him and said, "Until God sends us a boat."

Lala spoke up fearfully, "Do we have to get on a boat?"

"Yes, we do," Tut answered her seriously—he knew how afraid she was of the river. She was only six years old when their father drowned, and water terrified her after that. There was no making sense of it.

Tut said, "Do you remember the story that Jafaar told you the other day about Jesus and the boat?"

Lala nodded. "Yes, I remember. He and his friends were in a boat, and a great storm came up. It was so bad that the waves crashed over the bow of their boat and threatened to sink it. They were so afraid."

"I would have been, too," said Achan.

"Not me," said Ulan as he jumped to his feet and crossed his arms like a warrior.

Lala made a face at him and continued, "When they thought that they were going to die, they woke Jesus up."

"How could he sleep in a storm?" interrupted Ulan, still in his warrior stance.

Tut glanced up at him and then urged Lala to continue. "So—what happened, little sister?"

"He woke up and spoke to the wind and the rain—and it just stopped."

"How could that be?" asked Achan.

"That's what the disciples thought, too," said Tut. "They wondered how the winds and the sea obeyed him."

The group grew silent for a moment until Ulan spoke up in a confident voice, "Jesus will protect us, Sister. We are brave—we are his warriors."

Tut opened his mouth to say something when—at that moment, shots rang out from the river. Alarmed, he jumped to his feet as Achan grabbed hold of Zofa. "Mama, what's happening?"

Zofa hugged her close and sent Jafaar a worried glance.

"Luka, you must take Zofa and the children away from the river. Tut, come with me," said Jafaar.

Luka nodded, quickly doused the fire and gathered up Zofa and the frightened children.

Tut and Jafaar moved furtively behind the trees along the river bank. As voices echoed across the river, Jafaar motioned for Tut to hide behind one of the trees.

As several boatloads of soldiers floated by, shots rang out followed by raucous laughter.

"Got one!"

Another shot rang out. "Got two!"

Tut peeked out from behind the tree. He realized that the soldiers were shooting at the turtles that sunned themselves along the river bank. One shot hit way too close to his foot and he flattened himself up against the tree.

As the soldiers floated on by, Jafaar jerked his head for Tut to move back away from the river bank.

Several minutes later, they walked back to their doused campfire.

Luka and the family joined them a short time later.

His face solemn, Tut asked, "What do we do now?"

"We will wait one more day, and then we must come up with another plan," said Jafaar.

Only Tut noticed the troubled glance between Zofa, Jafaar, and Luka.

That night, something woke Tut from a light, fitful sleep. It was Jafaar. He had stoked up a small fire.

Tut sensed that something troubled Baba. "What's wrong?" he whispered.

"I had a bad dream—I do not know what to make of it."

Tut sat up on his pallet and asked, "What was it?" He recalled his own dream the other night.

Jafaar squatted down beside Tut and spoke quietly. "I was at the edge of the river, lying face down on the sand and praying when something caught my attention. The river began to bubble as if it was boiling—I couldn't turn away—steam was coming up out of it. At first, the water was brown, and then it turned into an appalling, black and green molten liquid. I . . . I . . . I was horrified and crawled away from the bank, but I couldn't take my eyes away from the foulness of it." Jafaar paused and tried to remember. "I got up off my knees and stood to my feet. A nauseating smell wafted through the air and caused me to gag. I started praying, 'In the name of Jesus . . . in the name of Jesus . . . in the name of Jesus.' Finally, I turned away, and that's when he appeared. He walked over to me and gently gripped both of my arms, gazed directly into my eyes, and moved me behind him. I'm not sure what happened next, but when Jesus stepped aside, the river flowed quietly once again to the east.

"Tut, Jesus spoke to me," Jafaar said in awe. "He told me what to do."

Tut gave a quick nod. He understood Jafaar's wonder. "What did he say, Baba?"

Jafaar closed his eyes and opened them slowly. "Jesus told me that we were to turn and travel a different way. I asked him, 'Lord, where?' He said to trust him and that he would show me." There was a pause, and Jafaar said, "I believe I know where he wants us to go."

A slow smile spread across Tut's face as Jafaar reached over and patted him on the arm and said, "Go to sleep, my son. Tomorrow we travel in a new direction."

Tut fell asleep that night with the buzz of mosquitos in his ear, but with the sweet peace of knowing Jesus watched over his family and him.

* * * *

The next morning, Tut woke early to the quiet voices of the adults. He listened in on their conversation.

"I'm worried, husband," said Zofa, her voice low so she wouldn't wake the children.

"Yes, so am I," said Jafaar.

"The children are already exhausted, and it has only been a couple of days . . . and Achan's leg wound—she doesn't complain, but I can tell that it has gotten worse."

"I know, I know. After watching and waiting at the White Nile yesterday, I believe that it may be too dangerous to escape that way." Jafaar paused. "I had a dream last night, Zofa. I believe that Jesus is directing us to go a different way. Across land toward the River Sobat. It will be a dangerous journey, also, but I trust that he is leading us in that direction. Our journey will follow the river as it drifts and curves toward Nasir and into Ethiopia and freedom. I have heard that there is a refugee camp in Gambella. Surely, we can find help at the camp and get in touch with the Knights."

Zofa reached over and took Jafaar's hand. "I have confidence in you, husband, because I know that you trust and hear the voice of God."

As Tut listened to the exchange between Jafaar and Zofa, he prayed a silent prayer. *Jesus, thank you. You placed Jafaar and Zofa across our path. I do not know where my family would be today without them.* At the end of his prayer, Tut finished aloud, "Amen." He sat up, stretched, and yawned.

Hearing his amen, Zofa called out, "Good morning, Tut, did you sleep well?"

Tut scratched both his arms and made a face. "All right, I guess, except for the mosquitos. They feasted on me all night long. I wish we had thought to bring mosquito nets with us."

As Tut spoke, the other three children stirred and then sat up, drowsy and still tired from the day before.

Zofa called out, "Good morning. Did the mosquitos bother you as well last night?"

All three scratched at their bites and grimaced.

"As we travel today, we will be on the lookout for herbs that we can rub on our skin to help with that," Zofa said.

"How do you know which ones?" Achan asked.

"My mama taught me many things. One of them was God's natural remedies for cuts and bruises—and biting bugs."

"Why did God create mosquitos?" Achan asked crossly.

Zofa walked over, gave her a quick hug and said, "Who knows? I'm sure God had a reason. Someday he will tell us." Changing the subject in her no-nonsense way, Zofa said, "Now, we must hunt for something to eat. Tut, I think I spotted some berries behind that copse of trees. They would taste good for our breakfast."

About an hour later, Jafaar gathered everyone together and told them about the change of plans.

"Where is Ethiopia, Baba?" asked Lala. "Is it far away?"

Not wanting to give false hope, Jafaar said, "Yes, it is a long journey, but we know that Jesus has directed our steps. Do you remember the story of Moses?"

Their eyes lit up—another story.

"God provided for the children of Israel for forty years," Jafaar began.

"Forty years?" said Lala. "I would be an old lady by then."

"No, it would not take us forty years to get to Ethiopia," said Jafaar.

"Will the Knights be there when we arrive?" asked Lala hopefully.

"I'm not sure," said Jafaar.

"Have they forgotten us, Baba?" asked Ulan.

"No, I promise you, they have not forgotten us."

CHAPTER NINETEEN

"Shelby . . . Miss Mercer . . . wake up."

With a start, Shelby realized that she had dozed off in class. Mr. Owen was standing over her.

She groaned inwardly, peeked up at him and then quickly down at her desk.

"Miss Mercer, if you continue to sleep in my class, I'll have to write you up."

"Yes, sir," she mumbled.

Shelby had been up late the last three nights working on the *Come and See* YouTube channel. She enjoyed the project even though she would never admit it to Grace.

Thankfully, the bell rang. As she left the room, Mr. Owen called out to her, "Get some sleep, young lady." With a quick nod, she ducked out the door.

Grace grabbed her as she walked down the hall.

"Are we ready to begin? Is the channel up and going? I couldn't stay awake any longer last night, and you were asleep when I left this morning."

Grace was a morning person who loved to "go to bed with the chickens and get up with them" as her grandmother used to say. Shelby, on the other hand, was a complete night owl. She would rather stay up late and then sleep late in the morning. Unfortunately, that did not bode well for school.

"Yes, I think we're good to go," Shelby said.

"Think?" Grace asked concerned.

"Well, some strange glitches happened as I worked on it last night."

"Glitches?" Grace asked.

"Yeah, it would work and format perfectly for a while, and then the computer would freeze up. It was so annoying. I'd never had that kind of difficulty before. I could *not* identify the problem."

"Well, hopefully, it's okay, and we can get together tonight and begin. This is really happening, Shel. Let's go tell Anna."

Shelby grumbled out loud as, arm in arm, Grace pulled her halfway down the hall. Grace spotted Anna over by the girl's restroom. She waved and called out to her. Yanking Shelby forward, she said, "Anna, Shelby said we're ready to go. I'm so excited." Shelby rolled her eyes.

"Great. What time should we get together tonight?" said Anna.

"Let's meet at my house at 6:00. It's Friday night and you know we always order pizza. It's our weekend tradition. I'll ask mom to be sure and order extra."

That evening the group gathered around Shelby's computer. Expectantly, they watched as she clicked on the opening sequence—an impressive animated graphic that she had created and paired with some cool music. As the music soared louder, the graphic bounced around the screen, circled in a spiral and then burst open as the words, "Come and see" pulsed in and out. Colors and light sprayed all over the screen. And then . . . it went black.

Perplexed, they stared at the screen.

"What happened?" Jonathan asked.

Shelby scowled at the screen. "I don't know . . . I told you there was a glitch. Sometimes it works, and sometimes it doesn't."

"So, what do we do now, Shel?" asked Grace.

Shelby said, "I told you—I don't know."

"Pizza's here," called out Ms. Maria.

"I'm starving," said David.

"You're always starved," Favor chided, hitting him on the shoulder. David shrugged sheepishly.

As they walked toward the kitchen, Shelby and Grace stayed behind at the computer. "You can fix this, Shel, I know you can."

Shelby grimaced and shook her head. "I'm not sure. It's so annoying."

Shelby and Grace stood and stared at the computer screen and wondered what could have gone wrong.

"What was that?" asked Shelby.

Behind her, Grace took a step closer and leaned over Shelby's shoulder. She narrowed and then blinked her eyes. "I don't know."

Shelby shivered as a chill ran up and down her spine. Something creepy was happening on the screen. The blackness began to move, bubble and shimmer. *What?*

"Shelby? . . . Guys?" Grace said, not taking her eyes off the screen. Then, turning her head toward the kitchen, she called out louder, "Hey, guys. You've got to come see this."

Jonathan was the first to walk back into the room. His face blanched as he stared. "Uh-oh. David . . . Favor, come in here."

The bubbling blackness had now turned into a disgusting, putrid green color. The phrase, *Stay away—Stay Away,* pulsated on the screen.

By that time, everyone crowded around the computer. Mesmerized, their eyes fixed on the words, "Stay away. Stay away."

"Evil," Favor said, "we stare at evil." She took a step back and began to pray in a strange language.

Bewildered, Shelby grabbed at her hand. "What are you saying?"

David and then Jonathan joined her, each praying in a different language—their eyes closed in concentration.

Shelby glanced from one to the other and then over at Grace, whose eyes were as big as saucers.

Grace whispered, "Shel, what's happening? I'm scared."

Grace grabbed Anna's hand, and they stood behind Shelby, transfixed. At last, the words faded out and the screen went black again.

Favor turned her back to the screen, focused on the group and said in her quiet voice, "We're in a battle—a spiritual—battle."

Shelby, her voice cross, said, "What do you mean?"

"Someone—something—doesn't want us to do this YouTube channel," said Favor.

"So, who's gonna stop us? Is there someone hacking into my computer?" Shelby countered. "I'll track him down, I promise." Her eyes flashed in defiance.

This is ridiculous, thought Shelby. *Who are these people?* Shelby didn't have much patience with all this spiritual or evil mumbo jumbo. Obviously, some yahoo out on the dark web was trying to hack her computer. It was as simple as that.

Favor said, "Yes, there is something hacking into our computer—a something, not a someone. There are powers who fight against us—powers between God's good and the forces of evil. Ephesians 6:12 says *we are not fighting against flesh-and-blood enemies, but against evil rulers and authorities of the unseen world, against mighty powers in this dark world, and against evil spirits in the heavenly places.*

Shelby just shook her head. She wasn't buying it.

"This is like a video game that I played once, but it's real, isn't it? What do we do?" said Grace. "I have to admit, guys, I'm scared."

Shelby opened her mouth to say something when Anna spoke up. "One of my grandmother's favorite scriptures comes from Psalm twenty-three." She quoted it from memory. *"Even when I walk through the darkest valley, I will not be afraid, for you are close beside me. Your rod and your staff protect and comfort me."*

Favor walked up beside her and said, "Yes, Anna, yes. *God has not given us a spirit of fear and timidity, but of power, love, and self-discipline."*

Shelby stared at Anna and then Favor, her face reflected a moment of confusion, vulnerability, even. What was it about that scripture? Why did it hit such a chord within her? Was it one that her dad quoted to her? She couldn't remember because thinking about her dad was just too painful. "So—what do we do now?" she said.

Favor began to pace with head down and her fists clenched tightly by her side. Finally, she stopped and raised her voice confidently. "Well, first, we pray. We can do nothing unless we pray for God's power and protection. We put on God's armor, and we fight. And then—we win. We make our voices known to those who can help us provide spiritual and financial help to get our kids back safely. We let people know that there is a real God in this universe who cares about our every need. A God who will accomplish great things through this effort. Satan is trying to thwart us because he knows this YouTube channel will help our kids as well as other teens."

Shelby wasn't convinced, but she decided to stay and not walk out like she tended to do sometimes.

"So," David interjected, "let's pray."

David began, his voice steady, powerful even, as he prayed, "Jesus, we need your help. We can't fix this on our own. We have no strength except what you give. Fight this battle for us, Lord. Send angels to the heavenly places to attack any who would come against our family, our kids, this project, and especially to those who will watch these videos. It's all too big for us, but not for you. You are the God of the Universe. We pray for miracles and manifestations of your power for our kids and for us. There is no limit to what you can do, Lord. We ask these things in your name—Jesus."

At his name, a saturating warmth and energy covered Shelby's body like a warm blanket on a frigid day in January. Closing her eyes, she *almost* allowed herself to go with it. But, as she opened her eyes, reality set in. In front of her was the blank computer screen. It was real—something tangible that she understood. She placed her fingers on the keyboard and then reached up to reboot the computer. She'd leave all that spiritual stuff to her friends—it was just too confusing to her. She took a deep breath and hit the power button.

CHAPTER TWENTY

"Are we lost, Baba?" Achan asked, her face pinched by worry and pain.

The longer she walked, the more she limped. Tut walked along beside her and helped her over troublesome obstacles such as logs or thick grass. Achan's soft groans tore at Tut's heart when she tripped or turned her leg a certain way. At times, he had to hoist her on his back and carry her.

Tut turned toward Jafaar and Zofa. They exchanged worried looks. "Let's stop and rest for a moment," said Jafaar. He placed his hand on Achan's shoulder and said, "No, we are not lost, my child. We will rest here for a while."

Many hours had passed since they'd left camp earlier that morning. They had to move slowly to accommodate Achan's deliberate and painful pace. The walk was difficult because they had left the road and any possible landmines and followed a narrow trail through the bush. Jafaar led them away from the White Nile toward the River Sobat. His compass was only the direction of the sun by day and the moon by night. Tut hoped that they would soon come close to the mouth of the river where the Sobat flowed into the mighty White Nile. The hike would be easier once they followed the River Sobat down to the town of Nasir. Since it was the dry season, there would be few boats, so they would have to walk the entire way.

Tut glanced worriedly at Achan's and the other children's brave but exhausted faces. "Baba said that we can rest," he said. Grateful for the respite, the children plopped down on the ground. With a sigh of relief, Achan curled up into a ball and fell asleep at once.

Concerned, Zofa reached over and laid her hand gently on Achan's forehead. She was warm, a sure sign of fever. Achan whimpered a little and then was quiet. Zofa stirred up a concoction of her herbal fever remedy and woke Achan and gave her a small dose. Soon she slipped back into sleep, Zofa motioned for Jafaar, Tut, and Luka to meet her away from the group.

She spoke to them in a muted whisper. "I'm not sure how much further Achan can walk. Her leg does not seem to be improving. What do we do?"

Tut nodded his head and said, "Yes, she is in great pain as she walks. She does not want us to know. She may be only seven, but Achan has always been the strongest one of all of us. She is very much like our mother."

"We will stop for the rest of the day. Let's make a pallet to carry her. Hopefully, after a few days, she will be well enough to walk once again on her own," said Jafaar.

There was a moment of silence—when Luka said, "Brother, let me travel on ahead. I can move quickly by myself. When I get to Ethiopia, I will somehow contact the Knights for help. Then, I will return the same way with food and supplies."

Jafaar glanced at Zofa and then raised his eyebrows at Tut. No one spoke until, finally, they all nodded their heads in affirmation.

Jafaar said, "That is good. We will wait for you in Nasir. I pray that He will bring you back to us soon."

Before he left, Luka knelt and they all laid their hands on him. Jafaar prayed, "Father, we pray for our brother. Go with him and bring him back to us safely." After hugs from everyone, Luka said, "I will be back, I promise." Zofa reached up and hugged her brother's neck. "God-speed, my brother." With one last wave, he disappeared into the trees.

"Now," Jafaar said, "we must find a couple of poles so that we can construct a pallet to carry Achan."

"I will hunt for small downed trees that we might turn into poles, Baba," said Tut.

"Yes, we passed such trees a little while ago. We'll attach our one blanket onto the poles. That way we can take turns carrying Achan without difficulty. Ulan and Lala, I need for you to search for vines that we can use to tie the poles together."

The children spread out and combed the woods for vines while Tut headed back the way they had come.

A short time later, Tut came upon a small copse of trees knocked to the ground by the last flood. Achan was so little that the makeshift bed wouldn't require huge poles to transport her. Pleased, he began to comb the woods for the perfect two trees. Spying one, he reached down to pick up the end of a small tree trunk—and froze—he knew that sound. A hiss . . . A growl. A Naja haje, otherwise known as an Egyptian cobra, raised its ugly hooded head and weaved back and forth in warning. Transfixed, Tut stared into the vast black pupils of the snake's demonic eyes. Snakes terrified him. In the bush, snakes often meant a paralyzing death. He'd heard that the bite of a cobra could even kill an elephant. His heart thudded in his chest, and he didn't know which way to turn. He took a shallow breath, held it, and then cautiously backed away and stopped. The snake reared up even higher. Its tongue flicked in and out of its mouth as if to hypnotize him. There was no way that he could outrun the snake, so immobilized, he began to pray.

As he prayed, a strong hot wind tore at his clothes and stung his skin. It swirled the leaves and debris at his feet. Limbs rained down on his head. He closed his eyes and tried to ignore the pain as a small branch hit his shoulder. Tut stood absolutely still. Finally, he opened his eyes. A large limb fell with a crash onto the cobra. The snake convulsed and then, writhing and squirming, slithered away. Tut tried to take a ragged breath. He shivered and wrapped his arms around himself still paralyzed with fear. The wind calmed as quickly as it raged. Quiet, except for a gentle breeze whispering through the trees. Tut slowly inhaled and exhaled, inhaled and exhaled. He moved his head and his eyes at the same time scoping for anymore snakes.

After one more cleansing breath, Tut said a quick prayer of thanks. He remembered his task and once again grabbed hold of the small tree trunk, a little more carefully this time. He dragged it out into a clearing and returned for one more tree. After stripping the leaves from the branches, he dragged the small poles back to the camp.

When Tut arrived, Zofa sensed that something had happened. Concerned, she walked over and put her arm around his shoulder.

Wincing, he couldn't help but cry out, "Oww."

She quickly removed her arm. "What's wrong? What happened to you?"

Tut told her about the snake and the wind.

"Praise God," said Zofa. "Let me see your shoulder."

Gingerly, Tut removed his shirt so that Zofa could place a poultice on the bruise. She smiled at him. "You will be as good as new before long. You're a brave young man, Tut."

Later that day, as they were working on the pallet, Jafaar again commented on Tut's bravery.

Tut lowered his head. "No, I was not brave at all. The snake terrified me. I *hate* snakes."

"The snake could have struck and killed you. You had a right to be fearful of it."

"Yes, but sometimes I am too fearful—like a girl," Tut confessed.

He bent down close to the pallet. He couldn't look Jafaar in the eyes. Tut knew that there was more to this story than what he had admitted to Jafaar. But how could he acknowledge his fear and not lose face before this man that he respected so much?

Tut turned toward Jafaar. "Look at you, Baba. You are the brave one. You have the scars to prove it. I was too fearful to earn the scars."

Unconsciously, Jafaar raised his fingers to his face and traced the familiar line of bumps that crossed his forehead and swirled across his cheekbones.

Tut bowed his head in shame. "I ran away," whispered Tut. Tears filled his eyes. "I ran away," he repeated. "Mama and my brother and sisters were going to be so proud of me. We had traveled back to my mother's village to perform the ceremony. I remember my mama proudly introducing me to the village chieftain, one of her relatives. We were to spend the night, and the ceremony was to take place the next morning. That evening, I sat around the fire with the men as they told their stories and explained what was to happen to me. They said the ceremony signified my journey from boyhood to manhood." Tut eyed Jafaar and said, "You know what was to happen, Baba. I had to stand during the 10-minute ceremony and show absolutely no pain as they used a razor blade to cut my face and then a thorn to pull the skin out. If my baba had been alive, he would have performed the ceremony on me, but of course, he . . ." Tut's voice broke off.

"I didn't fully understand what it was all about, but that night as I sat around the fire listening to the others tell their stories, I became frightened. I couldn't go through with it, Baba. I ran away. I ran away."

Tut turned his back on Jafaar, placed his hands to his face and sobbed. The memories were just too much for him. He was so ashamed. Jafaar walked over and put his hand on Tut's shoulder, turned him around and said, "Tut, listen to me, listen carefully."

Tut forced himself to raise his head and stared unblinking into Jafaar's steady gaze.

"Scarification has fallen out of favor. Very few go through that ceremony anymore. Jesus does not need an outward, physical sign of your bravery. The bravery that he gives is on the inside. That is where it matters. Jesus hasn't given us a cowardly spirit but a spirit of power, love, and good judgment. You have been very brave today." Jafaar placed his hand on Tut's shoulder and prayed a scripture from Psalms 81,

"I lift the burden off your shoulders. Your hands are free of the brick basket."

At that moment, the weight of those bricks lifted out of his hands, off his shoulders and his chest, replaced by a lightness of spirit. Tut inhaled deep and long, and then let his breath out—smooth and easy. It streamed from his chest without the constriction of the usual twisted knot at his throat. He breathed in and out, in and out, relishing the easiness of it. He was released, liberated, and set free.

Tut sucked in one last deep, satisfying breath. "Come on, Baba, let's finish this pallet."

CHAPTER TWENTY-ONE

Ms. Maria called out for the third time, "Pizza's here. Y'all ready to eat? It's getting cold."

The group didn't move. Shelby turned toward her mother's voice, hesitated, and then reached over to reboot the computer. Thankfully, the computer buzzed to life displaying the home screen like nothing had happened.

David let out his breath with a loud whoosh and said, "Okay, let's eat and then we've got our work set out for us."

They sat around the big kitchen table, munched on pizza and drank orange soda, each one distracted in their own way. Shelby broke the silence. "I don't understand what happened, but I promise y'all that I *will* fix this."

Surprised by her determination, Grace said, "Yes, Shel, we know you will."

A shot of adrenaline surged through Anna. "All right, guys, we've got to start thinking big—God-sized big." Anna stared intently at her friends. She sensed the same electrifying power had begun to work its way into the group. A thought came to her mind, where it came from, she didn't know, but she blurted out, "Okay, our God is a creative God, right? He created the world by speaking it into being. We serve that God. Why can't we tap into his creativity?"

"Yes, you're so right," said Favor. "*No eye has seen, no ear has heard, and no mind has imagined what God has prepared for those who love him.* God has revealed these things to us through the Spirit."

"So, obviously, there are powers in the universe that want us to fail," said David. "Let's brain-storm—no—let me call it something else—let's *God-storm.*"

Anna pulled out her iPhone and held it up to the group. "I'll record our ideas." She pressed record and waited expectantly.

Jonathan spoke first. "Okay, we need money. How do we bring in donations to help our kids?"

The group was quiet for a moment when abruptly Grace shot up from the table and began to pace up and down. "What about a concert?" she asked.

"Here in Johnson?" Anna asked skeptically. "Who would come to our little town?"

"Hey, we're God-storming, remember?" Jonathan said, grinning at her.

Embarrassed, she said— "Of course, why not?"

"So," said Grace, "who do we get to come?"

"This is where we pray," said David. "We've got to pray that God will do a miracle here. We don't aspire to some ordinary group—we want God's group."

They were silent for a moment as each prayed in their own way.

"Wait—I've got it." Grace's eyes were huge. She sat down and grabbed hold of Anna's hand. Pausing after each word, she said, "What . . . about . . . the . . . Righteous . . . Descendants? They are like *the* most popular Christian rock band."

Anna's first response was, "No way. They'd never . . ." she clapped her hand over her mouth and finished with . . . "Well, maybe they would." Anna's eyes were now as big as Grace's. "Yes—why not?"

Righteous Descendants were her very favorite Christian rock band. She and Grace were members of their fan club and followed them on social media. They had several of the band's cool posters plastered on their walls. A couple of months ago, Anna even entered a contest to win an all-expense paid trip to their next concert in Frisco, Texas.

Everyone spoke at once, throwing out all kinds of ideas. Who would contact them? When would it happen? Where would it be? How would we get the word out?

"Okay . . . everybody, listen up." Grace raised her voice and said, "This is where our *Come and See* YouTube channel comes in. Somehow, we can involve our audience in this by sending it out there—and see what happens. Now, the question is, what do we say and how do we present it?"

After a pause, everyone started talking at the same time once again. Breaking into the cacophony, David raised his hand. "All right, this calls for serious prayer and fasting. Jesus told us that sometimes our prayers needed to be paired with fasting."

"Fasting?" Anna gulped. Food was extremely important to her—well, let's just say, she loved to eat.

"Yes, this is what we need to do. Instead of eating lunch next week at school, let's meet at our table and pray for God to do a miracle here."

Excited, they finished their pizza and began to make plans for the week. Even Shelby seemed caught up in the excitement—well, as much as Shelby would allow herself to be.

That night Anna sat cross-legged on her bed. She pulled Max in close, bowed her head and prayed, "Jesus, fasting is not going to be easy for me. I'm not sure that I can do this."

A quiet voice broke in from the corner of her room, "Yes, you can, Anna."

Anna slowly raised her head. He sat all comfortable in her chair with his legs crossed. Her scruffy teddy bear, now missing one eye, sat on his lap and Sally Primrose, Anna's old American Girl doll, leaned up against him, her frizzed hair squashed up against his arm. An incredible, mind-blowing joy flooded through Anna. The corners of his eyes crinkled, and his smile lit up his whole face. She so wanted to jump up and give him a big hug, but she stayed on the bed. Instead, a metaphysical sensation of love streamed around her body as if his arms encircled her in a hug. Anna had no words in her vocabulary to describe it. Max lifted his head, wagged his tail, and then settled back into the covers.

Embarrassed, Anna asked, "I guess you heard me talking to you, huh?"

He chuckled out loud and said, "Yes, I hear everything you say."

Mortified, she ducked her head.

"You can tell me anything. You never have to be ashamed."

"Well, you know, food is kind of a big deal for me. I'm not sure that I know how to fast or why," Anna said.

"There's no magic in fasting, Anna. It helps you to put your total trust in me. Fasting takes you to a different level. There's nothing wrong with food. When I created you, I placed that desire in you for many reasons—survival was one."

"Well, I know I won't starve, but I get so hungry when I don't eat."

"I went 40 days without eating once. I know exactly the feeling." He smiled fondly at her.

"40 days?" Anna asked in disbelief. "How did you do that? I would simply die of hunger."

He laughed out loud and then said, "Well, I didn't die. I was in a battle, and it was necessary at the time."

Anna thought for a moment. "We're in a battle, too, aren't we?"

Jesus gave her a sad smile. "Yes, you are. I need for you to be on your guard. There is an enemy who thinks he can still get to me by disguising himself as one of the good guys and lead the unsuspecting in the wrong direction. He will do everything in his power to keep you and your friends from this mission. I will give you the spiritual eyes to see him."

Confused, Anna asked, "See him? . . . Who *is* he?"

"He is the same one that I battled in the wilderness for forty days. You call him Lou. I call him Lucifer."

Her eyes opened wide and she gasped, "Lou? Lou, you say? No way . . . I've got to warn Shelby."

"She won't believe you, Anna. You must wait for me to show her."

"But Jesus . . . what do I do in the meantime?"

Her heart hammered in her chest to the point that she moved off the bed and paced up and down the room. She had to know what to do about Lou, Shelby, the kids—everyone.

"That's why you're fasting. Shelby and a group of children from half way around the world need my help. I'm here to show you and your friends the way." His voice calmed her, and she sat back down on the bed.

"Lord, I'm afraid. What if I fail you?" A tear trickled down her cheek and she swiped at it.

Jesus' eyes warmed, and his voice swirled into her like liquid honey. "There's no need for you to be afraid. Just listen for my voice, take one step at a time, and you will know what to do."

Anna took a deep breath and then let it out. "With your help, I can do this, Lord."

"I'm with you, Anna, I'm with you. I'll never leave you." At that, the light faded and dimmed from the corner of the room and he disappeared.

She sat for a while and stared at the chair where he'd been sitting. Her teddy bear leaned forlornly over on his side against Sally Primrose. *What do I do with this information? Tonight? Nothing,* she decided. Anna yawned. *I'll deal with it tomorrow.* With that thought in her mind, she crawled under the covers and whispered, "Good night, Jesus."

The weekend flew by and Anna kept busy by finally cleaning out her room, a job that she had put off long enough. It had gotten a bit out of control. Well, to rephrase that—it was a mess. Dad had been after her for some time to clean her room, so, today seemed like as good a day as ever. Sometimes she did her best thinking while she cleaned. Max followed her around, as usual, and Anna kept up a running conversation with him. She loved the way he cocked his head when she asked him questions.

"Max, what do you think about all of this?"

Max tilted his head and wagged his tail.

Anna reached down and rubbed his velvety ears. "I know, I think so, too."

It was when she pulled out the junk drawer of her desk that Anna found a stack of papers that she'd stuffed in the drawer about a week ago in a vain attempt to *neaten* up as her grandmother used to say. In the middle of the stash was a letter that she'd received in the mail about two weeks earlier. Thinking it was junk mail at the time, she added it to the stack of magazines and mail in the drawer. Honestly, she'd forgotten about it.

Anna grabbed the letter opener and neatly sliced open the top of the envelope. She admitted that she was a *bit* OCD about things like that.

"Hmm, I wonder what this is, Max?" She opened the letter and began to read. Anna caught her breath and whispered at first and then said out loud, "No way . . . Oh—my—goodness—Oh, my goodness . . . OMG . . . No way. No way." She read through it again. "Max . . . I've won a trip to the Righteous Descendants concert."

Anna held the letter to her chest and kneeled beside him. He licked her face as she bowed her head and breathed a prayer of unbelievable thanks.

Monday at noon, Anna and Grace walked outside and sat down at the lunch table and waited for everyone to join them. Anna's stomach growled, and she tried her best to ignore it. She was about to burst with excitement to show everyone what she'd found in her junk drawer. Anna wanted everyone to be together when she shared her good news. Her friends were never, ever going to believe this.

CHAPTER TWENTY-TWO

Tut's stomach rumbled loudly. He had picked up the poles of the pallet about an hour ago. It was his turn to help Jafaar transport his little sister. He was so tired and hungry—it had been many hours since they had eaten breakfast. There was nothing for lunch, and it didn't appear that they would have much to eat that evening. As he walked along, he had been daydreaming of a huge bowl of his mother's fish stew and hunks of warm, moist kisra. He could almost taste it. At that moment, his foot caught on a root and he almost tripped, taking the pallet with Achan down with him. She did not even make a sound as he jostled her.

Jafaar stopped to allow Tut to get a better grip on the poles.

A few minutes later, Lala whimpered, "I am so hungry."

Tut turned his head to the side and called back over his shoulder, "I know, little sister."

"Jafaar, can we stop soon and see if we can find anything to eat?" asked Zofa.

"Hopefully, there is a village up ahead of us," he said.

They had been walking at a snail's pace all day. Scratches and insect bites covered their legs and they constantly reached down to slap or scratch. It was hard going, and they were all hungry and exhausted.

Lala walked up beside Zofa. Her face pinched with hunger and fatigue, she asked hopefully, "Will they have food, Mama?"

"Yes," she said as she placed her arm around the little girl's skinny shoulders. "Surely, they will have food."

Finally, Jafaar stopped and said, "Let's rest here for a while." He motioned for Tut to lay the pallet down.

Grateful for the respite, Tut gently laid his end of the pallet on the ground, stretched his back and wiggled his numb fingers.

"Tut, I want you to go with me. Perhaps, we will come across a place up ahead where we might find food and shelter."

Tut's face split into a weary smile. "Yes, we will find something, I'm sure of it," Tut answered a little more confidently than he felt.

Jafaar turned to Zofa and said, "Stay here with the children. I promise we will not be long."

Ulan spoke up, "Baba, may I go with you?"

"Son, you must stay here and take care of Zofa and your sisters."

Ulan's thin seven-year-old chest swelled, and he stood up proudly. "Yes, Baba, I will."

Jafaar gathered the group close and prayed. "Father, we ask that you guide our steps to a place of protection and nourishment. In Jesus name. Amen."

Zofa reached out and patted each child. "We will wait here and pray."

Satisfied that Zofa and the children were in a relatively safe place, Jafaar and Tut took off to the east. They walked in silence. About an hour into their hike, Tut stopped in the middle of the path. "Do you hear that, Baba?"

Jafaar nodded, placed his finger to his lips and motioned for Tut to be silent. Noiselessly they crept forward. They hid behind a thick copse of bushes and watched as a group of Nuer women and girls gathered up fronds and sticks. They talked and giggled amongst themselves, oblivious to any danger. Aware that it might frighten them less if the young Tut approached, Jafaar signaled for him to walk out and greet the women.

Without hesitation, Tut walked from behind the bushes toward the group and bowed in respect. Curious, the women and girls stopped talking and just stared at him.

He held up a hand in greeting. "Sisters, my name is Tut. My family and I need help. My little sister is not well, and we are so hungry. Can you help us?"

The group gawked at him—not saying a word—until a young girl broke the silence. She placed her hand across her mouth and giggled. An elderly woman stepped forward. "Welcome, Tut. Yes, we will help your family."

Tut cracked a huge smile and bowed to the old woman. "My baba is behind the trees. May he greet you?"

"Yes, he may," the old woman said.

After listening to the exchange, Jafaar walked into the clearing. "My humble thanks to you, old mama. My name is Jafaar. My wife and three other children are waiting as we speak. We had to leave them several kilometers away so that we might find help. As Tut explained, one of the children is very ill, and the others are hungry and thirsty. We will go back and fetch them. Thank you—thank you for helping us."

"We have water. Are you thirsty?"

"Yes," said Tut, licking his parched and cracked lips.

Motioning to the young girl that had giggled before, the woman ordered, "Nyamin, please fetch water for our friends." Nyamin was about Tut's age, dressed in bright colors that shone against her beautiful, polished black skin. Around her neck were brilliantly colored beads which indicated that she was a chieftain's daughter.

Shyly, she picked up the heavy water bucket and struggled to bring it to Jafaar and Tut. Tut smiled at her as he took the bucket from her. He quickly ladled out water and gulped down the wonderful cool liquid. After he drank his fill, Tut gave the ladle to Jafaar who also drank until he quenched his thirst. Jafaar wiped at his mouth. "Thank you again. We will return soon with our family."

As they turned to leave, Nyamin called out, "Wait. I have a few small desert dates that I will gladly share with you."

Surprised, Tut turned around and said, "Thank you, little sister."

Nyamin ran up boldly, pushed the treats into Tut's hands and then hurried back to the women. Tut smiled after her and then took a small bite of one of the delicious desert dates. He decided to save the rest for the other children. His face wreathed in a smile, Jafaar patted Tut on the back and said, "Come, let's hurry. We have good news for Zofa and the kids."

When they returned to the family an hour later, Zofa sat on the ground rocking Achan. The little girl was asleep, limp in her arms.

Tut walked over and kneeled beside them both. Her voice low so that the other children could not hear, Zofa said, "She is burning up with fever. Do you have good news?"

"Yes, we found a village," Tut said. He told her about the women who had been gathering in the woods. "They have food and water for us. Baba said we will stay with them for a while until Achan begins to feel better." Tut reached down and gently placed his hand on Achan's forehead and gave Zofa a worried glance. He then walked over and squatted down in front of the other two children offering each of them a desert date. Surprised and grateful, the children savored their small treat, sucking the date, then rolling it around in their mouth slowly to make it last.

"We will go to the village," said Jafaar. Tut reached down and tenderly picked up Achan out of Zofa's arms. She was so light that he had no trouble carrying her over to the makeshift pallet. As he carefully placed Achan back on the pallet, she whimpered a little but then settled back into her feverish sleep. Grateful for that, Tut laid his hand on her hot brow and prayed that God would keep her safe until they arrived at the village. He nodded at Jafaar, and they picked up the pallet and began to walk. The trek was slow as they trudged through the brush until they found the path to the village.

When they returned to the clearing where they'd previously met the women, they laid Achan's pallet on the ground to rest.

"It can't be far from here," said Tut.

At his words, Nyamin walked out from behind a tree and bowed. "Welcome, I will take you to my village."

Tut could not take his eyes off her. He had never seen a girl so beautiful. She smiled shyly at him and pointed down the path.

"Tut," said Jafaar trying to get his attention.

Tut tore his eyes away from Nyamin and focused on Jafaar.

"Pick up the pallet," he urged.

Tut blinked his eyes and reached down for the poles. They followed Nyamin through a maze of trees and then along a river bank.

"Could this be the River Sobat?" Tut asked. "We have traveled a long way to find it."

"Of course," said Nyamin. "We live along the river during the dry season."

An hour later, the entire group sat together around one big bowl. They ate fried perch and drank from a gourd of rich, fresh cak (milk) pulled straight from a favorite cow. Never had food or drink tasted so delicious. Zofa helped Achan sit up so that she might get something to eat, also. Her eyes glazed from the fever, but she allowed Zofa to feed her some of the fish and give her several sips of the refreshing, sweet milk.

"Take your time," warned Jafaar. "I know you are all so hungry, but you do not want to get sick to your stomach and lose your meal."

Tut closed his eyes and forced himself to chew slowly. It tasted heavenly, or at least what he thought food in Heaven might taste like. He noticed Nyamin and a group of village children. They stood at a distance and gawked at Tut's family. Tut grinned at them, and they all smiled back, especially Nyamin.

After their meal, the village chief walked over to Jafaar and invited him and Tut to come and sit a while under the tribal heglig tree. The tree perched high on a small rise with the village on one side and the river on the other. This tree was unique and mystical to the village because one like this did not typically grow so close to the river, preferring the dry more than the wet. The village elders said the gods planted this tree on elevated ground for protection. Whatever the reason, the tree's branches stretched out wide and provided welcome shade during the heat of the day. The chief motioned for someone to bring an animal skin for Jafaar and Tut to sit upon, a sign of honor.

"It is peace, my brothers?" asked the chief.

"It is peace," answered Jafaar.

Tut bowed his head in respect.

"You are welcome to our village," said the chief. "Another young man came through a few days ago. He told us that his family was close behind."

Relieved, Jafaar said, "Yes, our brother, Luka, goes before us to Ethiopia."

The chief lit his pipe and inhaled, bringing the smoke deep into his lungs, and then leisurely exhaled. He watched the smoke curl and float in the air. "Yes, it is good. My daughter, Nyamin, will serve you. Ask her if you need anything at all."

Tut's skin warmed as he pictured Nyamin. So beautiful. He looked forward to meeting her again.

CHAPTER TWENTY-THREE

Grace leaned over and whispered in Anna's ear, "Are you hungry?"

Grimacing, Anna nodded her head and whispered back, "Yes, we're in for a long afternoon."

She wondered out loud, "Do you think Shelby will join us?"

"Who knows?" said Grace.

"Anyone hungry?" Jonathan grinned as he walked up and straddled the bench.

Behind him were Favor and David.

As they sat down, Anna asked, "Have y'all seen Shelby?"

"Not since this morning," said Favor.

Shaking off a feeling of disquiet, Anna turned to Jonathan and asked, "So, what do we do now? I'm kind of new to this fasting and prayer thing."

"Well," said Jonathan, "Jesus told us that when you fast, don't put on a gloomy face like the hypocrites or make a big deal about it around others—like taking a picture of your sad self and posting it on Instagram. He said that's reward enough for those people. Act like everything's normal, brush your hair and teeth, wash your face, and God will see what you're doing in that secret place."

Anna's heart skipped a beat when he mentioned the secret place, remembering the words that Jesus spoke in her room last Friday night. Should she tell them about her "visits"?

She knew that the Knights would understand, but not her friends—at least not yet.

Jonathan continued, "It's not anything mystical or magical."

Hmmm, Anna thought to herself, *pretty much the same thing Jesus said to me the other night.*

"Fasting helps us focus on God and his plan for us without worrying about things like food. It's never easy, I admit that." Jonathan grinned and said, "So, let's stop talking and start praying."

She glanced around to see if anyone was watching. *Anna, why are you worried about other people?* She chastised herself. She twisted around and turned her back to the courtyard, bowed her head and closed her eyes.

First Jonathan, David, and then Favor prayed out loud. They prayed for their family, the children and their safety, and God's creative hand to help them come up with some extraordinary way to make money to help them reunite with the four kids.

After Favor finished her prayer, they sat silently, heads still bowed before the Lord. Anna's grandmother told her once that if you're going to pray and talk to God, you've got to give him time to answer. The courtyard noise seemed to dim as the friends continued to sit and listen for God's voice.

Antsy, Anna decided to get up and walk around. She made her way over by the band room, a short distance from the picnic tables. She sat down on the steps and closed her eyes.

"Hey, Anna," a voice whispered in her ear.

An acrid smell hit her nose, and Anna's eyes popped open. She flinched and turned to the sound of the voice. Lou stood right behind her. His face was so close to hers that she jerked back.

"May I?" Without her consent, he sat down beside her on the steps.

With a furtive glance at him, Anna was about to call out to her friends for help but stopped when she noticed that they were still praying, paying no attention to her.

Anna scowled and narrowed her eyes. "Where'd you come from?"

"Oh, just hanging out. I noticed you over here, so I thought I would come by and say hey. Talking to God, are you? Hmmm, what's up with that?"

Anna squirmed on the step as her stomach growled and rumbled. "Yeah, I am—so what of it?"

"You must be hungry. I could help you, too—without all that fasting nonsense. All you have to do is fill me in."

She narrowed her eyes and scooted away from him. "I don't think I have anything to say to you."

"Oh, come on, Anna. Who do you think you are? Trying to be all Christian-like, fasting and all that. Why would he listen to your prayers? I know you have your doubts. Who wouldn't? Where was he when your mother left? Huh? Or when your grandmother died? You called out to him, didn't you, Anna? But, she died anyway, didn't she? Admit it—you don't really trust him, do you? Your God has disappointed you, hasn't he? There's so much that I could help you experience in the world. Your family and friends and your Jesus only want to hold you back. You don't need any of them."

"Stop it. Stop talking to me. Stop asking me questions. Get out of my mind. I have nothing to say to you."

"Anna, Anna," his voice was soft and appealing. "Nothing's going to come of all this fasting and prayer nonsense. It's all in your imagination." He pointed toward Favor and the others. "They're just making all of this up."

Were they? She stared over at each bowed head. Anna didn't speak for a moment—she didn't know what to say. Admittedly, she did have doubts sometimes. There were a lot of things in her life that didn't go the way she wanted them to go even after she prayed. But then Anna remembered Jesus sitting in her chair. He wasn't a figment of her imagination. She saw him—talked to him. No one could convince her otherwise. Anna recalled the smile on his face and the indescribable love that flowed through her when she spoke to him. At that moment, a surge of energy raced through her body and she knew—she got it. Her mind was clear now. Lou's words were all lies. Suddenly, the courage that Jesus told her about welled up inside of her. She would fight back.

Lou kept on talking, oblivious to her change of attitude. "Shelby understands. Now, that girl knows her mind. She knows who to turn to when something needs to happen. She knows who will listen to her."

Anna jumped to her feet. "No—no, Lou," she said fiercely. "Shelby does *not* understand. She's miserable. You can't make her happy. Only God can do that."

Lou peered at her. The insidious grin was gone, replaced by a malevolent sneer. "Oh, Anna—what am I going to do with you? You have no idea what Shelby understands or wants. She's mine."

At the picnic table, all three Knights raised their heads and opened their eyes at the same time. David sensed something was wrong. He stood up and started to walk toward Anna. She glanced over at him and then turned back to tell Lou to leave, but he was gone—completely vanished from sight.

Where did he go? Anna ran over to David and the others. "Did you see him, David? Jonathan? Favor?" . . . Frantic, her voice squeaked, "Grace?"

"No," said David, "but as I prayed, God warned me of danger."

Grace spoke up, "Anna, are you all right? What—who did you see? I didn't see anyone."

"It was Lou. What was he doing here?" A bit hysterical, she did a 360-degree turn. "Why did y'all not see or hear him? I don't get it."

Favor walked around the table and put her arm around Anna's shoulders and gave her a hug. "We believe you. Come on and sit down. What did he say to you?"

Anna explained about their short conversation but left out the part about her doubts *and* what Jesus had told her about Lou—she wasn't sure if they would understand.

"We know him." Favor said. "We already know about Lou."

"But how? How do you know him?"

"We fight him and his minions everywhere we go. He was in South Sudan with us and now he is here," she said matter-of-factly.

Bewildered, Grace didn't speak until—"Okay, I am *completely* freaked out now. So much has happened in this last month, and I don't get any of it. I'm scared—scared of the things that I don't understand. Y'all have got to help me out here. First, Shelby and Lou, then the weird computer thing, then all of this. I . . . I . . ." Grace stuttered, not finding the right words to say anything more.

Jonathan reached out across the table and took her hand. "We get it, Grace. It's okay. It's okay."

Grace blushed and wiped tears off her face with her other hand. "I'm sorry. I'm so not like you guys."

"Here's the thing, everyone," said Favor. "When we move closer to God's will, there's a lot of flak that we have to endure. But, we must remember that God is on our side. We can't lose. The fact that Lou was here is reason enough for us to believe we're on the right track."

"But why me?" Anna asked. "Favor, why me?"

"Because—you're a threat."

There was a long pause, and then David said, "All right, forget Lou. This is where our God-storming kicks in. He has it all laid out for us. We just have to listen to him."

Now even more determined to come up with some great ideas, they spent the next twenty minutes throwing out ways that they might raise money for the kids and the orphanage. When there was a lull in the conversation, Anna said out loud, "Hmm—so—what else?"

That's when it hit her—Anna remembered what she'd found in her drawer after she'd cleaned her room last night.

"Oh, my goodness, in all this craziness, I forgot to tell y'all about what I found in my desk drawer last night."

Curious, everyone stared and waited for her to continue.

"Well, my desk drawer was full of junk mail . . . so I decided to go through it and throw it out. And that's when I . . ." Anna stopped mid-sentence.

"Anna, the suspense is killing me here. What did you find?" asked Grace.

"A letter. I found a letter."

"So . . . go on . . ." Grace said impatiently.

"Well—I so happened—to have won—an all-expense paid trip to the Righteous Descendants concert at the Toyota Field in Frisco, Texas—airline, hotel, meals—the works. But . . ." she paused for the drama of it, "the best part is that I can take three more people with me *plus* one parent."

CHAPTER TWENTY-FOUR

The sun shimmered, hot and stifling. The scorching rays peeked through the leaves of the heglig tree like a magnifying glass. Tut reached over and picked up several fragrant flowers from the tree that had dropped on the ground. He handed one to Jafaar and popped the other into his mouth and sucked out the sweet nectar. They both sat respectfully waiting for the chief to speak.

"My name is Luthrial. I was named after my beautiful black and white ox that my baba gave to me when I received my cuttings and became a man."

"He was very important to you?" asked Tut respectfully.

"Yes, all of my herd originated with him. He made me very wealthy."

Tut gazed out at the cattle. Some grazed on the sparse grass while others lay down between the dung fires around the village. He was very impressed. Jafaar had explained to him the importance of cattle to his people.

What must it be like to live free?

Tut knew that Jafaar grew up in a village just like this. "Baba, do you regret leaving your village and moving to the city?" Tut asked.

"Yes, I do—sometimes. I was very young when I left. It was right after my cutting and the world and adventure called out to me." He hesitated, closed his eyes and smiled. "I admit, though, when the rains dry up every year and the air is sweet with the smells of summer, I remember and sometimes yearn for the life that I missed."

Tut and the men sat silent for a moment and enjoyed the sights, sounds, and smells of the village. Finally, the chief asked, "Tell me, friends, what brings you to our village?"

"We come from Malakal, but civil war has destroyed our city. We search for a place of peace and safety," said Jafaar. "We travel toward Ethiopia. One of our children is very sick. While escaping from the refugee camp in Malakal, a stray bullet hit her in the leg. It has become infected and causes her great pain. We carried her here hoping to rest and give her time to heal," said Jafaar.

Luthrial shrugged his shoulder and said frankly, "Yes, it is good to rest. Perhaps she will live, but, many children die each day in South Sudan."

"My sister will not die," Tut said fiercely.

"Do you want me to call the healer?" asked Luthrial.

Tut recoiled at the thought. He didn't want the healer anywhere near his little sister. He had a very frightening experience with a healer when he was a little boy. He had gotten very sick at his stomach, his bowels were like water, and he kept throwing up over and over. His mama called on the healer to come and pray for him. A man covered with colored beads, feathers, and tattoos walked into their hut and hovered over his bed. He sang and prayed to a god named Kwoth. Tut could only remember panic as the healer bent low and peered searchingly into his very soul. The healer's eyes blazed and lit up his contorted face like a scary mask. The man's prayers did no good, and finally, his mama took him to the missionary hospital and begged that they would see him. Not only did their medicine heal him, but through the kindness of the missionaries, his mama met Jesus for the first time.

Respectfully, Tut answered the chief, "Sir, thank you, but we are praying to Jesus that he might heal her."

Luthrial shrugged and didn't say anything, but once again inhaled and blew smoke into the air and watched it float away, caught by a hot breeze off the river.

"What can we do for you, brother, in exchange for your hospitality?" said Jafaar. "We are very grateful for your protection."

"We could use your help in the building of a temporary tukul (hut) for my son, Rolnyang, and his new wife. We are in the process now of negotiating the number of cows in exchange for his bride. The wedding will happen soon. The tuk is temporary, of course, because when the season of rains come, we will move our cows away from the river and back to our village."

Jafaar smiled at Tut and said to the chief, "It is good. The women that we met yesterday were gathering grass for the building. They told us about the new tuk. We will be happy to help you."

The chief grunted, stood up, and dismissed Jafaar and Tut with a wave of his hand. They bowed their heads in respect, backed away, and returned to Zofa and the children.

Ulan and Lala sat under a tree beside Zofa and Achan; their eyes rounded with worry and fear. Achan lay with her head in Zofa's lap.

Zofa smiled up at Jafaar as he approached. "It is good, my husband?"

"It is good."

Later that day, the chief sent Nyamin to show the family to an empty tuk. "You may stay here," she said.

Zofa, Tut, and Lala followed her inside.

"Look Tut," Lala said excitedly, "mosquito nets."

"Thank you, Nyamin," said Zofa. "We have all been miserable. Sleep has been difficult without the protection of the nets."

Naymin smiled shyly, bowed her head and left.

Jafaar told them about their conversation with Chief Luthrial. He grinned at his brother and sister. "Will you help us?"

Excited, they bobbed their heads in unison.

The next morning, Zofa woke Tut and the children up early. She had been awake off and on most of the night placing cool cloths on Achan's forehead. Her fever always spiked at night. Finally, near dawn, her fever broke. Exhausted, Zofa moved over as Jafaar sat down beside her.

Troubled, Tut asked, "She sleeps?"

"Yes," said Zofa.

"Is she better?" asked Jafaar.

"I don't think so." Zofa leaned her head on Jafaar's shoulder. "Her body is cool this morning, but her leg is still on fire with the infection."

Jafaar heard a rustle at the door and motioned for Tut to see who was there. He crawled out the low opening to see Nyamin holding a gourd in each hand, one of fresh milk and one of durra porridge. Her pretty smile lit up her face before she ducked her head. She wore a beautiful African print dress that accented her gorgeous skin. Tut's heart flipped a little as he stared at her because Nyamin was just so lovely. He'd never had that kind of reaction before to a girl, and he was unsure as to why he was feeling that way.

Nyamin offered him the gourds. "Brother, this morning I milked the cow and pounded the dura for your family. My mama cooked some porridge."

Embarrassed and not knowing why, he took the gourd and mumbled a thank you.

"We begin work in a short time. Will you tell your baba?"

"I will tell him."

Bowing her head, Nyamin turned to go but then hesitated, spun back around and gave Tut a quick smile. She then giggled and hurried away.

Tut stared dumbly as she walked off, shook himself and crawled back into the tuk, holding onto the large gourds of milk and porridge.

Tut and the other children gathered around as Jafaar gave thanks to God for the generous breakfast. They each took turns, drinking deep and savoring the sweet taste of the warm, rich milk. They made sure to save a good portion for Achan who was still asleep on her mat.

"Let me try and wake her," said Zofa.

Zofa whispered her name and ever so gently placed her hand on the child's forehead. "She is still feverish. Tut would you pour a little milk for her?"

Tut carefully poured the milk and set it down beside Zofa. He couldn't take his worried eyes off his little sister, willing her to get better. He had to admit, she was a favorite. Her spunk and tenaciousness filled a void that his mother had left. What would he do if Achan died? That thought intruded, and he quickly pushed it away. If Achan died, his heart would break. He had tried to be so efficacious by taking good care of his younger siblings. His mama had asked him one day to do so, shortly before she disappeared. He remembered her face, what she wore, and especially what she said on that day—her words were etched into his memory forever. He had gone with his mama to the river bank to wash clothes. His job was to stand guard and watch for snakes or crocodiles. When she had finished her wash, Tut helped her to pile the wet clothes into a woven basket and then balance them on her head. They walked back to their shack in silence, the only sound the swish of his mama's long skirt. Tut could tell that his mama had something on her mind. She was usually bubbly, full of chitchat and laughter, but on this day, she was quiet. A short distance from their shack, she stopped, grasped the basket from her head and set it down at her feet.

"Tut, if something happens to me, you must take care of your brother and sisters. Will you promise me that?"

He studied his mama's beautiful face for a moment and said, "You know that I will."

She sighed, reached over and kissed his cheek. Pulling back, she said, "Yes, I know, my son."

Several weeks later, she was gone.

Zofa broke into his thoughts. "Lala, would you get me a cool cloth?"

Lala jumped up and did as Zofa asked, her forehead creased in worry. "Is she going to get well, Mama? I have prayed every day to Jesus that he would heal her."

Zofa smiled up at her as Lala handed over the moistened cloth. "Keep praying, my child."

Lala smiled back at Zofa, and then suddenly grabbed Tut's hand and said, "Tut, come pray with us."

As he knelt beside Achan and Zofa, Lala placed her small hand in his and her other hand on Achan's head. Tut bowed his head and listened as Lala prayed. "Jesus, sir, please heal my sister. I know you can. Baba tells me that you are the healer. Thank you for hearing my prayer." She sat for a moment, her hand still on Achan's head, and then remembered, "Oh, in Jesus' name. Amen."

Tut repeated, "In Jesus' name."

He sat in silence beside Zofa and Lala, whispering that prayer over and over. Unknown to them, Achan's eyes popped open. She noticed the three of them beside her with their eyes closed. "Lala? Zofa? Tut," she whispered. She spoke louder this time, "Lala. Zofa. Tut. Why do you sit with your eyes shut? I'm hungry."

The three opened their eyes at the same time as Achan tried to sit up, still tangled in her mosquito net. "Please get me out of this," said Achan.

Quickly, Tut unwrapped the net from around her. She sat up straight and smiled at him, her first one in many days. Puzzled, she noted the surprised and joyful expressions on her family's faces. "Why are you staring at me like that?"

They all spoke at once until Jafaar raised his hand to quiet everyone. "Lala, will you get your sister some milk? Zofa . . . please examine Achan's leg."

The entire group huddled around Zofa as she removed the bandages from Achan's wounded and infected leg. Tut held his breath as Zofa unwrapped the last dressing. They gasped at the same time. Stunned, they locked eyes and then turned back to Achan's leg.

"Tut," she whispered. Louder this time, "Praise God!"

Achan's leg was completely, perfectly, and totally healed.

CHAPTER TWENTY-FIVE

Mouths gaped open and eyes widened as the group reacted to Anna's news.

Grace jumped up and squealed, "*What*? Are you kidding me? No way. No way."

Laughing at the expressions on all their faces, Anna said, "Yes, it's true. Can you believe it? We actually get to see the Righteous Descendants in person." She raised both hands in the air for emphasis. "Oh, there's one more thing. We also have back-stage passes to meet the band before the concert—and have a pre-concert dinner with them."

Grace grabbed at her heart and sat down hard on the picnic bench. "I think—I'm—going—to—faint. Do you know what this *means*?" She squeezed her eyes shut and said one more time, "Do you *know* what this means?" Grace tended to repeat herself when she's excited.

"Yes, yes, this is our answer," said Favor in an awed voice. "Our answer."

Always the voice of reason, Jonathan said, "This could be our chance to invite the band to our town for a concert. Surely, it's God's plan for us."

The five grabbed hands as the good news soaked into their addled brains. Anna noticed they were getting strange looks from some of the other students in the courtyard. Even the resource officer walked by a couple of times.

Disregarding all of that, Anna broke the silence by saying, "Okay, now, how do we decide who gets to go?"

David joined in. "Well, of course, you'll go to Frisco, Anna. I mean, you're the one with the letter, and I think it needs to be your dad as the parent. In the Bible, they often drew lots to decide who God chose. Why don't we do that to decide who goes with Anna and her dad?"

* * * *

"Why are you drawing lots?" A dour Shelby walked up to the group.

Grace jumped up and hugged her. "Shel, you're never going to guess. Always the eternal optimist, Grace assumed that Shelby would be as excited as they were. "Where've you been? We've been looking for you."

Shelby didn't bother to answer. She didn't want to tell Grace that she'd been on the other side of the school talking to Lou. There was an alcove on the west side of the grounds where no one ever gathered. She'd go there sometimes to eat her lunch when she wanted to get away from people. No way was she fasting with the group—she didn't see any reason for it. She'd just finished her ham sandwich when Lou appeared out of nowhere.

She glared at him. "Where'd you come from? The last time I saw you, you jumped in the car and left me with that crazy lady, Ms. Ruby."

Lou pursed his mouth in an annoying smirk and said, "Yeah, I guess I did, didn't I? Forgive me?" He reached out and gave her a hug. Lou could be very charming when he wanted to. "So, what have you been up to lately?"

Shelby didn't mention the YouTube channel or the Knights because she figured that Lou would just make fun of her. "Nothing much."

Lou raised his eyebrows and smiled like he knew she wasn't telling him the truth, but he didn't say anything. "Well, then—guess I'll see you around. Let's go for a ride one of these days, okay?"

"Sure, why not?" She reached into her lunch bag for her drink. When she glanced up, he was gone. She shrugged her shoulders and sipped her Gatorade. Shelby finished her lunch and checked the time on her phone. She had just walked up when she heard her sister mention something about drawing lots and a concert.

* * * *

Grace filled Shelby in on the concert details and the trip to Frisco. Even though she tried to hide it, Anna could tell that Shelby would like to go, also.

"Do you want to put your name in the hat, Shel?" Anna asked.

She lowered her backpack to the ground and said, "Sure, if I don't have anything better to do, I guess."

"Okay, then, everyone," said David, "write your name on a piece of paper and we'll draw."

Anna yanked open her backpack and grabbed an old algebra test paper and unfolded it. She grimaced at the "D" that she'd made on the test and dismissed it with a shrug. She tore the paper into five equal pieces. After each one wrote their name, they wadded their piece up and gave it to David to put in his baseball hat. He glanced around and called out to a girl sitting at the next picnic table. "Would you come over and draw for us?" Blushing, she got up and walked over to the table. She reached into the hat and pulled out three pieces of paper.

Smiling that cute smile of his, David said, "Thank you."

The girl smiled back and went back to sit down, her eyes still on David.

"Well, okay," said David, trying to ignore the pretty girl. "Let's see who God has chosen." He opened each piece of paper and called out the names: "Grace . . . Jonathan . . . and . . . Shelby."

Grace beamed. Anna knew that her friend was about to burst with excitement; she just didn't want to show it. Shelby plopped down on the bench, stunned, while Jonathan's lips split into a huge smile.

"So, we're good then?" asked David.

At that, the friends stood up, cheered, and gave each other a high five.

As soon as everyone had quieted down, Anna said, "You know, I was just thinking—this would be the perfect way to launch our *Come and See* YouTube channel. We'd tell our audience all about the trip, and they'd *virtually* travel with us. If we posted the videos on the Righteous Descendant's Fan Club Facebook page and their Instagram, we could really get the word out."

"Of course," said Jonathan, studying Anna's face until she blushed and dipped her head, "that's brilliant, Anna."

She wasn't sure what to say to that, so she mumbled something—stupid, she was sure. Right then the bell rang, and all Anna could say was, "Uh . . . guess we better go to class."

She was in such a hurry to pick up her backpack that she stumbled over one of the straps. Jonathan was right behind and grabbed her arm to keep her from falling face first in the grass.

"Hey, careful there," he said.

Doubly mortified, Anna regained her balance, gave him a weak smile and breathed out, "Oh, thanks." She was so embarrassed. He must think she was the biggest klutz. Anna gathered her bag along with her wits and walked quickly to class, thankful that they did not have fifth period together.

That afternoon, Anna and Max waited for Dad to come home from work, impatient to tell him the good news.

"Anna? Ben? I'm home."

Max jumped up, wagged his tail and barked out a greeting.

"We're in the kitchen, Dad—at least Max and I are. Ben is still at baseball practice."

Dad stuck his head through the door and said, "Hey, you. Let me put my stuff in the office and I'll be right back."

A few minutes later, he walked into the kitchen. "What's going on? You seem happy about something."

"So," she began nonchalantly, "what do you have on your calendar for the second weekend in April?"

Dad pulled out his phone and glanced down at it for a minute. "Looks like I'm free. What's up?"

With a dramatic flair, Anna pulled out the Righteous Descendants' invitation letter from her backpack and gave it to him to read.

Raising his eyebrows, he took the letter from her, reached for his glasses and began to read. When he finished, he peered up over his glasses, slowly shook his head back and forth and said, "Anna, are you sure this is legit? This is hard to believe."

"I know, I know. It *is* hard to believe, but . . . let me explain." Anna told him everything. She began with her friends' desire to help the Knights get their kids back. "Dad, we brainstormed, or rather, Godstormed and came up with the idea for a YouTube channel. We even prayed that God would help us bring the Righteous Descendant's back to Johnson. We believe this trip is an answer to our prayer."

Dad listened and nodded his head at appropriate times, not saying anything at all until finally, Anna couldn't stand it anymore.

"So, what do you think, Dad?"

He read the letter one more time and then said cautiously, "Well, this seems to be legitimate, but of course, we need to check it out to make sure it's not a hoax."

Noticing the dismay on Anna's face, he said, "I'm sure it's okay, hon. I'll email the address on their website to verify." He walked over, put his arm around her shoulder and said, "Anna, you amaze me. It's like you have a direct line to Jesus or something. If this checks out, then of course, I'll go with you. We'll need to find a place for Ben and Max to stay."

At the sound of his name, Max wagged his tail, jumped up on dad's leg and whined.

"What do you think, Max? What do you think?" Dad asked as he reached down to rub his head.

That night as Anna and Max got ready for bed, an Instagram popped up from Grace. She had taken a selfie of Shelby and her in front of the Righteous Descendants poster that hung up on her wall. They both had huge grins on their faces—yes, even Shelby. Under the picture were the words—*No Way.*

Anna answered her. "Yes, still can't believe that God is sending us to this concert."

Changing over to text, she wrote, *"What do we wear?"*

Grace: "Hmm, got to be thinking about that."

Anna: "Maybe we can go shopping. :-)"

Grace: "Always a good idea!"

Anna: "I could use a pair of new shoes, of course."

Grace: "Let's wear our matching RD T-shirts."

Anna: "Perfect!"

Grace: "So, we've got to have a plan. Like—how do we go about even asking the band to come to Johnson?"

Anna: "Hmm—I guess we could say, 'So, what are y'all doing in May? Have any free nights open? Coming our way anytime soon?'"

Grace: LOL

Anna: "I bet Jonathan could take charge of that. He's got a way with words."

Grace: "Yes, he does, doesn't he?" Grace ended her text with the smiling and blushing emoticon.

She had a bit of a crush on Jonathan—well, okay, so did Anna—who wouldn't? He was cute—totally unaware of his looks. Always sweet and respectful—what more could a girl ask for?

Anna: "Hey, I'm bushed. Let's call it a night. Hope I can sleep after all this excitement."

Grace: "Yeah, me, too."

CHAPTER TWENTY-SIX

Achan grabbed the gourd and drank with great thirsty gulps. Gently, Zofa pulled the vessel away from her mouth. "That's enough for now, my child. You must drink just a little so that you do not get sick."

"But, I am so thirsty, Mama."

"Yes, I know. I'll stir some of the milk into the dura porridge. That will help fill your stomach with nourishment and quench your thirst."

As Zofa stirred, Lala and Ulan sat cow-eyed, still not understanding—or believing, what had happened to their sister. Tut stood nearby, frozen in place, stunned at what had happened. He watched as Achan straightened her leg, examined it, and reached down and rubbed the place where the wound had been.

"It's a miracle, isn't it, Tut? Tut? Tut!" said Achan.

Tut had to physically shake himself out of his daze. He took a deep breath, blowing it out as he sat down beside her. He picked up one of her small hands and bowed his head as sweet relief and joy flushed through him; filling him with thanksgiving and praises to God.

"Yes, little one, the world has become right again."

"Ulan and Lala," she said, still in awe, "Do you see what Jesus has done for me?" Speechless, they just blinked and nodded their heads.

"Lala was the one who prayed for you, Achan," said Tut.

Achan's face lit up, and she turned toward Lala. "It is good. Thank you, sister."

Embarrassed, Lala bent her head down. Then—glancing back up, she said in a confident voice, "It was Jesus who told me to pray for you, Achan—Jesus."

A joy-filled silence floated in the air until Jafaar broke into their thoughts and said, "So—all of you must breakfast well this morning because we will not have nourishment again until evening."

There was a quiet grumbling noise from Ulan, but the others said nothing.

Sympathetic, Jafaar placed his hand on Ulan's shoulder and continued, "I promised the chief that we would help in the building of the new hut."

Ulan narrowed his eyes at Jafaar and said in his honest way, "We do not know how to build, Baba. We come from the city."

Jafaar smiled at him and said, "There will be many things for you to learn, and it will be good for you to know the ways of your tribe."

"How long will we be staying in the village?" asked Tut.

"I don't know for sure. Now that Achan is well, we will leave within a few days. I promised the chief that we would help in exchange for his hospitality, so we must do that. We will continue our journey to Ethiopia as soon as possible—before the rains begin. There is still much danger in front of us."

Tut ate a little breakfast, saving most of it for his brother and sisters. When he had finished, he crawled out of the hut into the bright sunlight. The village was stirring with men and women walking toward the river. They carried sticks and grasses on their heads and had huge smiles on their faces. The children were laughing and running around between the adults.

Tut weaved his way around the dung fires, built to give the cattle relief from the irritating insects that tended to suck the very blood out of them. He walked up to a tall young man, gently and lovingly rubbing ash on the back of his ox.

Curious, Tut asked, "Why do you put ashes on your ox?"

"To keep the insects away."

"What is your name?"

"I was given the name, Rolnyang," he said proudly. "Named after this beautiful creature."

He patted the ox and said, "My father, Luthrial, gave him to me when I received my cuttings—he is special." Rolnyang rubbed the ox's back one more time and said, "I thought I would have to give him up to my bride's family, but after my father negotiated the cattle price, my bride and I will get to keep him."

"So, you are the one who is getting married?"

"I am."

"My family has been asked to help build your bridal tuk. Will you be married soon?"

"Yes, tonight we kill the bull for the feast. Then we will dance to celebrate. You must come. You and your family must come."

"We would like that very much."

"Do you hear the call of the drum?" asked Rolnyang.

Tut tilted his head to one side to listen. He glanced around and spotted a tribe member beating loudly on the bul. Each beat called out an invitation to all within hearing distance. The man seemed oddly familiar. Tut tried to think where he might have seen him.

"Who is that?" he asked.

"The drummer?" asked Rolnyang. "He is the healer, the holy man."

Tut stared back at the man one more time. As he did, the drum stopped, and the drummer stood up and ambled toward them, slowly threading his way through the cows and the dung fires. Transfixed, a kaleidoscope of images spun around in Tut's mind as the man approached—he recognized him—it was the man in his dream. But, there was a difference—this man was black, and the man in his dream was white, but they were the same. A shiver curled up his neck as he noticed a ragged scar on the man's forehead ending with a star tattoo at his temple. How could that be?

"Good morning, young friends," he said pleasantly.

Rolnyang bowed and hit Tut on the shoulder, motioning for him to bow, also. Tut couldn't swallow; fear threatened to crush him as his chest constricted. Reluctantly, he bent low before the man. Unaware, Rolnyang said to the healer, "You will come to my celebration tonight, sir?"

Not taking his eyes off Tut, the healer's face twisted into a mocking smile and he said, "Yes, I will, of course . . . and your friend?"

Tut raised his chin and forced himself to look the man in his eyes. "Yes, I will be there." With a curt nod, the healer turned and sauntered away. He disappeared behind the smoky fires. A short time later, the slow beat of the drum began once again.

At the sound of the drum, Rolnyang said, "So, until tonight . . . I look forward to meeting your family."

Bewildered, Tut rubbed his eyes and turned toward Rolnyang, "What . . . what was that you said?"

"I said I looked forward to meeting your family," he repeated.

"Yes . . . yes, of course."

Tut left Rolnyang and weaved back around to the tuk where his family slept the night before. His brother and sisters stood outside, wide-eyed and a little bewildered by all the commotion. Soon, Zofa and Jafaar crawled out of the tuk and joined them.

"We go to the river, Baba," said Tut.

When the family arrived at the building site, the men had already laid the strings showing the round shape of the foundation. Joyfully, the women sang as they tied the bundles of straw together for the walls. Nyamin waved to Zofa and the girls to join them.

"Come help." A man gestured to Jafaar as he carried a long pole and laid it beside the foundation.

Jafaar nodded at the man and then motioned to Tut and Ulan for help. The three of them walked over and picked up a pole together and added it to the pile. After they had the right number of poles, the men began digging holes in the dry earth to place them in. It was sweltering, and the work was back-breaking because the ground was so hard. The heat did not deter the men at all. They often stopped to drink water from the gourds and then quickly got back to work. By afternoon, the skeleton of the walls stood tall and straight. After a time of rest, the men began laying the poles for the roof. The tribesmen kept up a loud banter as they labored, told wild stories and laughed hilariously at themselves. Tut laughed, too. He enjoyed the time with these Nuer men—his kinsmen. With no father, he had missed this as a child, growing up in the arms of his mother.

By evening, the men had finished framing the tuk. Now it would be women's work to place the thatch on top and mud the walls. The men stood back proudly and admired their efforts. At the sound of the drums, the men and women dispersed to their tuks to get ready for the dance. It was time to celebrate.

The family spoke of their day as they walked slowly back toward their tuk.

"I am tired, Baba," said Lala.

"You did well today, my child. Everyone worked hard. Tonight, we celebrate with our new friends."

The children ran on ahead, and Jafaar, Zofa, and Tut strolled behind.

"When do we leave?" asked Zofa.

"In two days' time. That will give the young ones time to rest and prepare for the journey," said Jafaar.

A smiling Nyamin waited for them back at the tuk. She had prepared a meal of fish, kisra, and milk. Tut's mouth watered as the aroma filled his nostrils and made his stomach growl. All the children were hungry since they had not eaten since breakfast. Patiently, they held hands as Jafaar blessed the food.

While they ate, Zofa said, "Nyamin, tell us about the celebration tonight."

Her eyes danced with excitement as she explained. "It is much fun. Everyone has been preparing for the evening. They have painted their bodies and put on their most colorful beads." She smiled at the girls. "I have beads for you if you would like to wear them."

Lala and Achan bowed to Zofa for permission. She smiled back at them and they nodded their heads eagerly.

"There will be a big fire and so much dancing. My brother, Kuac, is preparing for the dance now." Nyamin pointed to a young man about Tut's age in the next tuk who was oiling his body and covering his face with designs made of ash and chalk. He had bleached his hair a strawberry blonde in preparation for this night.

"Tut, you must come. Kuac will show you how to prepare for the dance."

Heat rushed to his face as he stared at Nyamin like a love-struck puppy. Finally, he broke his gaze and asked, "Baba? May I?"

"Yes, you may go."

Tut scrambled to his feet. As he walked away he turned back and grinned at Jafaar and followed Nyamin to the next hut.

CHAPTER TWENTY-SEVEN

"Have we got it all?" asked Anna. At that moment, she tripped over a load of equipment getting out of the car. "Ouch! Grace, who put that tripod there?" Anna grumbled as she made her way around it on the ground, her arms full of gear.

Anna and Grace had just returned from a trip to Home Depot and Hobby Lobby where they'd bought all the essentials that they would need to film the *Come and See* videos. The group gathered at Grace's house. Ms. Maria had told them that they could use the basement for their studio. Shelby stood at the bottom of the basement stairs, clipboard in hand, and checked off her list as they filed by her.

"Lights. . . check."

"Movie camera . . . check."

"Tripod . . . check."

"Green screen . . . check."

Shelby stopped and glanced up. "Where did you get the cool green material?"

"Went to Hobby Lobby," Anna said, smugly.

"Okay, that'll work," Shelby said. That was a compliment, coming from her.

Curious, Anna asked, "How did you learn how to do all this stuff?"

With a dismissive flip of her hand, she said, "Oh, I just watched a YouTube video called, *Green Screen on the Cheap*. It seemed easy enough."

"Hey, supper's here," said David as he walked down the stairs, balancing four boxes of pizza above his head.

"I'm starving," said Ben, coming right behind him. "Do I smell pizza?" Ben always showed up when there was food involved.

"Oh, yeah—Let's eat before we get started," said Jonathan. "I could do with some pizza right now."

Everyone agreed and sat down on the old couch as Jonathan said a short blessing. "Lord, thanks for this food." With a chorus of *amens*, they all reached at once for the pizza.

As they ate, the conversation jumped from one topic to the other until, during a lull, Ben said, "Hey, Anna and I were talking the other night, and she told me about the little boy who hurt his knee. What's up with that? I have to admit that I wasn't with y'all, but I figured there must be a good explanation."

Favor and Jonathan exchanged glances and then deferred to David who said, "Yes, it happened."

"But how?" asked Ben.

An uncomfortable silence fell around the table as they waited for David to answer. Shelby jutted her chin out, crossed her arms and leaned back against her chair. Anna caught Grace's eye and quirked an eyebrow at her. They both had the same question.

"Do you believe that miracles happened when Jesus was here on earth?" asked David.

"Sure, I believe that," Ben admitted.

"Well, the Bible says that Jesus is the same yesterday, today, and tomorrow. So—if we believe that Jesus performed miracles yesterday, could he not perform those same miracles today?"

"Yeah, but . . ."

"We experienced some amazing miracles while we were in South Sudan." David turned toward Favor and said, "Tell them about Kamal."

"Let me show you his picture," said Favor as she reached for her phone and scrolled through her photos until she came to the one that she was searching for. She held up the phone, and they all leaned in to get a closer look. "This is Kamal," she said. "I think he was about six years old in this picture."

The photo showed a little boy grinning from ear to ear. He had a bright red ball in his hands. Favor turned the phone back to herself and studied the photo for a moment as tears welled up in her eyes.

"Kamal's father was a freedom fighter. His name was Abdol. One night, Dinka rebel soldiers came to his house hunting for him. They broke down the door and started shooting. They killed Kamal's mother, little brother, and Abdol. A stray bullet hit Kamal in the back and paralyzed him. After an extended stay in the hospital, they placed him in the same orphanage where Tut and his brother and sisters lived. Kamal was in a wheelchair—he wouldn't talk to anyone. He'd just sit in his little chair and stare at everyone mutely, as they came and went."

David continued the story. "One day an evangelist came to Malakal to hold a series of tent meetings. Jafaar and Zofa decided to take Kamal and several other children to the service. David flashed a smile. "I wish all of you could experience one of these services—the music—the joy—the praise—you wouldn't believe it. I can only describe it as pure heaven. At the end of the service, the evangelist invited people to come forward who needed healing. Jafaar rolled Kamal up to the front, and at once people surrounded him and prayed. I don't know how to say this except, Kamal stood up from his wheelchair and ran around the stage—completely healed."

No one said anything. Ben reached for another slice of pizza and chewed thoughtfully. Covering his mouth, he raised his eyebrow and interjected, "Huh."

Favor smiled at him and said, "We took that photo of Kamal holding the red ball several months later. He was adopted soon after that."

The conversation then turned back to the YouTube channel. "So, Anna, you and Grace will be in front of the camera," said David. "Jonathan, you be our cameraman and Favor will be the director. Shelby's our tech princess and Ben—you're our gopher."

"I can do that." Ben grinned and gave David a high-five.

"Shelby, how does that green screen thingy work?" Anna asked.

"Well, basically, it's a large sheet of solid color material pinned up behind the people on screen. Chroma Keying allows me to easily separate the green screen from you and Grace and replace it with a new background."

The way she described the process seemed so simple, but Anna didn't have a clue. "Okay, so—what will be our new background?" she asked.

Favor said in her quiet way, "What about a photo of South Sudan and then switch over to one at a Righteous Descendants' concert?"

"Of course, that would be perfect," Anna agreed.

Ideas bounced around that basement for the next couple of hours. Since it was a school night, Anna suggested that they call it quits about 9:00 and get back together that weekend.

The spicy fragrance of the warm spring air wrapped itself around Anna and Ben as they walked toward home. They conversed quietly.

"Anna," Ben said seriously, "what do you really think?"

"What do you mean?" she asked. It wasn't like Ben to voice his thoughts very often. He was always kidding around. Rarely serious.

"Do you think God is in all of this? It's crazy, you know?"

Anna chose her words carefully. "Ben, it's real, I promise."

"But how do you know what God wants, Anna? It's not like he talks to us or anything."

"But, he does, Ben—talks to us, I mean."

Ben stopped walking for a moment under a street lamp and studied her face. "It's just—where was he when we were little kids and mom left? Why would he allow that? Our dad didn't deserve any of it." There was a touch of bitterness in his voice.

"He didn't leave us, Ben," Anna said quietly.

"Well, it felt like he did."

"Yes, I know."

They continued to walk quietly for a few minutes. Hesitant, Anna stopped under the next street lamp and laid her hand on Ben's arm. The streetlight cast a shadow on his face so that she couldn't read his expression.

"Ben . . . I talk to him. I talk to Jesus."

"Oh, yeah? You mean when you pray?"

"Yes, I talk to him when I pray, but there's more."

"What do you mean?"

"I mean—I actually talk to him. I know you're going to think I'm making this up, but I really do."

"Dad always said you had a wild imagination, Anna."

"I know, I know—but let me tell you what happened."

As they walked, Anna told Ben about the night their mom left and how Jesus appeared in her room.

Ben didn't say a thing, so she continued. "And then," she paused, "well, I talked to him the other night . . . he was there, right there in my room."

When they arrived at their house, they stopped at the porch and sat down on the steps.

"Talk to me, Ben. What do you think about what I just told you?"

"I don't know, Anna. I don't know—I don't know what to think. It all seems like a fantasy, you know? Jesus doesn't appear to people like that."

"Yeah—I don't understand why he appeared to me, but yes, it happened. I'm not making it up, I promise."

"But—why would he appear to you and not me?"

"Well, the first time I saw him, you were just four years old," she said gently. "Maybe, that's why."

"This is all a bit much for me. First, the situation with the little boy and the healed knee, and then the story that Favor and David told tonight about the paralyzed boy walking. I don't know—I've got to think about everything. I need time to process all of this."

"I get it," she said. "Sometimes I feel like I could totally go with my heart—believe, you know? Then, my head gets in the way, and I talk myself out of it. It's easy to believe when I'm at church or around the Knights—their faith is so infectious. But, then other times, like when we're at Mom's for the week-end? It's like I completely lose my religion. Tom gets on my last nerve. He makes me so angry at the way he treats us—treats Mom, too. I know I act like a spoiled teenager when I'm at Mom's, but I can't help myself. I want to be the same person around Mom that I am around Dad, but I'm not."

Ben grinned at her and said, "Yeah, I agree, you're a brat at Mom's sometimes."

She swatted at him and they both laughed.

At that moment, the porch light came on, and dad opened the door and stuck his head out. "Hey, guys, what's up? You have school tomorrow, remember?"

"Okay. We're coming in, Dad," Anna said.

That night after getting ready for bed, she sat down on the floor, leaned her back against her bed and had a long talk with Max.

"Hey Max, you know me better than most anyone."

Max cocked his head and whined.

"Am I the girl who talks to Jesus or am I the spoiled brat who makes my mother miserable? Who am I?"

Max wagged his tail, leaned against her and stretched his neck out for a good scratch. As she rubbed the sweet spot behind his ears, Max closed his eyes and totally slipped into a state of doggie bliss. Anna leaned over and laid her head on his soft head and whispered, "You love me no matter what, don't you?" Then a thought crossed the threshold of her tired and exhausted mind—so did Jesus.

Anna turned on some upbeat Righteous Descendant's music and crawled into bed. She fell asleep at once, dreaming of a technicolor dance with people swirling and swirling around a huge bonfire.

CHAPTER TWENTY-EIGHT

The full moon glowed, a soft, buttery orb slung low in the African sky. The hot and oppressive air vibrated with the drone of millions of mosquitos. The drums beat hypnotically out into the night, drawing and beckoning to all within range of the rhythmic music.

Tut paced outside the tuk. Impatiently, he waited for the family so they could all walk together to the river and join the celebration. He placed his hand on his heart. It pulsed to the rhythm of the drums. He had never experienced anything like this. He was excited for the celebration, yet anxious.

Why am I so uneasy?

He shivered and shook out his arms as he recalled the strange encounter with the healer or the drummer—or whoever he was. Tut was grateful when Jafaar and Zofa crawled out of the tuk and gathered everyone together. Zofa's hands held a gourd full of ash mixed with citronella oil.

"We must cover ourselves with this," she said. "It will help keep the mosquitos away."

The children reached in and smeared the smelly stuff all over their arms and legs.

"You will be happy that you did this," said Zofa, laughing at their grimacing faces.

"We need to stay together," Jafaar warned. "As the drums beat, my spirit warns me of possible danger."

"What do you mean, Jafaar?" asked Zofa, concerned. She reached out and placed her hand gently on his arm.

"I'm not sure," he explained. "Perhaps it's a warning from God, but hopefully, it isn't." He shrugged and patted her hand on his arm. "I'm sure we will be fine."

The little girls were beautiful in their colorful dresses and beads. Their eyes danced with excitement. Impatient, they grabbed Tut's hands, pulled him forward and said, "Come, Tut. Let's go!"

When they arrived at the river, Tut held tightly to his sister's hands. They stood and watched as people milled around and chatted with each other, their voices high pitched and excited. A towering bonfire blazed and crackled, sending sparks high up into the air. Some people walked in and out of the smoke, trying to get relief from the mosquitos.

The chief sat in a place of honor and the family walked up to pay their respects.

"Welcome, my friends," he said. "It is an important night for our family. Enjoy yourselves."

Jafaar bowed and led the family away to the other side of the bonfire.

Tut spied Rolnyang among a group of young men, laughing and cutting up as young men will do.

"Baba," said Tut, "may I join them?"

"Yes, but do not leave the campfire area."

"May I go with Tut?" pleaded Ulan.

"I will watch him, Baba," said Tut.

Jafaar gave his reluctant consent. Tut grinned and turned to go just as Nyamin ran up to them. They stood and stared at each other, until finally, she giggled, grabbed Achan and Lala's hands and called out happily, "Come, let's dance. Let's dance." The girls entreated Jafaar, and he smiled and said, "Go—go have fun, but, stay close," he warned.

"Yes, Baba."

Tut watched, pie-eyed, as Nayamin escorted the girls away to join the dance. The bride led a group of women zigzagging around the fire. An old woman sat to the side. She played traditional wedding songs on the dallooka drum as the party danced and sang. Tut stood spellbound until Ulan pulled on his shirt. "Come, brother," he said impatiently.

For the next hour, Tut and Ulan joined Rolnyang and the other men as they watched the women dance and chant to the mesmerizing beat of the dallooka drums. The intricate wedding dance captivated Tut. As the drums got louder and faster, Ulan motioned and then shouted out to Tut that he was going to the other side of the bonfire to sit with Jafaar and Zofa. Tut waved at him and joined the other young people as they encircled the women, shouting out songs into the night.

At once, the dallooka drum stopped its beat. At first, the dancers continued to dance and sing, seemingly unaware of the silence. Then, everyone paused like statues, silent except for the doves cooing in the distance and the crackling fire.

After a short time, a single drum, different from the one before, began to beat once again. The beat was slow . . . ominous . . . and caused Tut to shiver involuntarily. Something was wrong. The women and then the men began to move slowly and purposely, hypnotized to the beat of the drum. Tut glanced over at the drummer, and his heart clenched in sickening fear. He could not see the drummer's face in the shadows, but only the man's hands on top of the drums. *What?* He took a step closer. The drummer's hands glowed and burned—they were on fire. Even though he could not see the drummer's face, he knew—it was the healer—the disturbing man in his dreams.

Terrified, he backed away and walked ever so slowly around the fire until he reached Jafaar and Zofa. Jafaar grabbed hold of him and whispered, "Where is your brother? Your sisters?"

"I thought Ulan was with you," said Tut. "He left me a little while ago and said he was going to sit with you to watch the dancers."

Jafaar worriedly scanned the crowd. "We have not seen him."

Zofa stepped to the right and stretched to her tiptoes, squinting through the smoke. Relieved, she spotted the girls over to the side of the circle. They were holding hands, their eyes as big as saucers; too terrified to move. "I see the girls."

"Let's get them," said Jafaar.

They walked through the smoke to the side of the bonfire, and Zofa grabbed hold of each girl's hands. There was no sign of Ulan.

Tut kneeled in front of the little girls and said, "Have you seen our brother?"

"He was just here with Nyamin a little while ago. She pulled him out to the circle to dance with her," said Lala.

His voice low and steady, Jafaar said to Zofa, "Take the girls back to the tuk. We will join you when we find Ulan. Tut, go with me."

Tut raised his eyes to the sky and prayed, "Jesus, where are they? Where are they?"

He and Jafaar walked along the path to the river and away from the sound of the menacing drum. They stopped when they reached the river.

Tut called out, "Ulan. Nyamin. Where are you?" Nothing—nothing but the faint sound of the distant drum and the water of the Sobat lapping up against the bank.

At once, the sound of the drum stopped. The reeds along the bank parted, and the healer, dressed all in black, stepped out in front of them. The air, heavy with a rotten stench, radiated from him. Repulsed, Tut grimaced and took a step backward, almost falling over Jafaar who reached out to steady him.

"Friends, who do you seek?" the man asked.

His voice was a deep bass. It vibrated and echoed into the quiet. Tut shivered and wrapped his arms around his stomach. "A beautiful, bright night, isn't it?" the man continued. "It would be difficult to get lost on a night like this, now wouldn't it? Such beautiful children—where could they be? Hmmm—where could they be?"

The drum beat once again, slow and steady. *Brrum . . . Brrum . . . Brrumm . . .* The man closed his eyes and swayed to the pulsing rhythm. *Brrum . . .brrum . . . Brrummm . . .* Out of the corner of Tut's eye, Jafaar raised his hands and prayed loudly. He shouted above the sound of the drum, "Jesus, Jesus, Jesus—help us. Send an angel to fight for us—help us find Ulan and Nyamin." The man's eyes flew open, and he laughed, a hideous, spine-chilling sound that reverberated across the river and back. Jafaar prayed even louder, "Jesus, Jesus, Jesus." Tut reached out and put his hand on Jafaar's shoulder and joined him in the prayer. Now they both roared at the top of their lungs, "Je—sus. Je—sus!"

The drums stopped. Unexpectedly, the air around Tut and Jafaar grew thick with a fragrance that was so pleasing and enjoyable that they inhaled deep cleansing breaths. The horrible stench disappeared, replaced by the sweet, delicious smell of a bouquet of a million flowers. They couldn't get enough of it. A wondrous, joyful presence swelled in their hearts as the sweet fragrance flowed in and out of their lungs and then visibly over their bodies from the top of their heads to the soles of their feet. Beautiful, stunning beings materialized around them. They glowed with love and shouted out their praises to Jesus. Tut and Jafaar fell to their knees, unable to stand in the presence of the holy angels. And then—he appeared—Jesus. A brilliant light shimmered out from around Him. He reached down and lightly touched Tut and Jafaar each on the shoulder. He smiled at them. He slowly turned toward the darkness and pointed out past the light. The light swirled through the darkness, engulfing the man in black. He began to pixelate in front of them.

The man eyed Tut and mouthed, "I'll be back for you," and then dissolved in front of them, his face twisted into an ugly, hideous grin.

Tut had absolutely no fear—how could he in the presence of God? His Bible told him that perfect love cast out fear. Now he understood.

Jesus turned back toward them and said, "Remember, I will never leave you or forsake you." At that, the light slowly dimmed.

Tut and Jafaar were alone, still on their knees. For a moment, they were physically unable to stand up on their trembling legs. Finally, they grabbed hold of each other's arms and slowly stood.

"Baba . . ." Tut had no words. He swallowed, took a deep breath, and then tried one more time to speak. "Baba . . . I . . ." Words still would not come to him.

"You do not need to speak," said Jafaar.

They stood for a few more moments letting their hearts slow down. Finally, Jafaar said, "All right . . . let's find Ulan and Nyamin. Jesus will show us the way."

Tut's lips curved into an ever-slight smile and he turned back toward the river, "This way, Baba—I think they are this way."

CHAPTER TWENTY-NINE

A thick, noxious fog swirled above and below her. Anna placed her hands in front of her face for protection and tried to run through the hot, soupy cloud but could barely put one foot in front of the other. She wanted to scream out a warning but couldn't make a sound. Anna began to pray. As she did so, she came upon two children ensnared by a massive thorn bush.

They reached out to her and cried, "Anna, help us."

She tried to get to them, but her limbs would not move. Terrified, she glanced down. Brambles crawled up and encircle her legs. The thorns scratched at her ankles and blood trickled to the ground. She tried to move away but couldn't. The clawing continued until, thankfully, Anna opened her eyes. It was Max. He pawed repeatedly at her leg and whined for her to wake up. She squinted at him and tried to focus but her eyes would not stay open.

He continued to whine, so she reached over, pulled him close and hugged him. "I'm okay, Max. I'm okay."

He wagged his tail and gave Anna a great, sloppy kiss.

"Yuck, Max, you know I don't like your kisses."

Anna tried, unsuccessfully, to reconstruct the dream in her mind. She could only remember bits and pieces of it. It left her with a sense of uneasiness that she couldn't shake. She uttered a quick prayer, sat up in bed and glanced at the clock.

"Uh oh, check out the time. Max, we've got to get up. I'm going to be late for school."

As Anna scrounged through her closet to find something to wear, she thought about the conversation that she had with Ben last night. Wishing now that she hadn't said anything, Anna wondered what questions he might ask her next. She stood in front of her clothes for a moment and finally picked out a favorite white t-shirt and paired it with bright colored leggings.

Holding them up in front of her in the mirror, Anna raised her eyebrows toward Max and asked, "What do you think?"

Max shook his head and rolled over on his back. She went back to the closet. Three outfits later, Max finally wagged his tail in approval. Anna dressed quickly and ran down the stairs. Dad and Ben had already left. She glanced at her phone and realized she'd be too late to get breakfast at school, so she grabbed a piece of toast and bacon and ran out the door.

The thunderous sound of several hundred voices hit Anna as she walked into the gym. She spotted the group in their usual spot with their heads together. Grace was gesturing wildly as the others nodded.

Grace spotted her as she walked across the gym floor. She jumped down from the bleachers and ran over, grabbed Anna's hand and pulled her toward the group. They all greeted her with smiles. "Hey, Anna." Her friends were excited about something. She sat down and waited for someone to tell her.

"What's up?" she asked.

"We have very good news," said Favor.

"What?"

"We have news of Jafaar, Zofa, and our kids."

"Really?"

"Yes, Zofa's brother, Luka, crossed over into Ethiopia and arrived at a transit site in Burblei several days ago. They evacuated him by helicopter yesterday, and he is now at a way station in Matar. Luka spoke to a missionary when he arrived who contacted our parents."

Anna remembered her unsettling dream and blurted out, "Are they okay?"

Favor reached out and gave her a reassuring hug. "Yes, other than Achan, Luka told the missionary that they were fine."

"Achan? What's wrong with Achan?" Anna asked, remembering that sweet, beautiful smile.

"The missionary told us that they had escaped from the UN camp in Malakal about a month ago. A stray bullet hit and wounded Achan's leg, so the family had to move slowly. Luka journeyed on ahead to get provisions to take back to them. He hoped to return to them as soon as he gathered his supplies."

The din in the gym seemed to amplify as Anna thought about all that Favor had said. At eight o'clock, the bell rang and the group gathered their backpacks and climbed down from the bleachers.

"Let's meet at lunch, okay?" Anna asked.

They all agreed.

Three hours later, Anna claimed their favorite lunch table in the courtyard. The weatherman had called for rain around noon, so they'd have the place to themselves. Jonathan was the first to sit down beside her.

"Hey," he said. He opened his lunch sack and took out a sandwich and chips. He took a large bite of his sandwich, chewed and eyed her. "You eating today?"

Anna smiled sheepishly. She was always hungry but sitting here beside Jonathan took away her appetite. She didn't know if she could eat in front of him, so she said, "Yeah . . . I . . . ah . . ." Mercifully, before she could explain, the rest of the group walked out together and sat down.

As they ate, Jonathan said, "Our timeline is critical now. We have only a short time to raise the money to buy the things Luka and the family need when they arrive in Ethiopia. We've got to get our video on-line and solicit followers to help us. Once we have our video channel up and running, we can also use social media to gain even more followers."

"And—hopefully, bring the Righteous Descendants to Johnson for a concert," added David. "We'd use the money to help us reconnect with the kids in Ethiopia. We would need funds to travel and rent a home there for them. Our dream is to provide a home in Ethiopia for many children just like ours."

"Okay," said Anna, "let's do it. Tonight, will be our first video online. Grace and I have been talking about our dialogue. What we're going to wear and all that stuff. Are we agreed?"

They huddled in with a team hand stack and cheered loudly. "Come and See!" At that, a crack of thunder sent the group scurrying inside for their fifth-period class.

That night they gathered once again in Grace and Shelby's basement. David tacked the green screen up on the wall while Jonathan centered the lights. Everything was ready to go, that is, except Shelby.

"Where's your sister, Grace?" asked David. He plopped down on the couch.

"Shel said she had something to do after school, but she promised that she would be here tonight," Grace said.

She glanced over at the stairs willing her sister to walk down them.

"It's okay," said David reassuring her. "We can start recording. If Shelby is here in time to edit the video and download it to YouTube, we'll be fine. She's already created an amazing trailer for us."

Anna pictured the trailer—so cool with bright colored shapes that zoomed in and out and circled like colorful, African beads. She especially liked the part where the beads dissolved into a spectacular backdrop of South Sudan and then faded out to the words, *Come and See*. Impressive.

"Is everyone ready?" asked Favor. "Let's take it to the Father before we begin." They bowed their heads. "Father God, this is yours. Make it good. Make it real. Make it awesome. In Jesus' name—amen."

Anna and Grace took a deep breath, smiled at each other, nodded at Favor and then sat down at the table. Their first video had begun.

"Hey, guys. I'm Grace and this is Anna. Welcome to our *Come and See* channel. We're so glad that you joined us. We think you'll be totally amazed and a lot inspired by a group of kids that you've never met—yet. You're going to love them as we do."

Anna waved and jumped in. "You won't believe all the things that are happening to us. We can't wait to share with you. It's all *very* real and *very* exciting. When you follow Jesus, you're in for the adventure of your life. This journey is not a virtual, imaginary-world adventure, but one so real that you'll be shaking your head and saying, 'No way.'"

The ten minutes they had allotted for the video went by very quickly. There was so much they wanted to say, and the girls didn't have time to say it all. Anna explained how the Righteous Descendants had chosen her to attend their concert. "Six of us are flying to Dallas in April. We want y'all to join us! By the miracle of technology, you can. We're going live on Instagram," she said. "The most important thing that we have to tell you is that we're raising money to reunite the South Sudanese kids with the Knight family. It's going to be awesome. We need to get the word out. Please share this video with all your social media friends. We love y'all!"

"Cut." Favor called out. She laughed. "I always wanted to do that. You two were awesome. I think we have a great beginning. Now, we must get the word out on social media."

"After Shelby comes home and edits it, that is," Grace said. "She's so in and then so out. Sometimes I just want to give up on her."

David walked over and put his arm around her shoulders. "You know you won't."

Frustrated, tears pooled in her eyes. "I know—I know, but, where is she? I get so angry at her one minute, but then I worry that she's caught up in something that's bad for her the next. It's such a confusing feeling, you know? I guess it's a twin thing."

"So—let's pray," said David in his obvious, matter-of-fact, tone of voice. "Lord, we need your help. We lift Shelby up to you for the protection of her heart. She's hurting, Lord. Only you know why. Place angels around her to keep her safe. In Jesus name, Amen."

As Anna bowed her head, she shivered involuntarily and remembered her dream—something about brambles, her legs bleeding and two kids calling out her name.

CHAPTER THIRTY

Jafaar and Tut called out into the night, "Nyamin. Ulan." They walked down the banks of the river and didn't see or hear anything except for a couple of frogs splashing into the water. With the drum silent, the night was curiously soft and quiet, replaced by a peace that was unimaginable moments before the angels appeared.

"We need to be very still and listen," said Jafaar.

Motionless, moments passed, their ears tuned to the sounds of the night.

"What was that? Did you hear something?" Tut asked.

"Yes, I did."

Tut cocked his head. "I think it's that way." Tentative, they both turned and walked toward the sound. As they drew nearer, they found Nyamin and Ulan entangled in a thicket of bramble bushes, unable to move or free themselves.

"Baba. Tut. Help us. Help us."

"We're here," said Tut. "Be very still."

The two sat side by side, scratched and bleeding from the thorns. Terrified, their eyes pleaded silently as tears of pain streamed down their cheeks.

"How do we get them out?" asked Tut.

Jafaar glanced around, thankful for the light of the full moon.

"You must go back to the village for a knife and a light."

Tut didn't hesitate. "Yes, I will."

Tut hurried away and quickly found a man from the village who loaned him a knife and a torch. With the light from his torch bobbing through the darkness, he made his way back to them.

As Tut held up the light, Jafaar started at the bottom of the thorny bush. Very, very carefully, he cut it away from Nyamin and Ulan. Stoically, they did not make a sound.

After an interminable amount of time, they freed the two from the bush. Nyamin and then Ulan gingerly moved away. They stretched their arms away from their thorn-covered bodies and clothes.

"You've been very brave," said Jafaar. "We will go to Zofa—she will help get these thorns out of you."

Everyone greeted Ulan and Nyamin with cries of joy when they returned to the tuk. Zofa *tsked* to herself as she pulled the thorns out of their tender skin, one by one. Trying to get their minds off the pain, Tut asked them what had happened.

"It was the drummer," said Ulan.

"Yes," said Nyamin, "he walked up to us as we stood by the fire and told Ulan and me that he could teach us how to play the drum. We thought that sounded like fun, so he told us to close our eyes and hold on to each other. He would lead us. It *was* fun at first as we followed and danced blindly to the sound of his drum. We laughed and bumped into each other."

Ulan made a wry face. "We thought we were dancing around the campfire, but when we opened our eyes, we realized that he had led us down the trail instead. So, Nyamin and I turned around to go back."

"He told us that we weren't going anywhere," said Nyamin.

"Tut," said Ulan, "his face changed. It was his eyes—they started to glow. He frightened us, so we panicked and ran away from him as fast as we could. It was so foggy and dark that we couldn't see. That's when we ran right into that terrible bush. We couldn't move because of the thorns." Tears pooled in Ulan's eyes as he glanced down at his scratched arms and legs.

In an awed voice, Nyamin spoke once again, "But then, a cool, refreshing wind began to blow. It caressed my skin like a chilled rag that my mother would have place on my forehead when I had a fever. The thorns still hurt, but not so bad. Where did that come from?"

Jafaar raised his eyebrows at Tut, and they both smiled.

The next morning, Jafaar, Zofa, and Tut sat outside the tuk and talked, their voices low so that they would not wake the children. The sun streaked through the leaves, brushing their faces with splashes of light. *This morning is so quiet and peaceful,* thought Tut. *So different from last night . . .*

"We must leave," said Jafaar. His eyes moved from Tut to Zofa and then back to Tut. "I don't think the town of Nasir is that far away. Hopefully, Luka waits for us there.

"Yes, you are right. It is not safe for us here," Zofa agreed. "I will wake the children and pack up our belongings."

"Baba, we have no food—no water."

"Perhaps the chief will be kind enough to provide us with some provisions for our journey. We will go and speak with him."

Several hours later, after they had packed their meager belongings, Nyamin appeared. She gracefully balanced a basket on her head and carried two baskets in her arms.

"My father has provided food and drink for your journey." She lowered her eyes to the ground, but her mouth curved in a shy smile.

Tut walked over to her and took the two baskets from her arms. Nyamin giggled and reached for the basket on her head and placed it on the ground.

She pointed to each basket. "There is kisra . . . corn . . . and . . . beans."

"Thank you, sister."

Tut stood quietly for a moment and gazed at Nyamin until, embarrassed, she bowed her head and walked away. As he watched her, Zofa moved over and placed her hand on his shoulder.

"Perhaps—someday, if God wills, you will see her again, my son. I will carry one of the baskets if you will bring the other two. Come, Jafaar calls to us."

With a resigned sigh, Tut picked up the baskets and followed Zofa over to where Jafaar had gathered the rest of the family. He smiled at them when they walked up.

"Tut, would you call on the Lord for our protection?"

With a nod, Tut prayed, "Lord, be with us for the rest of our journey. Send your angels to guide us and keep us safe. In Jesus' name, amen."

Jafaar lead the way and Tut followed up at the rear. They walked along a path by the river, one created by tribesmen and cattle who had trod back and forth along the bank year after year. Tut glanced back over his shoulder one more time, stopped abruptly and did an about-face. Nyamin stood a short distance away from him on a rock that jutted out of the river. She stood as still as the shimmering air that rose just above the surface of the slow-moving water. The sweltering breeze gently stirred her colorful dress. She slowly lifted her hand in a pensive wave and smiled her good-bye. Transfixed, Tut returned her wave and walked backwards down the trail until Nyamin was out of sight.

* * * *

The trek was easy at first until the path disappeared, possibly because of last year's flooding. Forced to walk for miles through the brush, the family often stopped to rest to take a small sip of water. Tut stepped wide over many snake holes in the ground. He was grateful that it was hot, and the snakes were not out in the open like they were during the rainy season. The younger children continually swatted at mosquitos and flies which buzzed and bit unmercifully around their necks and faces. Ulan was especially miserable because of the sores left by the thorn bush from the night before.

That evening, exhausted from the day, they made camp. Jafaar sent Tut and Achan out to gather firewood. Later, sitting around the fire, they laughed and shared stories.

"Baba, tell us the story of the boy and the slingshot," said Ulan.

Tut smiled. They all loved Baba's Bible stories; especially that one.

"Once there was a young boy who took care of the sheep. His tribe was at war with another tribe."

"The Dinkas, Baba?" asked Lala. "Our Nuer tribe is always at war with the Dinkas."

"No—no, my child. This tribe is the Israelites, and they were at war with the Philistines. The Philistines had a warrior named Goliath. He was a huge giant, and no one dared fight against him."

"Except David," said Ulan.

Achan pouted. "Let Baba tell the story, brother."

Jafaar laughed out loud. "Yes, David said he would kill the giant. Everyone laughed at him because he was just a boy. When he approached Goliath, David shouted out that if he could kill a bear or a lion, he could kill him. The giant almost fell to the ground laughing when he saw David and said, *I'll feed you to the birds.*"

Lala's eyes widened. "Oh, no, Baba."

Tut reached over and patted her on the arm. "Lala, Lala, you know what happens. You've heard this story many times."

Her eyes snapped. "I know. I know. Go on, Baba."

"David told that giant, *you come at me with sword, spear and javelin, but I come to you in the name of the Lord of Heaven's Armies—the God of the armies of Israel, whom you have defied.* He took a rock and placed it in his slingshot, twirled it around his head, let it go and hit that giant right between his eyes, and he fell down dead."

Achan and Lala clapped their hands and cheered. They always did that at the end of the story.

"I want you all to know that we still follow the Lord of Heaven's Armies. He will continue to fight for us. Do you believe it?"

"Yes, Baba, we do," said the children.

The fire died down to glowing embers. Zofa smiled over at the exhausted faces of Ulan and the girls. "It has been a very long day. It's time to sleep."

The younger children did not argue but curled up together under the stars.

Tut couldn't sleep. He turned on his side for a while and then flopped over on his back. He had experienced so much in the last couple of days that his mind skipped from one thought to another as he recalled all that had happened. *What did God want from him*? Tut thought about Baba's story. David was not much older than himself when he killed the giant. He wondered if David had been afraid—even a little bit. How could he not have? Baba had told him that fear paralleled courage. He could not have one without the other.

His thoughts then turned to the beautiful Nyamin. He pictured her as she waved at him from the rock on the river. He smiled and ever so slowly relaxed and drifted off to sleep.

CHAPTER THIRTY-ONE

Shelby sauntered nonchalantly down the stairs to the basement, oblivious to the fact that her sister had been worried about her.

Relieved and then irritated, Grace jumped up. "Where have you been, Shel?"

"Out."

"Out? What do you mean, out?"

"Out, just out."

Shelby yanked back a chair and sat down in front of the computer, turned it on, and demanded, "Give me the video—I'll download it."

Grace stood for a moment, stared at her and then asked sarcastically— "Please?"

"Pu—lease," said Shelby.

Grace glanced over at Favor. She raised her eyebrows, pulled the flash drive out of the camera and walked it over to Shelby.

"Thank you," Shelby mumbled.

She quickly and easily downloaded and then edited the video by adding the intro and the background.

About thirty minutes later, the group gathered around the computer to view the final video. At the end, no one spoke until finally, Grace broke the silence and said, "That was so cool."

"Way to go, Shelby," said Jonathan.

"That was amazing," said Anna.

"What do you think, guys?" asked Jonathan. "Are we ready to go live?"

After they all agreed, David said, "Let's pray first, okay? Lord, this video and the YouTube channel is yours. First, we pray that somehow, someway, supernaturally this video will go viral. Don't know how you're gonna do that, Lord, but, hey, nothing is too hard for you. Then"—David paused a moment— "we pray that you will use it to expand your kingdom here on earth. God, we ask that you touch people's lives in your mighty way—and especially—" David's voice caught—"we pray for our family in South Sudan that you will reunite us very soon. In Jesus' name. Amen."

Shelby sat impatiently as David prayed. *If these kids think that prayer helps, well, so be it.* She tapped her finger on the top of the keyboard, itching to continue.

After a chorus of *amens*, Favor took a deep breath and said, "So, Shelby, let's do it."

Shelby turned back to the computer, opened YouTube and began uploading the video.

Anticipation in the room built as they waited for the video to upload. A few minutes later, Shelby said, "Okay, that part's done. Do you want me to add a CTA overlay?"

"What's that?" asked Grace.

"CTA means a call to action. It's like a final handshake on a video. It encourages your visitors to take action," she said.

"That's a great idea," said David.

Shelby shrugged. His compliment meant nothing to her.

David said, "After doing some research on the internet, I learned that videos ending with a CTA received more views, shares and comments. So, what do we want people to do after they watch the videos?"

After a pause, Jonathan spoke up. "We could send them to our *Come and See* website *or* to our *Go Fund Me* page—*or* even to sign up for a text message to let them know when our next video comes out before the Righteous Descendants concert."

"I can do that. Give me a minute." A short time later, Shelby said, "Okay, I'm done. You want to see it?"

Everyone crowded in close behind her. Shelby clicked on the video and watched with the others. Admittedly, she was proud of the video, but she'd never let Grace or her friends know that. When it finished, she pushed her chair back and said, "Yeah, well—I've got to go." At that, Shelby got up and started toward the stairs.

Grace called after her, "Where are you going now, Shel?"

"I'm meeting a friend."

"Who?"

"I'll see you later, Grace."

* * * *

Grace watched her walk up the stairs and then turned toward Anna, clinched her fists and mouthed silently, "She—makes—me—so—mad."

"I know. I know." What else could she say?

Jonathan gathered everyone back together and said, "We've prayed that God will multiply our work, so now—we post the YouTube URL to all our social media accounts and ask that our friends share with their friends. That way the videos will be widely circulated."

Immediately, they each opened YouTube on their phones and began to share with every person on their friend's list. They knew that many kids at school were on their phone this time of night, so they'd get the message. Every time Anna hit *share*, her heart thumped hard against her ribs.

They all agreed to meet the next morning before school.

That night after Anna had showered and let Max out to do his business, they both crawled up on her bed. She picked up her phone and opened YouTube.

"Max, this is so, so cool. Do you want to see it?" Max cocked his ears and laid his head on her leg. Of course, as they watched, Max fell fast asleep. At the end, Anna breathed a quick prayer and burrowed down in the covers beside him.

The next morning, the entire school was buzzing about the YouTube video. Grace ran up to Anna when she got to the gym. "Have you seen how many hits we had since last night?" she said. "Everyone is talking about it."

"No, I was running late, as usual."

"Well, as of 8:00 this morning, we had 500 likes."

"Are you serious?"

"Yes, I promise. Come sit down." She tugged Anna over to the bleachers where everyone had gathered in their usual spot. Jake and Mary, two kids from their church, came over and asked about the video and the concert.

"Are y'all really getting to go to the Righteous Descendants concert?" asked Jake.

"Yes," said Grace.

"How'd *that* happen?"

Grace pointed to Anna. She smiled and explained about the contest. It was all over school by the end of the day.

* * * *

That afternoon, Shelby, Grace, Jonathan, and Anna decided to walk to the Dairy Bar and make their travel plans to Frisco. The concert was in two weeks, and they still needed to book hotel rooms.

Shelby was silent as she walked behind her sister and her two friends. She listened in on their conversation but didn't really care to be a part of any of it. They weren't going to ask her opinion anyway, not that she had one that she cared to give.

"I'll talk to Dad tonight. He can call the hotel and get us a couple of rooms. Jonathan, you and Dad can stay in one room and Shelby, Grace, and I can share the other one," Anna said. "The concert is on Saturday night, so, we can fly out Friday morning."

Hopeful, Grace asked, "Maybe get a little shopping in on Saturday morning?"

"Of course. Frisco has an amazing mall. Who goes to the Dallas area and not shop?"

Shelby groaned to herself. She wasn't into shopping that much. She was more a *Teen Rebel* brand kind of girl, than an *American Eagle* like Grace and Anna.

She tapped Grace on the shoulder and asked, "Are you sure you want me to go?"

They all stopped, turned around and stared at her.

"Of course, we want you to go," Grace said.

"I don't know."

"You don't know what?"

"I don't know if I should go—or—if I want to go."

"Shelby, God *chose* you," said Jonathan.

"Why would He choose me?"

"He has a reason for you to be there."

"Like what?"

"Sometimes we don't know until it happens."

"What happens? Jonathan, you talk in circles. None of it makes any sense to me."

"God orchestrates many opportunities in our lives. He doesn't force us to do what He wants us to do, but if we obey him . . ." He shrugged, "I just know that cool things take place."

"I don't know," she said for the third time.

When they got to the Dairy Bar, Anna ordered her usual—ice cream dipped in chocolate, Grace ordered her favorite, a chicken basket with French fries and cheese dip, and Shelby and Jonathan ordered milkshakes. They sat down on top of the picnic table to eat their snacks. Grace and Anna waved at some of their friends as they cruised around the Dairy Bar in their cars—a favorite pastime for the kids in Johnson.

Shelby's thoughts drifted as she sipped on her milkshake. She and Lou had gone for a ride the night before after she walked out on Grace. She smiled to herself as she remembered climbing on the bike behind him and holding on to his waist. Freedom. And that glorious sensation as the wind whipped through her hair and caressed her face. There was nothing like it. *I wonder what Lou is doing? I can't really see him cruising the Dairy Bar. Maybe . . . I should text him. He did say something about going for a ride . . .*

Bored, Shelby watched absently as Anna grabbed a bunch of napkins on the table, wrapped them around the cone and tilted her head to bite off a chunk of chocolate and ice-cream. Right at that moment, Jonathan accidentally hit her hand with his elbow, and her nose went straight into the ice cream.

"Anna, I'm sorry." He tried to keep a straight face but found it difficult with ice cream dripping off her nose. He couldn't help it; he burst out laughing.

"Just get me some more napkins," said Anna.

"Okay. Okay," Jonathan said as he reached out to wipe her nose with his napkin.

She pushed his hand away. "Jonathan, please, I've got this."

Grace, her mouth full of French-fries and cheese dip, shook her head and laughed. "You guys act like ten-year olds."

Shelby moved over a couple of seats to remove herself from their company. *Lou would never act immature like that.*

They headed back home about fifteen minutes later. Shelby joined Grace and Anna while Jonathan walked on ahead.

"I think you were flirting with Jonathan at the Dairy Bar, Anna," smirked Shelby.

"I was not."

"He *is* pretty cute," said Grace.

"I don't know what you're talking about," said Anna.

"You know I'm right. I think you have a crush on him and . . ." Shelby paused with a mischievous grin on her face, "you're looking forward to spending time with him in Frisco, aren't you?"

Anna swatted at her and then warned Shelby and Grace with her eyes to shut up as they caught up to Jonathan.

Shelby's phone pinged as she said goodbye to Jonathan and Anna and walked over to her house. She glanced down at the screen and paused at the steps to her front porch. A cryptic message had popped up from Lou. Shelby furrowed her brows as she read: "There's a way up, there's a way down, the fun's with me—I'll be around. Meet me tomorrow night."

She smiled to herself and typed back, "Maybe."

CHAPTER THIRTY-TWO

"Tut," called out Ulan. "I caught one. I caught one!" Grinning from ear to ear, he pulled a small perch out of the water. "We will have a feast."

"Yes. That is good. Let me take it off the hook for you."

"No, I can do it, Tut," Ulan said firmly.

Amused, Tut threw up his hands and backed away.

Ulan turned his back to Tut and gingerly pulled the hook out of the fish's mouth. With a proud smile, he turned around and held up the fish.

Tut grinned back. "We will eat well tonight."

The family had stopped for the evening and Tut and Ulan decided to go fishing with the hooks and string that the chief had given them before they left. Tut had dug some worms in the soft dirt of the river bank and had just baited and put his hook in the water when Ulan caught his first perch.

An hour later they had caught enough fish to provide an excellent meal for the family. Jafaar showed Tut and Ulan how to clean and dress the fish while Zofa and the girls prepared the fire.

Hungry from their long day, everyone ate quietly enjoying the delicious perch. Afterwards, they sat around the fire, stared into it and talked.

"I wonder where Luka is?" asked Zofa. "Do you think he has crossed the border?"

"Yes, knowing Luka, I'm sure he has found his way. Our plan is for him to contact Peter Knight in some way and then come back to us with food and supplies," said Jafaar.

"But how will he find us, Baba?" asked Achan.

Tut didn't voice it, but he wondered the same thing.

"Luka knows that we will travel along the River Sobat. We said we would meet at Nasir. He will find us. I'm sure of it."

* * * *

Luka was exhausted. He had traveled non-stop since he'd left his family. Finally, he crossed into Ethiopia where the River Sobat flowed into the Baro River. When he arrived at the transit site in Burbiey, Luka contacted the missionary in charge and gathered as many supplies as he could to begin the journey back to Jafaar and the family. Thankfully, he hitched a ride on an empty boat traveling back to Nasir on the River Sobat. The river was peaceful this time of the year, but it would be dangerous to cross once the rainy season arrived. He sat at the front of the bow and stared almost unblinking as the boat sliced through the murky, slow-moving river. The gentle, swaying motion soothed his tired and weary spirit.

A man walked up to him and sat down. The man was quiet for a time until, finally, he spoke. "Where do you travel, my friend?" asked the stranger.

Luka glanced at the man and then back at the water. "To Nasir," he said.

"That is very dangerous. Why would you travel back the way that you had come?"

Suspicious, Luka turned and regarded the man, not sure why this stranger was interested in his business. He was a giant of a man; his skin a rich, lustrous ebony. Luka searched the man's face—the eyes always gave someone away, but there was no deceit in them, only peace.

You can trust me," said the man.

Luka explained about his family and Achan's gunshot wound in the leg. "She could not travel on her own, so we had to carry her. The family sent me on ahead, hopefully, to get food and supplies for them."

"This is a perilous place for children," said the man. "Two weeks ago, a warring tribe crossed the border and kidnapped many women and children."

"Thank-you for the warning. We will be cautious. Even more reason for me to travel quickly." Luka questioned himself. *When will I find my family? Are they safe? Will they be in Nasir when I get there? Where will I find them?*

"My friend . . . when you get to Nasir, wait. You will find your family at the boat landing."

Suspicious, Luka narrowed his eyes and asked, "How do you know that?"

"Trust me, Luka. Trust me." At that, he got up and left.

Luka wandered over to the boat rail and gazed down at the muddy river. *I wonder how the stranger knew my name*?

He slept on board the boat that night, curled up against the bow, as it traveled up the river. When he woke the next morning, he found that they had docked at Nasir. He clutched his precious food and provisions and walked to the stern of the boat to thank the stranger but there was no sign of him. *Where could he have gone?* He dismissed the thought, said goodbye to the captain and disembarked the boat. His eyes flickered back and forth as he walked down the pier, but he didn't see a familiar or friendly face. People stared at him and wondered who he was, but he ignored them. It didn't matter. His family waited for him somewhere in Nasir. He would find them.

* * * *

"How far, Baba? Tut? How far?" Lala whimpered.

The family had traveled at least a week since their stopover at the Nuer camp. They continued to follow the river but had to hide at times when they suspected soldiers were nearby. The days passed, one after the other, tedious and grueling. Other than Lala, Ulan and Achan were mostly silent. They endured the trek by putting one leaden foot in front of the other. Tut didn't know how much more his family could take. Exhausted, he wanted to rest also, but he knew that he had to keep his spirits up so that he could encourage his brother and sisters.

"We will come to Nasir very soon," Tut said, as much to assure himself as his sister. "I'm sure of it."

He put his arm around Lala's shoulders and walked beside her. "Lala, when I am ready to give up, I think of a verse that Peter shared with me. He told me to memorize it, and I did."

Lala peered up at her brother; her small face pinched with exhaustion. She didn't say anything as she waited for Tut to continue.

"*For I can do everything through Christ who gives me strength,*" he said.

Lala's small body relaxed against Tut's as they continued to walk together.

Around noon, the family arrived at a dusty, well-traveled intersection. One road continued along the river bank and the other crisscrossed from the north. They joined other weary refugees walking in their direction alongside the river. The oppressive humid air enveloped their bodies and made it difficult to breathe. Tut reached up and touched the top of his head where the African sun seared into his scalp. He regarded the blank faces of the people who trudged along with them. Women carried silent babies strapped to their backs and held the hands of small children whose bellies swelled from hunger. Their eyes were unfocused and void of any hope.

Tut was grateful, and yet guilt-ridden that his family had someone waiting for them in Ethiopia—and these women and children didn't. Honestly, he didn't know what to do with those feelings as he observed the sadness around him. He could only send up a silent prayer that somehow God would take care of them.

They stopped at the next Nuer village to ask for directions. Tut and Jafaar approached an old man who sat in front of his tuk smoking his pipe. Tut stood respectfully behind Jafaar.

"Is it good peace, my brother?" asked Jafaar.

"Yes, it is peace."

"Kindly tell me—how far is it to Nasir?"

The man pointed toward the east and said, "A couple of kilometers. But there is much unrest in the town. You must be very careful because the soldiers are everywhere."

"Thank you, brother. The sun is small and my family is exhausted. May we rest here for the night?"

"Yes. You are welcome to stay."

That evening a sliver of moon smiled down at them from the eastern sky. Millions of stars flickered within a bed of thick ebony blackness. The family sat around the smoky fire, so tired that they could not even speak. The children stared into the flames, barely blinking until, exhausted, they curled up under their mosquito nets and fell asleep.

Tut sat across from Jafaar and Zofa and listened intently as the couple leaned against each other and talked.

"Where do we go from here, husband?"

"To be honest, I do not have a clear answer to your question. We told Luka that we would meet him in Nasir." He hesitated, "But I don't know where . . . or when. The villager said it was very dangerous." He glanced back and forth between Tut and Zofa. "Do we dare take the children into the town and risk running into soldiers?" Jafaar let out a long sigh and said, "I do not know."

Zofa took Jafaar's hand in hers and said, "God has guided us so far, husband. Do we still trust him?"

Tut spoke up, "Who else can we trust? So much has happened on our journey so far. We can't go back. Luka is out there somewhere, I just know it. He will be waiting for us to come. You have always taught us that when life sets up a barricade, you push through it and move forward—you don't turn around and go back."

Jafaar studied Tut's face for a long time and then a slow grinned spread across his own. "You have become a man on this journey, Tut. You have become a man."

CHAPTER THIRTY-THREE

Dad made all the arrangements for their hotel and flight to Dallas. They'd get an Uber when they arrived to take them to the hotel. He pulled up the hotel website to show Anna where they were staying in Frisco. She scrolled through the website. *This trip was really happening,* she thought. *Is it a dream?* They'd videoed several more episodes for the *Come and See* YouTube channel. Their following had grown to over 2,000. Anna still couldn't believe it.

The morning before the trip, Anna had just sat down for breakfast. *Ping. Ping. Ping.* She reached for her phone and smiled.

Grace: "Can you believe we're leaving tomorrow? Can you believe it????"

Anna: "Are you packed?"

Grace: "Of course. I've been packed for a week."

Grace: "Are you? Packed that is?"

Anna: "Of course not! You know me—leave everything to the last minute. Ugh!"

Grace: "I'm so tired! I can't believe we stayed up so late last night!"

Anna: "Me, too! I think it was one of our best!"

Anna and Grace did tend to overdo the exclamation points when they texted each other. But sometimes, it was just necessary.

Anna: "Is Shelby packed?"

Grace: "I dunno. She came in even later than I did last night, so I didn't get to talk to her."

The friends met at Grace and Shelby's house the night before to record one final video before they left for Frisco. Their followers from all over had caught the spirit of what God was doing in their lives and the lives of the family in South Sudan. This last video filled them in on plans for the concert. They would film several Instagram Live videos while they traveled and when they arrived at the concert. Anna wanted everyone to go with them on this incredible adventure. She hoped that the Righteous Descendants would allow them to video part of their meal with them, especially when the band found out about the kids in South Sudan. Mr. Peter checked on the *Gofundme* account that he had set up to collect donations for the family in South Sudan and the future orphanage. They had already collected two thousand dollars.

The morning dragged even slower than usual for Anna. Of course, Mr. Jones had to schedule an algebra test for that day of all days. Her one-track mind had a difficult time concentrating, so Anna didn't think she scored very high on the test. She winced when he handed her paper back: 65%. *Ugh.* She promised herself that she'd study harder and do better next time.

The group met at its usual place at lunch. They reviewed their plans for the trip and the concert.

"We have a lot of followers excited about this trip," Anna said.

"Yes, I think we should video clips for our Instagram Live story from the time we board the airplane until we return on Sunday," said Jonathan.

"Uh huh," Anna replied.

"What time do you leave?" asked Favor.

"Our plane takes off at 8:00. The school gave us all excused absences as long as we made up our work."

"We won't be able to be at the airport when you take off, but we'll be following you—along with hundreds, maybe thousands of others," said David.

"But, we'll be at the airport Sunday afternoon—for real—when you fly in," said Favor.

* * * *

Shelby was in over her head, but she couldn't stop herself. A swirling vortex coiled around her tighter and tighter until, like a spring, she thought she would shatter into a million pieces. The last couple of weeks, she'd met up with Lou without her mother or Grace knowing about it. He seemed so mature and totally got her. He didn't treat her as a child like her mother and Grace did. Yet, sometimes Lou caused a queasiness in her stomach. He'd say things that she didn't agree with. For instance, he thought the trip to Frisco was stupid and a waste of time. She wasn't sure about that. Last night they argued about it. He had previously texted her some ridiculous cryptic message about going up or down with him. She wasn't in the mood to play games.

"Stay here with me, Shelby. We'll have a great time. You don't need to go off to Frisco to have fun—that's for those Christian kids. I'll show you what a good time is," Lou said.

"I don't know—yeah, maybe—but I promised Grace I'd go."

"She's going to pull you in, you know it? She's all self-righteous with her friends talking Jesus this and Jesus that. What's he done for you, Shelby? Your dad died being the *good Samaritan,* didn't he? Where was your Jesus then? He didn't even care."

Shelby's face flushed with anger and her eyes filled with tears. Lou had hit a real sore spot with her. She did blame God for her dad's death. Why would God take him away from her? He was such a remarkable daddy—one of the good guys.

"I know. I know," she muttered.

Lou reached over and put his arm around her shoulders and drew her close to him. "I care for you, Shelby, even if God's forgotten you."

She stiffened and pulled away. Lou was so handsome, but he had this odd smell about him that sort of turned her off. She felt terrible about it, but . . .

Lou didn't notice. "Hey, tomorrow night we can hang out. I'll stash the motorcycle and borrow my friend's car."

She lifted her chin and quirked an eyebrow at him. "Yeah, well . . . maybe."

But here she was with Lou once again. She couldn't resist him. She'd told Grace that she was going to the store to buy some things for the trip the next day. Grace asked her to pick up shampoo and toothpaste for her.

Of course, instead of going to the store, here she was in Lou's car at the turnaround on Johnson Road, the place where the kids hung out on the weekend. She noticed several more cars parked around them. Smoke floated out the windows—marijuana, probably. The warm weather had brought out the mosquitos, so Lou kept their windows closed.

Lou pulled something out of his pocket. "Hey, why be miserable when you can feel great?" He held up a packet of pills.

"Instant relief," he said, placing them gently in her hand.

She closed her fingers around the packet and sat, numb inside. She thumbed the sharp side of the foil package and fingered the bumps of the pills, counting them one by one in her head. In the past, she'd always refused drugs when her friends offered them to her—up until now. Why not? Who even cares? She dropped the packet to her lap, covered her face with her hands and began to sob. She hated herself even more because of it.

Lou reached out and laid his hand on her shoulder. "It's okay, Shel. It's fine. Just let it go. I'm here for you." His honeyed voiced soothed her mind.

For a while, they both sat in silence except for her sniffs and a couple of mosquitos humming around inside the car. Shelby laid her head back against the seat rest and closed her eyes when . . . *rap, rap, rap*. Startled, she jumped, and her eyes flew open. Blue and red lights from a police car flashed beside them.

Lou said a curse word.

There was another rap, sharper this time. A towering, black police officer stood outside. He was so incredibly tall that he had to bend down to peer in. Lou hit the button and slowly let down the window. At the same time, Shelby palmed the med packet and stuck it in her pocket.

"May I see your driver's license and car registration, please," the police officer asked.

"Certainly, officer," said Lou. "Is there a problem?"

"Just wondered what was going on out here. A report came over the scanner of possible trouble.

"No trouble, officer."

"Hmm—well, it's late. You need to get this young lady home."

"Of course, officer."

The officer returned Lou's license and registration. "I'll follow you to make sure she gets home all right."

Shelby wrapped her arms around herself and slumped down in the seat.

When they got back to the house, she waved to the officer in his vehicle, pulled out her keys and unlocked the door. She walked in and flinched when the door slammed behind her.

"Is that you, Shel?" her mom called out from her bedroom.

"Yeah, good night, Mom."

"Good night."

Entering their bedroom, she knew Grace must be awake, too, so she quickly walked by her bed and into the bathroom. Shelby stared at herself in the mirror and remembered the packet of pills in her pocket. Without much thought, she quickly flushed them down the toilet, brushed her teeth, and put on her sleep t-shirt.

She crawled into bed a few minute later. Grace thumped her pillow and rolled over in bed.

“Don’t even ask,” Shelby said.

“Okay, I won’t. Did you get my shampoo and toothpaste?”

“No.”

Grace mumbled something and then turn back over in the bed. Shelby was not about to share this night’s adventure with her sister. She slipped beneath the covers, tried to go to sleep; tried to forget what had happened.

CHAPTER THIRTY-FOUR

The next morning, the family left the small village. Every day their pace had become slower and slower. They had little food and water, and the children could barely keep up. Until now, Zofa would try and sing a little song to lift their spirits, but this morning she had no energy.

"It can't be very much further," said Jafaar. "The old man said Nasir was only a couple of kilometers away."

"Will there be food, Baba?" asked Lala.

"I pray that we will find Luka soon. He will have food for us," he said with a little more confidence than he felt.

It was noon before they reached the outskirts of Nasir. Jafaar remembered the old man's warning. When they stopped beneath a shade tree, he said to Zofa, "I need for you to stay here. Tut and I will go into Nasir and search for Luka."

She reached for Jafaar's hand. "We will wait here."

* * * *

As they walked through the outskirts of Nasir, Tut and Jafaar noticed small clusters of tukels scattered here and there. At the town center, dirty white concrete buildings replaced the tuks. People were everywhere. Villagers hawked their wares, soldiers loitered beside their trucks, children begged, and refugees rested along the street. Compared to the fresh air of the country, it was hot, stinking, and suffocating. Overwhelmed, Tut held a hand up to his nose.

"Do you know where you are going, Baba?"

Jafaar stopped, checked out the surroundings and then motioned, "Let's go this way."

As they walked down the street, familiar music floated through the air. Could it be? Jafaar closed his eyes, smiled and said, "Come."

They followed the sound of the music to a church service held in a small building at the end of the street. Drawn by the joyful music flowing out the door, Tut and Jafaar walked in and stood alongside the wall. Women and children and a few men packed the room. The women wore snowy white dresses with white headscarves and colorful sashes. They sang joyfully, raising their hands and voices to the Lord.

A preacher man stood at the front. With a huge smile on his face, he called out, "Today we bring our gifts to the Lord. *Give generously to the poor, not grudgingly, for the Lord your God will bless you in everything you do."*

The women left their chairs one by one and danced down the aisle to the front of the church. Joyfully, they placed their small offering in the basket and danced back to their seats. One especially pretty girl smiled at Tut as she passed by him reminding him of Nyamin. He smiled back.

After the offering, the preacher man walked over and gave Tut and Jafaar the traditional Sudanese handshake. "Welcome, my friends. It is peace?"

"Yes," said Jafaar. "It is peace."

"What brings you to our town?"

"Our family waits at the outskirts. We search for a brother who traveled on ahead of us."

"May I pray for you?" asked the preacher.

"Of course," said Jafaar.

There was a reverent hush over the room as the preacher began to pray in a strange language that neither Tut nor Jafaar understood. When the preacher finished, the silence continued until a woman in the back of the room spoke up, interpreting in the Nuer language.

"This is what the Lord says to you, *I see you and your family. I have provided a way of peace and safety. You must go to the water, and I will meet you there.*"

As soon as the prayer was over, the people broke the silence with happy clapping and praised the Lord with shouts of "Thank you, Jesus."

The preacher enfolded both Jafaar and then Tut into a huge hug and said, "Go in peace, my brothers. If we do not meet again in this lifetime, we will someday meet in eternity."

Jafaar grasped his hand and smiled.

Back on the street, Tut said, "Where to, Baba?"

"We go to the water, Tut. We go to the water."

* * * *

Luka sat on the dock as the hot, African sun beat down on his shoulders and head. He watched as fishermen, out late last night fishing, pulled in their canoes for the morning. With huge grins on their faces, they called out to each other and bragged about their catch. Luka reached up to wipe sweat from his eyes as he searched the river and then the bank. The dock moved up and down as the water gently flowed by, almost lulling him to sleep. The man had told him that he would find his family at the boat landing. At the time, hope raised up within him, but today discouragement played tricks with his mind. *What in the world am I doing here?* Worn out and depleted after traveling so hastily for the last couple of weeks, he thought, *If I could just shut my eyes for a moment* . . . Luka leaned over and laid his head on his precious bag of food and fell fast asleep.

* * * *

Tut and Jafaar wove their way through the streets toward the river. Tut could smell it before they got there; the air thick with the scents of fish, mud, and water. Men and women, with large baskets of fish balanced on their heads, passed by them on their way to the market. Children weaved in and out begging for food. One little child stepped in front of Tut and almost tripped him.

"Do you have food, brother?" said the little boy.

As Tut gazed down at the child's filthy face, he had a flashback of himself digging through garbage bins and begging for food. He remembered how people had ignored him as if he were invisible.

He knelt at the little boy's eye level. "I'm sorry, little brother, I have no food. What is your name?"

The little boy stood up tall. "My name is Asim. It means protector."

"Do you have a family, Asim?"

"Yes, my mother and little sister."

"You are very brave, and your family is blessed because of you."

The little boy grinned from ear to ear as he reached out and touched Tut on the shoulder in a traditional Sudanese greeting. Tut grinned back and shook his hand. At that, someone called out to the little boy and he gave Tut a quick wave and ran off. Overcome by his memories, Tut watched until the little boy disappeared around the corner.

Jafaar gently laid a hand on his shoulder. "Are you ready to go, my son?"

Tut swiped at his face and turned around. "Yes, I am ready. Let's go."

When they arrived at the boat landing, Tut stopped, shaded his eyes with his hand and skimmed the crowd, searching for a familiar face. He and Jafaar paused for a few more minutes and then threaded their way through the hot, crowded landing. Ready to give up, Tut spied a curled up body at the end of the pier. He narrowed his eyes. *Could it be possible*?

"Baba, look—look there." Tut pointed toward the sleeping figure.

They raced each other to the end of the dock. When they reached the man, they stopped abruptly and stared in amazement.

Jafaar squatted and gently touched Luka on the shoulder.

"Luka . . . Luka—wake up. It's Tut and Jafaar."

Luka stirred and opened his eyes and squinted in the bright light. "Waa...? Jafaar? Tut? Can it be you? Am I dreaming?"

Tut bent down and then jumped on top of him. "Luka, it's Tut."

Luka reached up and pulled Tut down in a big hug. They both laughed and cried at the same time. Finally, Luka sat up. He drank in the smiling faces of Tut and Jafaar.

"How did you find me? How did you know?"

"How did you know to be here?" asked Tut.

Luka then glanced around and asked, "Where are Zofa and the children? Are they okay? How is Achan's leg?"

Tut pulled Luka to his feet. "They are good, Luka. Come, we will take you to them. We can talk on the way. Zofa and the children will be so excited to see you. We have much to tell you about our journey—and we have so many questions for you."

"Yes, I have much to tell you, also," Luka said. He placed his hand on the bag and said eagerly, "I have food—energy bars that were given to me by missionaries at the border. They will provide nourishment for everyone during the rest of the journey."

As they retraced their steps back to Zofa and the children, they each shared a little of their journey so far.

"Healed, you say? God healed Achan's leg?" Luka's nose and eyebrows wrinkled together as he scratched his head. "How is that possible?"

"There is so much more, brother," Tut added. "A lot has happened since you left us."

Luka slapped Tut on the shoulder and said, "God is good, my brother. Isn't he? God is good."

CHAPTER THIRTY-FIVE

Early the next morning, Anna and Dad picked up Grace, Shelby, and Jonathan and drove to the airport. They checked their bags and easily walked through security. When they arrived at the gate, Anna said, "Coffee, I need coffee."

"Me, too, I'll walk down to Starbucks with you," said Grace. "Anyone else?"

"Tall French roast for me," said Dad.

"I'll take a latte, extra whipped cream," said Jonathan, "—aaaand an orange scone, if you please."

"Shelby?" She was standing with them a minute ago. Anna turned around. "Where did she go, Grace? —Oh, there she is."

Shelby stood over by the window and watched the men load the airplane, her face reflected in the glass. Anna started to walk over to her, when—the strangest thing. For the briefest moment, Shelby's reflection transformed into a tall, thin figure, dressed all in black. Anna stopped, blinked her eyes, and it vanished—disappeared. *What? What was that?*

"Shelby? Shel." Anna called out to her to get her attention.

* * * *

Shelby shivered as she stared out the window toward the runway and thought about Lou's last words to her as he dropped her off at the door last night. She'd told him that she'd decided to go the concert in Frisco.

"Shelby, Shelby—I'm so disappointed in you," he said. "You're making a mistake, so—now I can't protect you. It could have been great, you know? We would have had such a good time together. It seems like I misjudged you—that's so sad." With a malevolent grin, he reached across her and opened her door. The car immediately filled with that noxious odor and she couldn't get out fast enough.

She crawled out, but before she shut the door, she leaned down and said, "Good-bye, Lou—it's been real."

"Yeah, see you around, Shelby."

As she stood at the window and stared at a blinking red light on the runway, she remembered—Lou's eyes. Before she had turned away from the car—his eyes glowed a malevolent red. That's when she had run up to the house and slammed the door.

Thankfully, something or someone called out her name and broke into her thoughts. She turned away from the window.

* * * *

Spooked, Anna called her name again, louder this time. "Shel?"

Shelby jerked and turned toward Anna. "Yeah?"

"Coffee? Do you want a Starbucks?"

"Yeah . . . sure," she said. "A vanilla Macchiato."

Anna glanced once more at the window and then back at Shelby. "Are you okay?"

She nodded her head and with a quick lift of her shoulders, turned backed toward the window.

Anna and Grace walked down the concourse to Starbucks and lined up behind four other people. Anna hesitated. "Okay, Grace, listen. The weirdest thing just happened."

"What's that?"

She told her about the reflection in the window in front of Shelby.

Puzzled, Grace asked, "What was it? Was there someone standing behind or beside her?"

"Noooo—she was all by herself. It made the hairs on the back of my neck stand straight up."

"There must be a good explanation for it."

"Yeah, I guess."

By that time, they stepped up to the register and placed their order.

Gathering back together at the gate, Anna said, "Let's record our first Instagram Live video. Dad, you're our cameraman. Come on, Shelby," she coaxed. "Get in the picture with us."

Shelby grudgingly agreed and sat down in the chair beside Anna.

Grace plopped cross-legged on the floor in front and said, "Who wants to say something?" Everyone except Shelby, of course, agreed.

"Anna, you start off, then I'll go, and Jonathan, you finish up. We have two minutes to do this. Shelby, just act like you're happy, okay?"

"You ready, Dad?" Anna asked. "Be sure and get some cool camera angles."

Dad nodded and got down on the floor beside Grace. "Y'all ready?" He pointed the phone at Anna and said, "You're live."

"Hey, everyone. I'm Anna, and this is our first live video on our super amazing trip to see the Righteous Descendants concert in Frisco, Texas. Here's a special shout-out to our friends at school and the RD Fan Club. We're so excited about our trip and all that's about to happen this weekend. Thanks for joining us. We promise that you will *almost* feel like you're at the concert with us. Here's Grace to tell you more."

Dad slowly panned the phone over to Grace. Her eyes danced, and she said, "Hi, guys. I'm Grace, and we're at the airport now, getting ready to hop on our plane to Dallas. I must admit that I'm a white-knuckle flyer, but it's all good. It'll be worth it when we get to Frisco. We've prayed so hard that God would provide not just an incredible weekend, but as Jonathan is about to tell you, one that will make a difference in the lives of some amazing kids. You're up, Jonathan."

Dad panned the phone back up to a grinning Jonathan and a subdued Shelby. "I'm Jonathan and this is Shelby. My family had to leave four incredible kids back in South Sudan. We want to get back to them as quickly as possible. God has a plan that you're going to get to be a part of. Thanks for hangin' in there with us. Your life will never be the same after this weekend. We promise. See you soon."

Shortly after, they boarded the plane and found their seats. Anna and Grace sat together. Hoping to get her mind off the ride, Anna said, "Let's watch the video before we take off."

As the flight attendant droned on about checking seat belts and where all the emergency exits were, Anna clicked on the video. They laughed at themselves, but then sobered as they noticed something strange behind Shelby.

"What is that?" asked Grace peering closely at the phone. "Play that part again."

Anna clicked one more time. A creepy shadowy mist floated behind Shelby. Wide-eyed, they gawked at each other just as the flight attendant finished her spiel and told everyone to turn off their electronic devices. Grace grabbed Anna's hand and said a quick prayer.

Thankfully, they had a smooth and uneventful flight to Dallas and landed in less than an hour. Grace barely breathed the entire trip. She gripped the left seat rest with one hand and Anna's right hand with the other. By the time the plane landed, Anna could barely feel her hand. She laughed and rubbed her tingling fingers. "Now I know what you mean by being a white-knuckle flyer."

Embarrassed, Grace let out a breath, reached over and gave her a big hug. "Thanks, friend."

They picked up their luggage at the carousel and Dad called for an Uber SUV. After stuffing everything into the vehicle, they all crawled in as Dad videoed once again.

"We're here everyone. We made it. Can you believe all of this craziness?" said Grace. "There's no traffic like this where we come from."

Dad turned the phone toward the front of the car and all the bumper to bumper traffic.

"Oh, my goodness—check out all of those cars," Anna said in the background.

Dad turned the phone back toward Anna. "We're headed to the hotel now. We'll check in with y'all soon." At the end of the video, they put their heads together in the back of the car and waved.

They registered at the hotel and pulled their suitcases up to their rooms. Afterwards, they met downstairs in the lobby.

"I'm starving," said Jonathan.

"Of course, you are. Me, too. Let's go eat," said Anna. She and Jonathan were always hungry.

"Where to?" asked Grace.

"Siri says there's a Cheesecake Factory in the mall close by our hotel."

"Sounds good to me," said Jonathan.

They ate lunch and spent the rest of the day wandering around the mall.

That night Anna got a call from the Righteous Descendant's tour manager. He told her where to go to pick up their backstage passes and what time to meet for supper before the concert.

They spent Saturday morning and early afternoon driving around from one shopping place to the other. Dad and Jonathan spent the day people watching while Anna, Grace and Shelby shopped.

They returned to the hotel about 3:00 to get ready for the concert. Anna and Grace had bought the cutest matching t-shirts at J-Crew to wear that night. Thankfully, Shelby put on a t-shirt that was bright and colorful instead of her usual black and depressing attire. After they dressed, Dad and Jonathan came over to the room. They all piled up on the bed as Dad videoed one more time.

Grace: "Hey everyone. We're ready for the concert. Come with us because we're getting ready to go eat supper with the guys from the Righteous Descendants."

Anna: "It's going to be amazing. They even said we could video while we eat."

Grace: "Meet up with us about 6:00. It's going to be so much fun. We want to introduce you to all of the guys."

Anna: "See you soon."

Oh—my—goodness—Anna thought. *Is this for real, Jesus?*

CHAPTER THIRTY-SIX

Tut and the two men quickly made their way back to Zofa and the children. They had not moved from under the tree since Tut and Jafaar left. When they came near, Jafaar and Tut paused and watched as Luka walked up to the family.

They all sat in a circle singing and clapping to the rhythm of the alphabet song. Zofa had her back to him, so she was completely unaware of his presence. Giggling along with the children, she didn't hear his footsteps until she noticed Ulan's eyes grow big. "Luka!" he yelled.

Zofa quickly turned around and threw her hand to her mouth. She squinted and blinked and then squinted again.

"Luka, is it you? Is it you? Oh, Lord God—thank you." She scrambled to her feet and ran to him, grabbed hold and wouldn't let go. She sobbed into his shoulder. "I didn't know if you were still alive, my brother."

Luka smiled and patted her on the back. "Shh—I'm here. Shh—Peace be unto you, Sister."

They held on to each other for a long moment. The children gathered around and jumped up and down. "It's Luka. It's Luka."

Luka broke his hold on Zofa and gave Ulan and Lala a big hug. Achan danced around him as she waited her turn.

Curious, he asked, "Achan? How is your leg?"

"Jesus healed me, Luka. I'm well. See?" Achan proudly showed him the place on her leg where the bullet had ricocheted into it. He bent down beside her. There was not even a sign of a scar.

Luka's brows drew together. His eyes questioned Zofa.

"It's true," she smiled.

By this time, Jafaar and Tut had joined the reunion.

Jafaar slapped Luka on the shoulder and motioned for everyone to sit down. Luka reached into his bag for an energy bar to give to each one of them. The children's eyes widened. They eagerly held out their hands.

"Take your time eating. Take your time," said Zofa.

The children carefully unwrapped their high-energy biscuit and slowly savored the sweet crunchiness of the treat. Luka pulled out a bottle of water and gave each one a long drink.

"I have a whole bag of these biscuits. They will last us until we get to the border. It is only a day away," said Luka.

The children could only smile at that.

After they had eaten, Luka, Tut, and Jafaar walked a short distance away from the family so that they could talk.

"How far is it to the border?" asked Jafaar.

"It is about 30 kilometers," said Luka

Luka told him about the thousands of refugees who had poured into Ethiopia. "We will cross the border at Burbiey where, hopefully, they will transfer us either by boat or bus to the refugee center in Gambella. We will contact the Knights when we arrive."

"The children are exhausted. Do you think we could go by boat to the border?" asked Jafaar.

"I will go back to the pier and see if I can find the captain who brought me up the river," said Luka. "Tut, come and go with me."

He and Tut left and promised to return as soon as they could. As they walked back to the pier, Tut filled Luka in on all that had happened since he left the family. Luka could only shake his head. He interrupted now and then with a question.

When they arrived back at the pier, Luka quickly spotted the captain. He was untangling the ropes that hung from the side of the hull.

Luka and Tut walked up to him. "Peace, my friend. It is peace?" said Luka.

The captain glanced up from his work, squinted at Luka and said, "Yes, it is peace."

"Sir, would you take my family up the river to the border? We have no money yet, but I promise that we will repay you. We have friends in Ethiopia who will reimburse you for your trouble."

The man bent back down and continued his work with the ropes. Luka and Tut waited respectfully until the man spoke once again. "Yes, I will. Meet me here in the morning at 6:00. You must not be late. We will leave then."

Luka said, "Thank you, my friend. Thank you."

Luka and Tut retraced their steps to the family to tell them the good news.

* * * *

That evening, the family joyfully sat around a small fire. They laughed and told stories, so thankful to God to once more be together. The children sang songs and danced around the fire until exhausted, they curled up together and fell fast asleep. Tut sat up with the adults and listened in on their conversation until he, too, yielded to fatigue and joined his brother and sisters.

In the middle of the night, Tut woke with a start, a nightmare still fresh on his mind. It was so dark. The fire had died down, and the only light came from the millions of stars flickering down on him from the sky. His heart still raced as he remembered the dream. It was all very confusing as dreams tend to be. He tried to piece it together in his mind. They were all together, his family, the Knights, and their friends—the teenagers that he had met on Skype. Unfamiliar music pulsated around them—western music—music that he had once heard when he was with the Knights. He knew that they were all in danger. There were two men in his dream, one dressed in white and the other in black. Everyone, except a girl, also in black, stood behind the man in white. The girl struggled to get away from the man dressed in black, but he held on to her arm. All the people behind the man in white yelled at her. Helpless, he watched as another girl left them and ran over to assist the girl in black, pulling at her to get her away. She resisted at first but finally broke loose; and then . . . a deafening explosion. At that point, Tut found himself back on the boat, but the Knights and their friends had disappeared. Someone wailed, and he walked toward the sound. It was Zofa. She had her arms wrapped tightly around his brother and sisters. She rocked them back and forth, back and forth. Where was Jafaar or Luka? He called out to them, but they didn't answer. Was it up to him to save his family? How? He began to pray, "Jesus, help us . . . help them."

Wide awake now, Tut replayed the dream over and over in his mind. What did it mean? Why did he dream about that girl? Troubled, Tut crawled up on his knees and began to pray. No words came to him, he just knelt and focused on God. A cool, refreshing wind began to blow. *What was that?* Unafraid, he sat back on his heels and noticed a beautiful light. It shimmered—pulsated around him. A man stood before him. *"So be strong and courageous! Do not be afraid and do not panic before them. For the Lord your God will personally go ahead of you. He will neither fail you nor abandon you."*

An inexpressible peace fell over Tut. He knew this man. He responded with only one word—he breathed it out like a prayer, "Lord."

"I will go before you and your family. There is still much danger ahead but be in peace. I will never leave you. Go back to sleep, my son."

At that, Tut laid down and closed his eyes.

The next morning, the family woke early and made their way to the pier. The captain waited for them on the boat. His face cracked into a friendly smile when they walked up. "It is a good day, my friends. It is a good day."

The early morning African sun peeked warm over the eastern horizon. It promised to be another blistering day. The family settled into the vessel, so grateful for the respite from the heat. Still nervous about the boat, Lala grabbed hold of Tut's hand and squeezed tightly. Tut smiled down at her. Lala finally relaxed a little and watched the beautiful, colorful birds flit along the banks of the river.

The morning's boat ride was calm and uneventful. But around noon, the captain spotted a cruiser full of soldiers moving toward them.

"We may have trouble, my friends," he said. "Let me speak."

CHAPTER THIRTY-SEVEN

The Uber driver dropped them off at the front gate. Anna and her entourage felt like rock stars when the Righteous Descendant's concert manager met the group at the ticket office to escort them backstage.

He grinned and shook hands with each one of them. "I'm Ray—welcome everyone. Follow me, and we'll go meet the guys."

Grace squeezed Anna's hand and said, "Okay—pinch me. Am I truly here in Texas with the Righteous Descendants?"

Anna's eyes were as wide as Grace's—taking everything in—totally in awe. All she could do was open her mouth and whisper, "Yes." Anna asked Ray if it was okay for Dad to video their meeting.

"Sure—have at it."

They followed Ray through a backstage door into a room filled with people. The room buzzed with excitement and anticipation. Ray left them for a moment and then returned with five smiling guys trailing behind him.

"This is Sam, Harry, Ed, Luke, and Isaac. Guys, these are the kids I told you about from the *Come and See* YouTube channel." They shook hands with each one of the guys while the band graciously allowed Dad to video. *They're so nice and friendly—just ordinary guys*, thought Anna.

Sam, the leader of the group, said, "Yeah, Ray filled us in on your channel, and we've watched a couple of your videos.

I must say we were impressed. The guys and I have talked, and we're going to give a shout out to the *Come and See* channel at the beginning of the concert. We want you to make yourself at home. We're very casual around here before a concert. Get something to eat and just enjoy. About thirty minutes before the concert starts, we'll all meet to pray, and we want you to join us."

Anna's jaws ached. She couldn't quit smiling—still could not believe she was here with these guys.

They got in line for the food, and Anna laughed when she noticed Jonathan's plate piled high with Texas BBQ and potato salad. "Are you *that* hungry?"

"I'm starving."

Anna thought she was hungry, too, but she was so excited that she could hardly choke down her barbeque—not like her at all.

For the next hour they walked around, videoed, and talked to the guys and the stagehands. Everyone was cordial and made them feel so welcome. Even Shelby joined in and chatted with Ed, the tattooed drummer. As Dad videoed, Anna explained to the guys about the YouTube channel and the kids in South Sudan. They were blown away by it all. They asked a lot of questions and wondered how they could help.

In the meantime, Jonathan watched the responses to the Instagram live videos. He held up his phone and said, "We have 500 likes, y'all. Can you believe it? People are going nuts over this."

At 7:30, Ray announced to everyone that it was time to pray. They gathered together in a big circle and held hands. Sam prayed, "Lord, this concert is yours. It has nothing to do with us. We ask that, through your Holy Spirit, you touch the hearts of the people throughout the arena. Speak to them through the music, God."

After a long pause, Ed continued, "God, we ask your protection on those who attend. Surround the arena with your angels." Another long pause. "Lord, for some reason, I sense a spirit of hatred somewhere near. We ask that you come against it in the name of Jesus."

What Anna's grandmother would have called a "rigor" shivered through her and made her skin crawl. She rubbed her arms and glanced over at Sam. He repeated Ed's prayer, "In the name of Jesus."

The band left soon after to finish getting ready for the show. Ray escorted the group to their seats, right down on the front row. It was awesome. Anna turned around and skimmed the crowd—thousands of people, laughing and excited, walked toward their seats. Someone familiar caught her eye. She stood on tiptoes to get a better look. *Who was that? Who would I know at this concert?* His back was to her, but he seemed so familiar. Shelby stood beside her, so Anna turned to ask if she knew that guy. Shelby's eyes widened in disbelief.

"Shelby?" Anna asked. "Who is that? Do we know him?"

Shelby visibly paled, turned around and dropped down in her seat. "It's Lou."

Anna gaped down at her and then back at the crowd. "What's he doing here?"

Before she could answer, Grace said, "Let's film a video of the crowd before the concert begins."

Dad videoed Anna and Grace with the arena and all the people behind them. "Can you believe it, everyone? We're at our seats, and the concert is just about ready to start. We're so excited. We can hardly stand it. Did y'all enjoy meeting the guys? They were awesome, weren't they?" said Grace.

"Yeah—these guys are the real deal," Anna said.

At that, the lights in the arena started to dim, and Anna said, "All right, here we go."

For one moment, the lights went completely dark, and then the stage burst into an explosion of brilliantly colored lights that streamed and pulsed all over the arena. People went crazy—clapped, raised their hands, jumped up and down and cheered—as the band opened with their Dove Award-winning song, "Jesus is Real."

Euphoria. Tears of joy swelled up inside of Anna as she joined in with the crowd and sang:

He's real. He's real.
I see Him, I feel Him
I know Him, I love Him
He's real.

The thought came to Anna as she joined arms with Jonathan and Grace, *This must be what Heaven is like.*

After the opening song, Sam walked up to the microphone and said, "We welcome all of you, in the name of Jesus. We dedicate this concert to an extraordinary group of kids on the other side of the world—South Sudan. These kids stand for all those oppressed in His name. As we gather here to praise God, we remember that it's not so easy for others to be Christ-followers. To these brave kids and all others who are persecuted, we dedicate this next song, *Be Strong, Don't Fear,* from Isaiah 25."

Tears streamed down Anna's face as she thought about Tut and his brother and sisters. She remembered her conversation with Jesus and his promise that he would watch over them.

For the next hour and a half, the band sang one song after another ending right before intermission with one of Anna's favorites, *Jesus—It's All About You.* When the lights finally came back up, she said, "O—my—goodness. Was that awesome or what?" Grace, her face wreathed in a huge smile, reached over and hugged Anna.

"Dad, did you get some video?" asked Anna.

"Yes—some great clips."

"Where's Shelby?"

"She told me she was going to get something to drink a little while ago. I wonder why she's not back?" asked Grace.

* * * *

Shelby could not believe it. What was Lou doing here? How did he get here? She had to go tell him to leave. He would spoil everything. She walked down to the end of the concourse to look for him. She stopped and turned around to go back the other way when—there he was—propped up against the wall just watching her. It creeped her out. She glared at him and marched up and stood right in front of him. "Why are you here, Lou? You hate everything about this. Just go away and leave me alone. I don't want anything to do with you anymore. Get out of my life."

With a mocking smile, Lou said, "Shelby, Shel—how could I miss this? We have important business here."

Shelby had a sick feeling in her stomach when she recalled their last conversation—and his eyes. An impending sense of danger flushed all over her, and she took several steps away from him.

For the first time, Shelby noticed someone standing a little behind Lou. Lou gestured back toward him. "This is my friend, Tim. He said he's got business here, too."

Tim gawked at her, unsmiling. A cold fear trickled down the back of her neck as she recognized that noxious odor again. She backed away even further and stuttered, "Uh—in . . . intermission is about over. I better go sit down."

"Yeah, you do that, Shelby. Tim and I will see you after the concert. A friend is meeting us outside the arena afterward. Sure you won't join us?"

Shelby didn't answer but turned around and walked quickly back the way she came. She felt their eyes drill into the back of her head. Their derisive laugh echoed down the concourse behind her. *Why are they here? What should I do?* Instinctively, she threw up a prayer. *Lord, help me.* When she got back to her seat, Grace asked, "You okay? You don't look so good. What's that smell?" Grace wrinkled her nose.

"Lou's here," Shelby hissed.

"What? Why is *he* here?" asked Grace.

"I don't know. But, I told him to leave."

As Shelby sat back down, she exhaled a sigh of relief. She was free. Her relationship with Lou had been all wrong—she knew that. He strangled her—controlled her, imprisoned her. She took another deep breath, let it out and then glanced at Grace. Her sister studied her with an expression of hope and curiosity. Shelby smiled and reached over and gave Grace's hand a squeeze.

CHAPTER THIRTY-EIGHT

Tut froze.

The boatload of soldiers barreled up the river toward them. They ran their boat alongside and called out, "Halt."

The boat captain turned off the engine and answered in a respectful voice. "It is peace, my friends."

The soldiers laughed, and one of them mocked back, "Yes, it is peace."

The lieutenant demanded, "Where do you go?"

"To the border, my friend."

"What business do you have at the border?"

"I have a load of maize to trade at the Boro River."

The lieutenant slowly ran his gaze over to Jafaar and the family and then stopped at Tut. "Who are these people? What business do they have with you?" Still staring at Tut, he said, "What a fine young man. The boy would make an excellent soldier, now wouldn't he? We need boys like him."

The other soldiers murmured in agreement.

He then noticed the girls peeking out from behind Zofa and said, "We always need girls to cook and fetch water for us, now don't we?"

Terrified, Tut's face and ears began to burn and his heart pounded. He backed up a step and bumped into someone. Jafaar steadied him with a comforting hand on his back. Tut took a couple of deep breaths to allow his heart to slow down. At once, God's reassuring peace engulfed him—a wave of peace that was beyond his understanding.

The lieutenant ordered the captain, "Drop your passengers off alongside this bank. We promise to take good care of them." He laughed.

Fearfully, the boat captain turned toward Jafaar who caught his eye and slowly nodded his head. At that moment, someone cried out to them from the riverbank. A tall man waved his arms frantically. "Help. I need help. Please help me."

The lieutenant pointed his finger at the captain and said, "You are forewarned. Do what I told you to do, and do not go anywhere. We will see what the man wants, and we will be back for you."

It was impossible to explain what happened next. In a blink of an eye, everything began to swirl around their boat. Terrified, the children screamed and Jafaar and Zofa grabbed hold of them and pulled them down to the bottom of the hull. The family held tightly to each other and crouched low as the boat began to move.

Tut closed his eyes and prayed, "Jesus help us."

As soon as the prayer left his lips, his body lifted like a feather in the wind—he was floating on air. Instinct kicked in, and he reached out for the closest thing to his hand—the anchor. He wrapped both hands and then his arms around it and braced himself at the bottom of the boat. He couldn't breathe—his chest constricted as he gasped for air. His stomach floated up to his throat, and he started to gag. Everything was happening so fast.

Shots rang out—but then—silence. Tut sat very, very still, afraid to move. It was so quiet, gentle waves lapped up against the sides of the boat. Doves cooed in the distance. Then—did he hear voices? Different voices? Who were these people calling out to each other?

Terrified, no one stirred until, finally, Tut raised his head and caught Luka's and Jafaar's eyes and whispered, "What happened? Where are we?"

Wide-eyed, Luka shook his head and said, "I don't know."

Jafaar didn't—couldn't say anything.

Hesitant, Tut stood up, his legs still trembling from the adrenaline. Jafaar grabbed Luka's hand and pulled him up beside him. Dazed, the three could not believe it—the soldiers had vanished. Tut closed his eyes for a moment and then slowly opened them again. *Where did they go?* He noticed that they had docked at a pier somewhere, but where? His mind could not process what his eyes were seeing. He spotted other boats pulled up to the bank. People were everywhere. His eyes slowly panned the scene—people selling water and food at the end of the dock—fishermen scooping their morning catch into baskets from their boats—a man walking by with a basket of fish balanced on his head.

Jafaar called out to him. "Where are we, friend?"

The man quirked his eyebrows at Jafaar as if he thought he was crazy, but he answered and said, "You are in Ethiopia."

Speechless, Tut and Jafaar both blinked simultaneously in disbelief.

Stunned, Jafaar walked back and squatted down beside Zofa huddled over the children at the bottom of the boat. He gently touched her shoulder and said in a quiet voice, "Zofa, get up. Get up. Praise God. He has given us a miracle."

Zofa lifted her head. She trembled uncontrollably. Tried desperately not to lose the fierce and protective grip that she had on the children. "Jafaar, what happened? Where are we?"

The children began to stir and protest trying to get out from under her arms.

"Mama, move," said Ulan backing out from under her left arm.

The other two girls backed away, also, and scrambled to their feet, weaving a little, still dizzy from the wild ride.

The captain of the boat had fainted dead away.

Jafaar walked over and shook him. "Wake up, my friend. Wake up."

The captain moaned and stirred, placing his hand over his eyes.

Jafaar helped the man sit up. "We're safe. We're safe. We're in Ethiopia."

The captain gazed around, disoriented and in complete shock.

Jafaar reassured him. "It is good. God has done a miracle—a miracle, my friend— a miracle."

In a daze, the captain wobbled and then stood to his feet grabbing hold of Jafaar and Luka as he did so. "This is impossible. This cannot be. Ethiopia, you say?" Stupefied, he stared with his mouth agape.

Tut eased over to Jafaar and Luka as they steadied the captain and asked, "What happened, Baba? How can this be?"

"I don't know—I really don't know, but we are safe, aren't we, my son?"

To reassure himself as well as Jafaar, Tut said, "Yes, Baba, we are safe."

Jafaar bowed to the captain. "Thank you. Thank you. We do not have the money to pay you now, but I promise we will get it back to you."

"No, no—you do not owe me a thing. I will never in my life forget this journey—ever."

Jafaar shook hands with the man and asked, "It is good?"

The man smiled and answered, "It is very good, my friend."

"*Our* God is *good*, sir. He did a miracle for us today. We are Christ-followers. It seems that he has transported this boat from Nasir to Ethiopia instantaneously and supernaturally as he did in the New Testament. Do you know him?" asked Jafaar.

"I know *of* him," said the captain. "But, I do not know him."

Jafaar reached over and placed his hand on the man's shoulder. "Today you have experienced his power and his glory. Now, if you choose, you can know of his forgiveness and his love."

The captain fell to his knees and cried out, "I am not a good man."

Jafaar kneeled beside him and said, "All you must do is confess your sins and ask Jesus to be the Lord of your life."

As the captain prayed the sinner's prayer, Tut and the family experienced another miracle on that day.

A short time later, Jafaar said to the family, "Let's help the captain unload his boat."

Happy to have a way to repay the captain, they hauled sacks of maize off the boat for the next two hours. The children sang and danced as they worked, laughing out loud for the first time in many weeks. After they had piled all the sacks of maize on the dock, the exhausted but still exuberant family stood proudly as the captain walked over and thanked them for their help.

"So, we part, my friend," said the captain.

"Yes, I pray God's blessing on you and your family," said Jafaar.

"I will never forget you or your God—now my God."

Shyly, Zofa and the children smiled at the captain and the family watched as he boarded his boat. They waved one more time as the man started the engine and pointed his boat back toward the River Sobat and South Sudan.

Tut, Luka, and Jafaar left the family at the pier and went searching for someone to tell them how they might arrange transportation to the refugee camp in Gambella. They asked a man selling water at the end of the pier. "That way." He pointed toward a long line of people waiting patiently at a tent set up a short distance away. They walked over and stood in line.

Several hours later, they stepped up to a man sitting at a desk inside the tent. "Where are you from?" he asked.

"We travel from Malakal," Jafaar said.

The man eyed him with respect. "That was a long and dangerous journey."

"Yes, but with God's help, we made it," said Tut.

The man nodded and said, "And where do you go?"

"We have missionary friends waiting for us in Gambella."

"Your family can travel by boat or a bus to Gambella. Which do you prefer?"

The men and Tut grinned at each other and answered simultaneously, "Bus." The man glanced up curiously from his paper. "You leave in two days. In the meantime, you can stay here." He gave them the number of a temporary tent. Jafaar thanked the man, and they walked back toward the pier to gather Zofa and the children.

CHAPTER THIRTY-NINE

As the crowd settled back into their seats, the lights dimmed, and the cheering rose for the second half. The rest of the concert was even better than the first half. Shelby let herself go and joined her friends as they jumped, clapped, raised their hands, and had a wonderful time praising God along with the music. At one point in time, as Anna's dad videoed live, Shelby joined her sister and friends as they sang along with the band.

Shelby laughed as Jonathan turned an ear to Anna and then her and teased, "Our audience might not appreciate our singing."

The girls giggled, hit him on the shoulder and sang even louder.

The concert ended with the song, *I AM*. The poignant melody floated around the arena and flooded Shelby with the words:

I Am
I Am He
The one who calmed and walked upon the sea.
I Am
I Am the one
The one and only—God's own Son.
I Am
I Am Real
To you I Am revealed

I Am
I Am
I Am

As the song continued, Shelby's heart broke open as the Spirit of God touched not only her but the hearts of so many in that arena. Tears streamed down faces; people kneeled, prayed—and reached out to God. Shelby found herself on her knees, sobbing. Anna motioned to Grace and they kneeled beside her, gently placed their hands on her shoulder and prayed. Tears streamed down her face.

She grabbed hold of Anna and said in awe, "Anna . . . it was . . .Jesus . . . up there . . . I saw Him." She then reached over and gathered Grace in a hug and whispered in her ear, "He told me where our dad is, Grace. He said he is good—he's happy—he's waiting for us to join him someday."

The girls smothered each other in a huge hug. When they did, Shelby caught Anna's eye over Grace's shoulder and then—they both blinked their eyes at the same time—it was Jesus. With arms crossed, he was leaning back against the apron of the stage—and smiling at them.

"Grace, turn around, look," Shelby whispered.

Grace turned around and gasped.

Pure love visibly radiated and shimmered from Jesus to Anna, to Grace, and then to Shelby. Shelby's heart cartwheeled, and she clutched at her chest and reached for Anna's clammy hand. Grace fainted.

The entire group, Jonathan and Anna's dad, included, kneeled beside Grace until she sufficiently revived. Everyone stayed until the lights came up and the concert was over. Shelby hugged each one and wiped her eyes. Emotionally sated, no one wanted to leave, so the group sat in their chairs and talked about the concert until the arena started to thin out.

Anna remembered Shelby's encounter with Lou and asked, "So tell me about Lou. Did you go talk to him? Find out why he was here?"

Shelby slowly nodded her head and then, inexplicably, her stomach lurched, and she jumped to her feet and grabbed

Anna's hand. "Anna, we're in danger." Her eyes darted around the arena. "Something's about to happen, and I don't know what it is."

"What's going on?" asked Anna's dad. He placed his hand on her shoulder to calm her down.

"Lou's here, Mr. John," said Shelby. "He had a friend with him, some guy named Tim. He told me they were meeting someone else after the concert. I talked to him at intermission. He said they would see me afterwards. I admit, Mr. John, he frightens me. Lou's evil—I *don't* want to be with him—I don't want him around."

Concerned, he asked, "Do you see him now?" He turned and scanned the crowd as they were filing out of the arena.

"No," she said. "Maybe he left. I hope so."

"It's okay," said Grace. "Hopefully, he's gone now. I'm sure everything's fine. Let's go back to the hotel."

They gathered all their belongings and joined the crowd streaming toward the exit doors that spilled out into the beautiful portico that encircled the entire stadium. Spaced equally around the circumference, colossal columns loomed majestically above them. Voices echoed as people walked in and around the columns toward the parking lot, stopping often to talk or take a selfie. It was a beautiful night. The moon had risen over the stadium bathing everything in a soft fuzzy glow.

The girls stopped a short distance from one of the beautiful columns. Shelby said, "Hey, let's take one last selfie."

Mr. John and Jonathan, deep in conversation, walked on ahead. "Okay," said Shelby, "move over here so that I can get the stadium behind us in the picture." She stood in the middle between Grace and Anna and held up the phone to get their faces. Suddenly, as Shelby was about to take the photo, she froze . . . It was Lou . . . in the camera's field of view. He stood behind them against one of the columns. Two guys were with him. She slowly lowered the phone.

Grace said, "Shel, are you going to take the picture or what?"

"Lou's behind us," Shelby whispered. Dread curled up her backbone.

"What do we do?" said Anna.

"We won't leave you, Shelby," said Grace.

The three slowly turned around. Lou and the other two guys stood about twenty feet away from them. Lou had a sick, twisted grin on his face.

Shelby's eyes narrowed. "Well, I've had enough of him," she said. "The guy to the left of Lou is Tim—but—I don't know who the other guy is. I'll go tell them to leave—leave us alone."

"I don't think that's a good idea, Shel," said Grace. "Something's not right. Wait."

It was too late. Determined, Shelby had already started walking toward them. Grace ran to catch up with her when it happened. As Shelby approached Lou, Grace dashed in front to stop her. Just as she put her hand out, a demonic and spine-chilling shriek pierced through the air and a horrified Grace turned toward the ungodly sound. Lou and the guy named Tim disappeared, vaporized into the shadows before her eyes. The other guy with them held a backpack in his arms. With blank eyes, he started to move toward Grace and Shelby. He pulled out his cellphone, closed his eyes for a moment and opened them. He reached down and . . . suddenly. . . a brilliant flash of white light and a muffled thud. A fiery concussion slammed into Grace and then dissipated. The explosion knocked Grace backward into Shelby and they both fell hard to the concrete. The guy with the bag crumpled unconscious in a heap on the ground. Pandemonium broke out as people around them cried out in terror, grabbed their family members and began to run.

Shelby screamed, "NOOOOO." She knelt beside Grace and began calling her name.

"Grace? Grace? Are you okay? Grace . . . Talk to me . . . Talk to me. Oh, God . . . Help her!"

Anna's dad and Jonathan ran back toward the girls, both yelling "Call 911!"

A security guard with a walkie-talkie had already done so.

Sirens wailed. Police poured in to secure the area.

When Jonathan and Mr. John reached the girls, Shelby stared up at them, her face white with shock. Jonathan and Anna kneeled beside them. With his voice steady and reassuring, Jonathan said, "Shelby . . . Anna . . . we're going to pray. We're going to pray for Grace."

Right in the middle of all that chaos, Jonathan, Anna, and Mr. John began to pray. "Jesus . . . Jesus . . . Jesus . . . Heal her, Lord."

Time appeared to stand still for Shelby as the cacophony of noise quieted as her friends laid hands on Grace and prayed. After what seemed like an eternity, Grace began to stir, moaning.

"Grace, open your eyes. Grace, look at me," Shelby sobbed.

"Wha-aa-t happened?" she asked.

"You're okay, Grace. You're okay. Thank God, you're okay," said Shelby.

The ambulance arrived soon after. The paramedics secured Grace to the gurney and carefully loaded her into the vehicle. Shelby climbed in behind her.

"Shelby, we'll follow you," said Anna's dad.

Shelby didn't answer. She was too busy attending to her sister.

* * * *

A policeman offered Anna, her dad, and Jonathan a ride to the hospital. Grateful, Dad accepted, and they piled into the police car. As they were driving out, another ambulance arrived for the young man who still lay motionless in the alcove. Dazed, Anna watched through the police car window as paramedics jumped out and began attending to him. The policeman turned on his sirens so that their car could move through the traffic, following close behind the ambulance.

"I need to let our families know what happened before they hear it on the news. They'll be frantic with worry," said

Dad. "Let me see if I can call Maria." After dialing, he shook his head, "Too many people are trying to call out. I can't get through. We'll try again when we get to the hospital."

The hospital was just a couple of blocks away. The policeman dropped them off at the emergency exit, and they ran in to find Shelby. They'd already taken Grace back to the ER. Dad rushed up to the desk and asked the nurse, "We're here to see Grace Mercer." She smiled and said, "Have a seat. They're attending to her now. You can see her in a little while."

They found a seat in the waiting room and—waited. Dad tried once more to get Grace's mom. Thankfully, the phone rang. He put the phone on speaker so that Anna could listen in on their conversation.

His voice calm, he said, "Maria . . . it's John. Listen to me . . . I don't know a lot, but there's been a bombing at the concert and Grace was injured." He continued quickly, "But, I think she's going to be fine. Shelby was with her, but she wasn't hurt—no one else was hurt. We're all with Grace at the hospital in Frisco now. This is one of the finest hospitals in the area. Don't worry. She's in good hands. Is someone with you? You don't need to be alone."

Maria's voice broke, "Yes, actually Peter and Ruth are with me now. We were having dinner."

Relieved, Dad said, "Good. Tell them that Jonathan is just fine." There was murmuring in the background as Maria relayed the information. She came back on line. "Ruth and I are going to catch the first flight to Dallas in the morning. We'll let you know when to pick us up."

"Great, we'll be there. We'll be in touch with you between now and then. Hey, I'm going to give the phone to Jonathan. He wants to talk to his parents. Maria—she's going to be okay. We'll see you tomorrow."

"Dad," said Anna, "I'll call Ben. I know he's worried sick right now." After she got off the phone with Ben, she told her dad that Ben had heard and had been desperately trying to get in touch with them.

The three paced the waiting room for the next two hours. Finally, a doctor and a smiling Shelby came out to let them know how Grace was doing.

"She had a concussion and a minor burn along the side of her right arm, but, thankfully, nothing too serious," he said. "We'll keep her here overnight to watch her, but she should be good to go home by tomorrow afternoon. She'll need a couple of weeks to recuperate, but, she's going to recover completely."

They let out a collective breath and sent up a prayer of thanks.

"Can we see her?" Anna asked hopefully.

"They're just finishing up. Give the nurses a few more minutes, and they'll come get you."

After that, Shelby said, "So—okay—I'd better check in with Mom."

About thirty minutes later, a nurse came out. "Mercer Family?" They all jumped up at once. "You can see her, but only two at a time," she warned.

Anna and Dad went in first. Anna pushed back the curtain to see a smiling, but wan Grace propped up drinking a Coke. "Hey, friend," she said.

"Hey." Anna walked over and stood beside her bed.

"Well, we had quite an adventure, didn't we?"

"A little more than we bargained for," Anna said.

"How's everybody doing?" It was just like Grace to worry about everyone else besides herself.

"We're all good. Dad talked to your Mom. She and Ms. Ruth are flying down here as soon as they can get a flight."

"I'm glad"—there was silence.

"I guess we're all still in shock, huh?" asked Anna.

"So, uh, we'll leave and send Jonathan in, okay?"

Anna reached over, gave her a gentle hug and said, "Grace, I was so scared."

She patted Anna on the back and whispered, her voice hoarse with tears, "I know. Jesus was with us, wasn't he?"

"Yes, he was."

CHAPTER FORTY

That night Tut tossed and turned on his pallet as the events of the last few days played over and over in his mind. Every time he closed his eyes, he was back on the boat—the faces of the angry soldiers, the boat swirling, the girl in his dream, even Jesus appearing to him. It had all come to a good end—except, what about that girl in black? As he pictured her face, a warm liquid peace radiated and pulsed inside of him, and he *knew* that she was out of harm's way. With a yawn, Tut turned over on his side and fell asleep.

The next morning, the family awoke to the hustle and bustle of the refugee camp.

"Tut—Ulan," called out Zofa. "Wake up sleepy heads. We need for you to go and fetch water for us this morning. There is a container by the front of the tent."

Tut groaned a little and then sat up rubbing his eyes.

"Luka, do we still have some of those high-energy biscuits?" asked Zofa.

Luka dug into his bag and pulled out enough for their breakfast.

"Good, but would you please go stand in line and get us more?" Zofa asked.

In good spirits, Tut, Luka, and Ulan left the tent to complete their errands. It was already hot and dusty as the hundreds of people in the camp began to stir.

The family settled in for the next two days, waiting for their chance to board the bus for the final leg of their journey. On the second morning, Tut went with Jafaar to talk with one of the missionaries in the camp about contacting the Knights.

"Come back tonight, my friends," said the man. "We have a satellite phone that you can use to call them."

"This is good, Baba," said Tut. Elated, he could hardly wait to get back and share the good news with the family.

That evening, they were all gathered together in front of the missionary's tent. Each face wreathed in a huge smile as the man dialed the number. Tut's chest tightened with anticipation as the phone rang. Finally, someone answered.

"Hello?"

"Peter, my friend. It is Jafaar." He held the phone out so that everyone could hear.

"Jafaar? Jafaar? Praise God." He called out excitedly, "Favor . . . David . . . come here. Jafaar is on the phone."

Tut smiled to himself as he pictured the two almost tripping over each other to get to the phone.

"Tell me, my friend," said Peter. "Are you well? Are the kids well?"

"Yes, yes. We are all good. The kids are here, too. They cannot wait to speak to you."

Tut got on the phone first and then everyone had a chance to say a quick hello. Afterwards, Jafaar returned to the phone.

"And you, my friend?" asked Jafaar. "Where is Ruth?"

"We have much to tell you," said Peter. "Too much to say now but know that God has done many miracles for us."

"Yes, as with us," said Jafaar. "We are boarding a bus in two days to take us to Gambella. We will contact you then."

"That's good. We'll make plans for you when you get to the camp. Call us when you arrive. We look forward to hearing from you."

The children skipped along and sang as they made their way back to the tent. Tut laughed out loud. It was so good to smile again and see the joy on the faces of his brother and sisters.

Two days later, they boarded the bus to Gambella. Refugees packed the bus so tightly that Luka, Tut, and Jafaar had to stand in the aisle beside Zofa and the children. Tut didn't care. He was happy that they were on their way—finally safe. As he held on to the rail above his head, swaying back and forth to the motion of the bus, Tut stared out the window and thought about their miraculous journey.

The family arrived in Gambella late that evening, met by kind and smiling aid workers who gave out water and food. They were so hungry and thirsty that Tut immediately sat his brother and sisters down and gave each a cup of water and an energy bar. He watched gratefully as they ate and drank their fill and then, finally, allowed himself to eat a little something. An aid worker came back soon after and showed them to their tent. The children were so tired. They could only smile wanly and walk sleepily behind Tut and the adults. It did not take long before everyone curled up together on the thin pallets strewn around the floor and promptly fell asleep.

The next morning, a man woke them by knocking on their tent. Jafaar and Tut walked out to meet him.

"Are you the man named Jafaar?"

"I am."

"I bring good news. A missionary named Peter Knight has been inquiring about you and your family."

"Yes, he is our friend—our good friend," said Jafaar.

"He has sent word that he is sending funds to your family."

Tut sent up a prayer of thanks and exchanged relieved smiles with Jafaar.

The man continued, "Come to the administration tent this evening, and you may speak with Peter and his family by Skype."

When they returned to the tent, Jafaar gathered the family in a circle.

Tut asked, "Baba, may I tell everyone?"

Jafaar smiled and nodded his head.

Bursting with the good news, Tut told the family about the funds that the Knights were sending to them.

They all spoke at once. They couldn't believe their good fortune.

"Wait," said Tut, "there is even more." He beamed at the excited faces of his brother and sisters. "We also get to skype with the Knights this evening."

That night, the family gathered in front of the small computer. The children could hardly sit still as they listened to Peter.

"God is so good. He has given a way for all of us to travel to Ethiopia. We have made reservations to fly to Addis Ababa and will seek transportation to Gambella from there. We leave in one month. There is so much more to tell you. We believe God has granted the funds to open an orphanage close to Gambella. Keep praying, my friends. We will see you soon."

* * * *

Something woke Shelby. *Where am I?* Eyes still closed, she reached out and touched the arm of a chair. She tried to straighten her legs and groaned out loud. She had a crick in her neck and her body felt like something had twisted it into a pretzel. Someone whispered her name.

"Psst—Hey, Shel, wake up."

She remembered.

Shelby slowly opened her eyes. "Is that you, Grace?" The room was dark except for the blinking light on the IV machine.

"Yes, you're snoring."

Shelby grunted and slowly disentangled her legs from the uncomfortable chair. "Man, what a night," she grumbled. "Are you okay? Do you need something?"

"Yes, I'm so thirsty. Would you get me some water, please?"

Shelby leaned over and turned on the light. It was so bright that they both blinked and covered their eyes. "Ouch," said Grace, grimacing. "That's not so good on the ol' headache."

"I'm sorry." Shelby whispered.

"It's okay." Grace whispered back.

Shelby reached over, picked up the cup and went to fill it with fresh water and ice. When she returned, Grace was sitting up in bed.

"Here you go." Shelby held the cup as Grace sipped.

"Thanks, Sister. Have you heard from Mom?"

"Yes, she's flying in this morning."

"Is she freaking out?" smiled Grace.

"She's very calm—for Mom, that is."

"That's a miracle, isn't it?" laughed Grace. She grimaced and put her hand to her head.

Concerned, Shelby said, "Can I get you anything else?"

"No, I'm good. Just have a pretty bad headache."

After an awkward pause, Shelby said, "So have you talked to Anna?"

"No—she, Mr. John, and Jonathan were outside in the waiting room until about four this morning. The nurse told me that she persuaded them to go back to the hotel to get some sleep."

"Grace . . . I'm so sorry about Lou and everything that happened. He filled my mind with lies and half-truths. I was so angry with God, you know? I didn't understand how a good God allowed our dad to die like that—helping someone else."

Grace's eyes filled with tears. "I know, Shel."

"But, my anger only got you hurt—and I don't know what to think about that. You could have died."

"But, I didn't," Grace said. "God protected all of us from evil." Shelby took Grace's hand in hers and said, "Grace, you know what I discovered? It wasn't evil that caused our dad to die. He gave his life to save someone else . . . just like Jesus did for us. The Bible says *don't let evil conquer you but conquer evil by doing good.* That's what happened."

Shelby reached over and gave Grace a gentle hug, and they both held on to each other and cried, cleansing tears of relief and joy.

Finally, they broke away from each other. Shelby grabbed a bunch of tissues and shared them with Grace. "Are you hungry?" she asked.

Grace swiped at the tears on her face and smiled. "You know I'm always hungry."

CHAPTER FORTY-ONE

About ten o'clock, Anna, Dad, and Jonathan caught an Uber to pick up Ms. Maria and Ms. Ruth at the airport.

"How'd you sleep?" asked Dad.

"Not very well," Anna admitted. "I kept playing everything over and over in my mind."

"Me, too," said Jonathan. "It just seems surreal, doesn't it?"

They waited on the concourse for the two ladies to arrive. "There they are." Jonathan ran toward his mother, picked her up, spun her around and gave her a big hug. She took his face in her hands and said, "Praise God. You're okay."

Ms. Maria smiled and waited. When Anna walked up to her, Ms. Maria grabbed hold of her and burst into tears. They both held on to each other. "I was so scared," she said. Anna patted her on the back and murmured, "I know, but she's fine. They're both just fine."

As they walked back down the concourse together, Anna thought about her two friends. Grace's injuries would heal quickly, but the true miracle of healing had already occurred in Shelby. Anna was privileged to see it with her own eyes. Jesus had healed Shelby's broken heart and restored her crushed spirit. Her mom was in for a wonderful surprise.

What about me, thought Anna. *How has all of this changed me?* Anna didn't think she'd been angry at God, just disappointed. She'd stuffed it all down deep inside. She tried to act the part of the good daughter and the good sister. Anna knew now that her disappointment in God affected her as much as Shelby's anger at him had affected Shelby. Anna's mom left her dad, but Jesus never left her—he never left any of them. He was with her all the time; working for her good. She didn't see it—until now.

When they got in the Uber, the driver said, "Hey, you're those guys my daughter told me about from the concert. She was following you on Instagram Live last night when all of that happened. She couldn't believe that video. She showed me. I saw it—I mean *Him—with* my very own eyes."

"What do you mean?" asked Anna.

"I'll show you when we get to the hospital," he said.

When they arrived at the hospital, Dad tried to pay the driver. "Nope," he insisted, "save it for those kids."

Reporters and people were everywhere. They skirted around all the commotion and made their way through the crowd to the elevator. Grace's room was on the third floor right in front of the nurse's station. A new nurse was on duty. She glared at Anna and the others when they walked up, not knowing who they were.

Dad introduced everyone, and the nurse's tone of voice changed. "She's doing well this morning and waiting for you."

When they opened the door, Grace and Shelby greeted them with huge smiles. They were both propped up in bed and watching TV. Ms. Maria walked over and engulfed the girls in an enormous hug. They embraced for several minutes, until Shelby said, "Mom, we're fine. We love you." Their mom hadn't heard that word from Shelby in such a long time. Tears streamed down her face as she gave Shelby another hug.

In the meantime, Jonathan had his phone out. Anna happened to glance over and noticed a curious expression on his face.

"What's up, Jonathan?"

"I remembered what the Uber driver had told us, so I thought I would check it out. Listen to some of these comments on Instagram Live."

"I saw Him!"

"That's so cool, how did you do that?"

"Where did He come from?"

"Who was the enormous black man dressed in white?"

"What are they talking about?" Anna asked.

"I'm not sure. Let's go back and watch the videos."

Jonathan walked over and held the phone out for all of them to see.

He clicked on the video that Anna's dad had filmed when the band sang, *I Am*. They all crowded in to watch. Suddenly, Anna gasped, "Look, do you see?"

"Oh, my goodness," said Grace."

"What?" asked Shelby leaning in to get a closer look.

"Jonathan, play it again," said Anna.

As Jonathan replayed the video, Anna could only stare in amazement. Behind Ed, playing the drums, stood a colossal black man dressed in white and beside Sam . . . They all leaned in even closer and gasped at the same time. "It's Jesus!" whispered Anna.

She smiled. Yes, they had seen Jesus. There he was—as real as life. Anna realized that not only had he appeared to Shelby and their group, but also, to all of those who had been watching. *Wow, what a gift.* Anna closed her eyes and sent him a prayer of thanks.

Later that morning, a detective arrived and gave them an update on the bomber. "We think he's a *lone wolf*," said the man. "Did you see anyone else?"

Shelby gave Anna a knowing smile. How did she even begin to explain? The girls knew that there was no finding Lou and his friend. They'd both disappeared back into the evil abyss where they'd come from. It was all so clear to Anna now. She realized that Lou was *Lucifer*—Satan himself— and Tim . . .? Just an evil minion. The poor boy with the backpack? Only some lost soul who allowed pure evil to manipulate him.

"Y . . . es," said Shelby to the detective, drawing out her words, "but . . . I . . . don't think you'll ever find them."

"Well, thankfully, his vest didn't fully detonate. Unfortunately for him, however, it was enough to kill him, but the blast didn't go far—just enough to knock you down, young lady."

"Was anyone else hurt?" asked Grace.

"No, since he was in front of that huge column, the blast was contained between you and the bomber."

After the detective left, there was a loud commotion in the hallway. Dad walked out of the room to check and came back in with a huge grin on his face. "You have visitors, Grace."

Behind Dad, walked in the five guys from the *Righteous Descendants* group. They circled the bed and Sam said, "You two are very brave. We want to do something for you and the *Come and See* ministry—so—we'd like to come to your town to perform a free concert."

* * * *

EPILOGUE
SIX WEEKS LATER

It was ten o'clock at night. Anna and Grace had been texting for about an hour. They were both too excited to sleep because tomorrow was the *Righteous Descendant's* concert at the high school football stadium. Max nosed around for his ball under the bed making his weird grunting noises. "Come on, Max—hop up—it's time to go to sleep." He backed out from under the bed and jumped up beside her, the smelly ball in his mouth. Anna grimaced and took it away from him. She knew he'd chew on it all night if she'd let him. He was a little obsessive like that. "Max, sometimes you just have to let things go. Okay?"

As Anna burrowed down in bed beside Max, she thought about all that had happened in the last six weeks. The Knights left about two weeks ago to fly to Ethiopia. It was hard to be sad because they were so excited about reuniting with their kids. Anna smiled and remembered the last conversation that she had with Jonathan. They'd sat on the front porch the night before they left.

"Anna, I'll miss you."

"I know, I can't believe you're leaving. Do you think you'll be back?"

"I don't know—that's all up to God."

"I'll email you, I promise, Jonathan," she said. "And we can skype."

"Maybe you could come see us?" he asked hopefully.

"Yeah, maybe." Anna could feel the tears spring to her eyes.

Jonathan took her hand in his and said sincerely, "Anna, God has so much planned for your life. Take time to grow up in him. Someday, somehow, some way—I believe that God will bring us back together, but in the meantime, we both have a lot of growing up to do." He leaned over and gave her a light kiss—her first. They sat together quietly side by side for a few minutes. Finally, he sighed and stood up to leave.

"Ma'alsalama, Anna." He smiled at her and said, "That means good-bye in South Sudan."

"Good-bye, Jonathan."

She'd never known anyone like Jonathan or David or Favor. They'd blessed her life so much. There's no doubt that they would see each other again someday—they had so many more adventures ahead of them with Jesus.

After the Knights arrived in Ethiopia, Anna, Grace, and Shelby skyped with Jonathan. He told about reuniting with Tut and his family. "When we saw them for the first time, they screamed so loud with joy that everyone around wondered what in the world had happened," he said, laughing out loud. "It was amazing to see them again."

So, tomorrow is the concert. People have volunteered to hold buckets at the door for donations. With those proceeds and the ones that they've already brought in from *Go Fund Me*, they will surely meet their goal of $200,000 to build the orphanage in Ethiopia.

As Anna reached over to turn off the light, there he was: Jesus, all comfortable in her chair and smiling at her. "Good job, Anna," he whispered. "Good job."

She returned his smile and whispered back, "Thanks."

"Oh, Anna?"

"Yes, Lord?"

My Word says, *"No eye has seen, no ear has heard, and no mind has imagined what God has prepared for those who love him."*—I Corinthians 2:9

He paused. "There's more."

A blissful warmth flooded through her. "That's what I thought, Lord."

At that, the light dimmed. Anna turned over, wrapped her arms around Max and fell asleep.

* * * *

Author's Notes
The Rest of the Story

In the preface of this book, I explained that God had given me a story, a story that I had never read, a story that spoke from my heart and my love for Jesus. One that would appeal to the young and the old. I knew that I wanted to show that Jesus was as real today as he was yesterday and would be tomorrow.

What would happen if Jesus appeared to Anna? It was so much fun to think about what he would look like to her. What would he be wearing? What would he say? How would Jesus use this ordinary sixteen-year-old girl in an extraordinary way? Over the centuries, artists have painted what they thought Jesus looked like. Why couldn't an author paint the same picture, only with words?

The narrative began to form in my mind and slowly appeared on the pages of Word. In January 2016, I came across a news article about missionaries, Kim and Brad Campbell, and their harrowing escape from Malakal, South Sudan with their two girls. Their story was riveting. I followed every link. What happened to them and the children that they protected? Finally, I read that the Campbells reluctantly evacuated, but their South Sudanese children were not allowed to leave.

The story continued to weave in my mind. What if Anna and her friends somehow connected spiritually and God-supernaturally with these South Sudanese children? At that point, I began to do extensive research about South Sudan and the people there. God guided me link after link to discover everything I could about the culture and the people. How did they dress, what were their customs, how did they speak to each other? Tut's story began to come together—a tale of a young man's journey into manhood.

That next September 2016, I wrote to Kim Campbell for the first time and told her how her family had inspired this story. I was trying to figure out the best route for Jafaar to lead his group to safety. I had researched the Sudd in South Sudan. The Sudd is twenty-two thousand square miles of marshlands dotted throughout by islands. I read where many South Sudanese people escaped to Uganda that way, but their journey was treacherous, and many died along the way. I asked Kim if that would be a possible escape route. She wrote me back and said, "*The Nile would flow North. So, to go from Malakal to Uganda (south)would be against the current. It could be done by boat but would take some time, and the boats they have are very primitive and not very river worthy. With the militia, bandits, and crocodiles, it would be a very long and dangerous journey.*" She told me that they had miraculously reunited with their kids somewhere in Ethiopia, but she did not tell me where or how they got there.

As I combed through maps, stories, and articles, it seemed probable that Tut and his family would go down the White Nile and over to the Baro River to Nasir and into Ethiopia. But where would their journey end? During 2017, as the story unfolded, providentially, God showed me that Tut's journey would end in Gambella. I did not know until March 2018, that the Campbells ended up there.

In the meantime, the story began to intertwine between Anna, her friends, and the missionary kids, David, Jonathan, and Favor. Not only does God place the American kids in Tut's story, but He also sets Tut in their story. Each one is vital to the other. There is no distance, space in time or place with God. He is omnipresent, and he was with both groups at the same time. God used Tut to fight supernaturally for Shelby, and he used Anna for Tut. Our prayers for those even around the world are just as effective as our prayers for those around us.

After completing the manuscript, it was time to find a beautiful cover. God led me to a woman by the name of Lisa Hainline. She told me that business had been slow, so she had taken down her website. However, she agreed to create my cover. After going back and forth many times, we decided on the beautiful picture of Anna. It still did not seem to be complete. I told Lisa about a favorite photo of a group of children that my daughter-in-law, Stephanie, had taken on a mission trip to Africa. Lisa included that photo on the cover, and I knew that God had placed his final stamp of approval.

Several other *God-incidences* happened during the writing of *Anna's Chair*. In the book, Anna and her friends decided that they would raise money for an orphanage in Gambella, Ethiopia. I wrote this part of the story sometime around the beginning of 2017. In March 2018, over a year later, the Campbells sent out an update of their ministry in Ethiopia. Stunned, I read that the Campbells were building a Children's Center for the orphans in Gambella . . . just like in the book.

In May 2018, I wrote to Kim and Brad to say that I had finished the book. I received an e-mail back, not from Kim, but from their daughter, one I did not know about. I remember just sitting there and staring at the signature. That daughter's name was—Anna.

At the beginning of September 2018, the Campbells sent out an email that they were back in the States and would be traveling in Iowa to raise money for their mission projects in Romania, Greece, and South Sudan. God spoke to my heart one morning and said he wanted me to go to meet them and take books to sell to help raise money for their Children's Center.

My friend D'Arylan and I flew to Des Moines, Iowa with a heavy suitcase load of books to meet the Campbells. Honestly, I was kind of nervous about meeting them, but I shouldn't have been, of course. There was an instant God-connection that confirmed everything. As Kim, Brad, and I spoke, and I shared with them how the book came to be written, we all had tears in our eyes. Our good God miraculously placed us together—three people who had nothing in common except Jesus and his redeeming love.

"Whatever is good and perfect is a gift coming down to us from God our Father, who created all the lights in the heavens." James 1:17
Our creative God allows us to tap into his creativity. He can use anyone if they are willing to be a vessel.

Anna's Chair

So many people to thank for helping me with *Anna's Chair.* Thank you, Shannon, Stephanie, Stacey, Starr, and Preston for reading and editing. To Steph for the beautiful photo that inspired Tut. Thank you to Shane for your blessing. To Kate and Saylor for being my teenage inspirations. To eleven-year-old Silas for being one of my first editors and making sure that I spelled "okay" the right way. To Slaton, Preston, Asher, and Patton—giving me the "boys" point of view. Thank you, Josie, for reading the proof. Your encouragement from a sixteen-year-old viewpoint was such a blessing. Thank you to Laurel and Julie—you both are an inspiration to me! Thank you to Josie and Cooper for the Instagram posts. Thank you to D'Arylan for your belief in this book. We had such an incredible adventure with Jesus, didn't we? And of course, thank you to Brad, Kim, Anna, Katie, and Cassidy for your inspiration and fearlessness as warriors for Jesus.

Most of all *Soli Deo Gloria. To God Be The Glory.*

ABOUT THE AUTHOR

Cindy Hamilton is a retired school counselor who has turned her love for Jesus, her grandkids and writing into a captivating story about the authentic supernatural. As a Bible teacher for many years, her imagination and the reality of being a Christ-follower have led to a unique relationship with Jesus, one she would like to share with teens and young adults. There's nothing boring about following Jesus—only a lifetime of wonder and adventure. She lives with her husband and two dogs, Max and Wynna, in the small town of Lonoke, Arkansas.

Made in the USA
Middletown, DE
06 December 2018